Riding
With
Ricardo

Grateful acknowledgment is made to D.A. Sele for permission to reprint the poem "The Ninth Day."

For my wife.

My inspiration and my destiny.

CHAPTER ONE

He looked down at the large, metallic food cart in front of him.

Rows of small, white paper cups adorned with smiling daffodils were neatly lined up on a plastic tray, their individual contents seeming to undulate mockingly at him under the harsh fluorescent lights.

Orange Jell-O.

God, he hated that stuff.

Just the sight of the tasteless, odorless, wriggling substance made his stomach reflexively tighten up. Even the optional dab of whipped cream on top to add some semblance of flavor couldn't save what he believed to be the world's most worthless excuse for a dessert item.

He realized that hate was probably too strong of an emotion to equate with something so innocuous. Yet, somewhere in the back of his mind, he couldn't help but think that there was obviously a long-repressed childhood memory associated with the gelatinous, culinary aberration.

Great, he thought sighing and shaking his head, now he was starting to view his "base feelings" with the "child-related trauma" observations of his life skills support counselor. Shit, he was even using the damn terms. And forget the silly, feel-good life skills support counselor title on the man's door or clinical psychiatrist designation imprinted on the obligatory office diploma hanging behind the desk -- the man was nothing more than a shrink. And at 280 pounds with a nervous stutter, he probably had more issues of his own to deal with than trying to help Scott figure out why he hated orange Jell-O.

Not that it would be worth a $150 session to try and discover the cause for his dislike -- that money was better spent on analyzing why the sight of his wife of 15 years made his stomach tighten up.

Perhaps his reaction to the mold-in-waiting was really due to an uncomfortable, repressed childhood experience -- after all, probably ninety-five percent of Jell-O consumers were either toddlers or senior citizens. They were the only ones whose partially-functioning taste buds wouldn't notice the distinct absence of flavor and whose soft gums and weak teeth would prefer the slimy goop. Either that or they had little room to argue as someone else made the stuff and usually spoon-fed it to them.

"Can I help you?"

For just a disoriented second, Scott had the panicked impression that the Jell-O was addressing him. It was long enough to make him seriously reconsider canceling that week's "life skills support" session.

He turned around to find an older, bespectacled gentleman in a white doctor's coat with a clipboard tucked under his arm.

"Oh good," Scott answered. "I'd hate to think these poor folks had to eat this stuff without trained medical help on the premises."

"Can I help you?" The man repeated; his expression unchanged.

"Oh, um, yeah," Scott replied, a bit embarrassed that his attempt at humor might have offended the man. "I, uh, I'm looking for one of your residents here, a Miss Eleanor Frost."

The man nodded slowly as his eyes narrowed the tiniest bit and his lips drew up into his mouth, as if sizing Scott up and finding him somewhat lacking.

Okay, so I don't look very professional, but he better not get a superior attitude with me, Scott thought in response. It's a Sunday afternoon -- there's nothing wrong with jeans and tennis shoes. Maybe the faded, black AC/DC T-Shirt was a little overly casual, and a little tight, for a 36-year-old, but in his defense, the visit to the nursing home had been unplanned. Well, not quite as much unplanned as simply forgotten – until his wife had called him in line at the corner Pump-N-Pay to remind him that the rest of "his" family was celebrating Gramma Eli's 85th birthday and wondering just where the hell he was…

He really hadn't meant to utter "Fuck" out loud as the cashier rang up his case of MGD Lite. A few folks nearby, dressed in their finest Church clothes, had given him much the same look as the old man in the nursing home had just done. But damn, he had known immediately that his quiet afternoon with the Broncos and Raiders was shot. At least he'd had the presence of mind to quickly add a bottle of wine for the special occasion, and made a deliberate show of placing a couple of crisp dollar bills into the Cub Scout donation jar at the end of the checkout lane.

"Ah yes, dear, sweet Eli," said the man in a hushed tone as he brought out the clipboard, used his index finger to push his glasses up above his nose and scanned the front page.

After an increasingly uncomfortable silence, in which the older man made no movement save for his eyes slowly drifting down the expanse of the page before him, Scott opened his mouth to repeat the question. Just then, however, the man flipped the page over on his clipboard with such a ferocity that it actually ripped the first sheet off the tablet and sent it fluttering to the glistening, tiled floor in front of Scott.

As the paper drifted to the ground, Scott noticed that it was completely blank on both sides. The old man appeared oblivious to the lost sheet as he now assumed an intent gaze at the second page. Jeez, thought Scott, this guy doesn't work here… he lives here.

Scott started slowly backing up as the other man continued to stare determinedly at the clipboard, seemingly unaware that Scott was now leaving him alone in the long, empty corridor, that is until his head suddenly jerked up and he yelled – "Save the Jell-O!"

Startled by the outburst, Scott, who was in mid-step, involuntarily jumped backwards and felt his butt come down on the handle of the food cart – lifting the back wheels a good two feet off the floor before sending it crashing back down. The Jell-O tray had slid toward Scott and now bounced back in the other direction, sending about a dozen cups over the edge and onto the floor. Scott turned and watched as they smacked the shiny linoleum, making sounds not unlike that of large bugs splattering against the windshield of a speeding car.

"Oh my goodness, look at what you've done," cried the old man rushing past Scott and dropping to his knees in the midst of the overturned Jell-O cups. He frantically began scooping them up in his arms.

"Whoa, geez, I'm sorry, let me help you," Scott said, getting down on one knee and reaching for a fallen cup, only to have his hand slapped away.

"Okay then," Scott remarked, more to himself than the distraught man on the floor. "I think I'll just go find her room myself. Thanks anyway."

He left the man sitting there moaning something about the injustice and atrocity of today's youth, which made Scott chuckle. It'd been a long time since anybody had referred to him in that regard.

As he made his way past the numbered doors down the hallway, he tried to remember which room his grandmother was in and realized that he hadn't been to see her since last Thanksgiving – almost a year ago. He felt a twinge of guilt at the thought, but life just had a way of getting busy and passing by. It certainly didn't seem that long ago. Anyhow, considering he had been laid off from his morning deejay job of 10 years right after Memorial Day and going from one temporary fill position to the next to help pay the bills, it's not like he didn't have enough else to worry about. Not to mention the widening chasm between him and Kate.

Hell, those are all just excuses, he thought. It's not like he was particularly close to his grandmother, but they always got along well and he should have taken the time to visit a little more.

"Scott! Scott! There you are!" He heard the voice of his sister from behind him and turned to see her and her husband coming out of one of the doors he had just passed.

"Oh, hey, good to see you," he said as he gave her a quick hug, then shook hands with her latest "soulmate" -- husband number three. Well, at least she was out there trying instead of slowly going down with the ship, he thought.

"Marcus, close gramma's door for a sec," Scott's sister whispered to the tall, blonde, athletic looking man next to her. Scott had never felt comfortable around the guy, perhaps because he reminded him of a third-generation Hitler youth. His features were definitely Aryan and his gleaming, perfect-toothed smile annoyed Scott. Or maybe it was just because he always felt like a short, balding, middle-aged doughboy next to Marcus.

"What's wrong? Is she okay, Sarah?" Scott asked his sister once the door was shut, adopting the same hushed tone as they stood outside the room.

"She's not doing well emotionally," Sarah answered. "She's just very depressed and crying a lot. Doesn't feel like having company, so you're in luck. You probably only have to go in and wish her a happy birthday for a few minutes."

"Come on, that's not right," Scott replied. "I don't mind seeing her."

"Yeah, that's why we had to call and find you," said Sarah. "It doesn't matter, for some reason she always liked you the best – even though you hide in the back and never say anything when we visit."

"Well, maybe that's why," said Scott. "I'm not feeding her a line of shit about how well she looks and how good she's doing and how nice it is in this place. She's here to die and everybody knows it, including her. So why make any pretenses about it?"

"God, you are just so fucking compassionate, you asshole," his sister said. "Well, you're gonna have to talk to her now, because there's nobody else left in there. Just try not to make her suicidal with your cheery attitude. Come on Marcus, let's go."

"Bye Marcus!" Scott called after them as they headed down the hall. Neither turned around.

He turned back toward the door and let out a huge sigh. This was going to be slightly uncomfortable. What the hell could he possibly talk to her about? He grasped at possible subjects – let's see, she had been here for almost three years now, her one child – his and Sarah's mother – had preceded her in death, and her husband had never returned from Korea where he gave his life on a cold, snowy field. Damn, no wonder she was depressed.

Suddenly Scott's unemployment and marital problems seemed minor in comparison to what his grandmother had lived through – and she was still hanging in there… sort of…

He didn't think any of those details would make for good conversation, but it did make him wonder about the fact that in the half century-plus following his grandfather's death why she had never remarried. Heck, even when he was young and she lived just down the street, he couldn't ever remember her having another man in her life. She had always been alone as far as he knew.

Okay, quit bringing yourself down and go in there with a smile and try to make her feel a little better, he thought.

He knocked lightly twice on the door and thought he heard her say "come in," although he wasn't quite sure. Still, he opened the door a crack and took a peek inside. She was sitting on her bed with her back to him and rocking slowly back and forth. He could hear her humming something, but didn't recognize the melody. He looked around the room and was struck by how sparse it appeared. Usually she had some family pictures on her dresser, some of her most meaningful possessions scattered around and whatever quilt she was working on at the time spread across the lone chair in the corner. But none of that was visible. It looked like she was ready to leave this place and Scott had a bad feeling that maybe his sister's callous remark about suicide wasn't so far off.

This is so not good, he thought. He was about to say something when she spoke.

"Are you just going to stand there or are you coming in Scottie?"

"Hey Gramma El, sorry," he said stepping into the small room and shutting the door behind him.

"You can leave the door open if you want, so it doesn't get so stuffy in here," said Eleanor, still sitting with her back to him.

"Oh, that's okay," Scott replied, closing the door. "I dumped a dessert tray of orange Jell-O, so I'm kinda hiding out so the angry hordes don't find me and beat me down with their canes."

Oh shit, he thought, I can't believe I just said that. How freakin' insensitive. But he was surprised to hear his grandmother laugh.

"Well, they probably wouldn't have enough strength to do you any serious harm," she said.

"Not necessarily because they're old," she continued, turning a little to face him, "but because you took away their nourishment."

"Ah ha, I knew it -- they're adding steroids to the Jell-O," he replied, trying to get the conversation off to a light start. He smiled and then went over to where she sat and leaned down to hug her softly. As he did so, he noticed that she was holding a framed 5x7 photo in her hands, but he couldn't tell what the picture was. At least she seemed in a fairly good mood, he thought.

As he straightened back up, he glimpsed an image of a handsome looking, silver-haired gentleman in the frame. He looked somewhat familiar, but Scott couldn't place him. Not wanting to appear overly curious about the photo, he turned to go to the tacky, green upholstered 1970's chair in the corner and heard his grandmother start sobbing.

That didn't take long, he thought, she's breaking down already. Just be a good listener, just be a good listener -- but when he looked back at her, he discovered that she had clasped a hand over her mouth and was actually trying to keep from laughing. Her eyes even had that bright sparkle to them that he recalled long ago from his childhood when he and his sister would visit her and always be greeted with a fresh-baked pan of oatmeal cookies.

Puzzled, he raised his eyebrows as if to question her shift in mood and wondered if maybe she hadn't popped a few happy pills just before he came in.

His grandmother simply pointed at him and lost her struggle to contain her emotions. She let out with a series of loud, laughing barks that diminished into spurts of giggling. All the while, she continued to point in Scott's direction.

Oh my God, she's laughing at me, he thought, feeling his face flush.

"Did you... did you..." his grandmother managed to stammer, before breaking into another uncontrollable peal of laughter.

Completely confused and embarrassed, he looked down to make sure his zipper was closed. No problem there, so why the hell was she laughing like a crazy... uh oh... that's it, he thought, she's finally snapped.

"Oh, don't worry, I'm not senile yet," she said catching her breath, as if reading his thoughts. "I was just wondering if you had run into Alfonso, our gay chef."

"Excuse me... what?" Scott answered, not sure if he had heard her correctly.

"Well, you've got this white cream smeared on your back and the crack of your butt," she managed to spit out before falling backwards onto her bed with laughter.

Scott tried to look down over his shoulder but couldn't see anything, so he reached his hands behind him and felt them slide into the soft, mushy remains of some stow-away whipped cream. He couldn't help but laugh as well. The orange fucking Jell-O had gotten him after all…

"That will certainly hurt the resale value of this vintage 1980's classic, black concert T-shirt," Scott said, wiping the small towel his grandmother had given him across his lower back and down the seat of his jeans.

"Yep," his grandmother nodded, "the E-bay listing will probably drop from two dollars to one fifty."

Scott gave her an appreciative glance and said, "You've got quite the little sarcastic streak going on gramma. Don't make me come over there and kick your ass."

"That's what I like about you Scott – you respect me enough to talk to me like a regular person," she said.

"What, by being rude and threatening you? Geez, I hope nobody talks to me that way when I'm oooooh… boy," he said, realizing that was a poor transition for what he was about to say.

"It's okay. I am old," she answered. "I'm a wrinkled, shriveled shell of a human being and quite frankly, it sucks, because it's not how I feel on the inside. But there's a lot that you don't know about me."

"Hey, you don't have any whips or handcuffs hidden under your bed, do ya?" Scott joked.

"Don't push it Scottie," his grandmother replied sternly.

"Sorry, ma'am," he said quickly, lowering his head apologetically.

"Oh please," she replied. "We're adults. How about you just call me Eli. I would like that."

"Uh, sure, as long as you don't call me Scottie anymore," he agreed, and they both laughed again.

They sat there looking at each other for a minute before Scott finally said, "So, um, happy birthday Eli. I got you a bottle of wine, but, uh, well, I left it in the car."

"You're such a funny boy," she answered. "But I was serious about what I said before. Everybody else is always so darn formal and uptight around me. Thank you for not treating me like some fragile, little schoolmarm whose turn-of-the-century sensibilities might be offended by some real-life, honest conversation."

"Are you alright gra... uh, Eli? I mean, are you doing okay?"

"Actually Scott, I haven't felt so good and so alive since... well, it's been so long that I can't even remember the last time I felt like this," she said, fidgeting a little with the neckline of the long, flowery gown she wore. The strong violets, blues and blacks of the dress complimented the clear blue of her eyes and her shoulder-length silver hair. Scott always envied her young appearance. Even now, at 85, he thought that she looked more like 60. Heck, he wouldn't be surprised if most of the old, single guys in the nursing home weren't trying to invite her to their rooms for Scrabble and tea. Wait a sec, nowadays with Viagra, they might be inviting her over for more than… yuch… eeew… say something quick, he thought.

"Got a boyfriend, huh?" Scott blurted teasingly. He wasn't prepared for the answer.

"Yes… yes I do…" Eli sighed, a shy little smile creasing the corners of her mouth.

"Um… say what… no wait, I don't want to know… that's cool… whatever…" he stammered, suddenly wishing he hadn't forgotten the wine in his car. He could use a drink after that unexpected revelation. God, please don't go into any intimate details, he implored inwardly. I don't want to be a good listener anymore, I don't want to be a good listener…

Eli just watched his reaction as if waiting to see what he'd say next.

"Sorry, just a little shocker there," he said, reigning in his overactive imagination. "You know what? I think that's great. Really I do. As long as you're happy, that's what really matters."

"Is it?" She asked. The question surprised him.

Damn, where the hell was this stuff coming from, he wondered? He felt like a featherweight being battered on the ropes by the heavyweight champ – and it was only the first round. And the referee, in the form of his sister, had abandoned him in the ring.

"Is what?" He managed to say, hoping to throw her off.

"Is being happy all that really matters? It's a simple question," she said, a little too innocently for Scott's liking.

"The question may be simple enough, but the answer is pretty darn complicated," he said, leaning forward in his chair to try and find some telltale signs of the alien that had obviously taken over his grandmother's frail form. "I mean, there is no universal definition of the state of happiness. It all depends on each single individual and what they perceive to be the one thing which can truly bring them…"

"Oh stop with the bullshit," Eli interrupted. "It's not that hard. People just over analyze it. Either you're happy or you're not. And whichever you are, you know it – right here."

She placed both her hands over her heart as she said it.

"But the question then becomes, is anybody ever truly happy?" Scott mused.

"Please, try to stay with me, I'm going somewhere with this," the alien heavyweight replied, knocking the air out of Scott's question, and then counterpunching with one of her own.

"Have you ever been in love? And before you tell me that you've been married for 15-something years, I want you to take a minute and think about it before you answer, because you don't want to lie to your dear, sweet old grandmother. Have you… ever truly been... out of control... nothing else matters... completely heart and soul... you'd do anything and give up everything... in love?"

Scott realized his mouth was agape like some Saturday morning cartoon character as he just stared at her, not quite knowing exactly how to respond.

"Well, I think that..." he started.

"You see," his grandmother interrupted again, "now *that* was a simple question that actually has a simple answer. It's either yes or anything else that comes out of your mouth, which equates to a no. I'm so sorry Scott."

"What? Why are you apologizing? What's going on here? How did you do that? What have you done with my grandmother?"

"Oh Scott," she said, getting up and crossing over to the chair in which he sat. She knelt down in front of him and gently placed a hand on his cheek. "I pray that one day you will be able to answer that question without hesitation, without having to think about it. Then you'll know what happiness is."

"It's your birthday Eli," he said softly. "So why am I the one who suddenly feels so depressed?"

"Now that's finally a question that you do have the answer to," she replied. "The answer is right here."

She took Scott's right hand with both of hers and placed it over his own chest.

"Have you ever been in love?" Scott asked after Eli had returned to her neatly made bed and sat back down.

"Yes," she said, looking directly at him. "Oh yes."

As soon as he saw the fierce resolve in her eyes, he couldn't help but envision what was coming next. He was going to be her sounding board, after all. Here comes the Titanic-style tale of once-in-a-lifetime romance cut short by unselfish heroic loss. Oh well, he really didn't have any plans for the afternoon and he certainly wasn't in a mood to go home now and face Kate. After all, as his grandmother just made painfully clear, he didn't really love her. He supposed he had always known that, but now that he had so much as openly admitted it to someone else, he would also have to face the fact that he was unhappy as well.

He couldn't help but smile at the thought that it had taken his grandmother five minutes to do what his shrink had been unable to in three months -- and a helluva lot cheaper. The only thing left now was for her to convince him that the root of it all was a latent homosexual gene and introduce him to Alfonso. Might as well face all his demons in one day…

"…on drugs?"

"Huh? You need your drugs?" He said jumping out of the chair.

"No, I asked if you were on drugs," Eli replied. "You keep getting this vacant gaze in your eyes like you're not all here."

"Oh, sorry, got a lot on my mind just now, as you can imagine," Scott said. "I'm sorry, you were gonna tell me about you and Grandpa."

"I was?" She asked, seemingly taken aback.

"Well yeah, your true love. I mean, you never even looked at another man after he, um, you know, didn't come back from the war."

"Died," she said matter-of-factly. "After he died. Why do people have such a hard time with this stuff? You really have some issues, but I can only work on one at a time, so let's get back to love. And, by the way, I slept with dozens of guys after Robert was killed. I just didn't love any of them."

This time Scott could feel his eyes nearly bug out of his head. Maybe he was a cartoon character after all. Hell, he didn't feel like he was living in the real world anymore.

"That was a joke, knucklehead," she said, laughing at his stunned expression.

No, he thought, that was a body blow. Round two to the wily octogenarian.

"But anyways," she continued. "There isn't just one kind of love. That would be pretty naïve to think, wouldn't it? There are different kinds. In addition to true love, there is passionate love, and comfortable love, and friendly love…"

"Whoa, so what exactly is true love then, if not any of those?" Scott asked.

"It's an equal part of all the others rolled into one," Eli said gently, as if explaining the obvious to a child. "I've had the truest love of all in my life and even though it doesn't seem fair sometimes to think I only had it for a couple of years, the truth is that once you have it, it's always with you. You can't lose the feeling of true love in your heart no matter what happens and that is what has gotten me through everything else. I'm blessed to have known it at all because so many people don't ever get to experience it in their lifetimes."

Scott cleared his throat loudly at that, as if to say: Yeah, one of those people is sitting right here, helloooo.

"Oops, sorry, Scott," his grandmother replied. "What were we talking about?"

"I think we were discussing the continuing procurement of nuclear components by North Korea, its progress in testing deliverable, rocket-propelled payload systems and how its genetic scientists were experimenting with impure biological matter to mutate us into a race of Pig-Humans," he answered.

"Oh yes," Eli said, completly ignoring him. "Different kinds of love... Now, I know that I will never have another true love like I did with your grandfather. But I've come to realize that doesn't mean I can't feel another type of love."

"Well, well," said Scott, serious again. "Who's the lucky guy and how long has this been going on?"

"His name is Wendell and we've been together other for quite a while now," Eli told him. "He's one of the kindest, sweetest, most caring men I've ever known."

"Alright then, I can't wait to meet him," Scott said, resisting the urge to laugh at the name.

"Neither can I," his grandmother remarked.

"You know," Scott managed after some silence, "why should anything you say surprise me anymore? Where did you meet this mystery man – in an online chat room for nursing home singles?"

"As a matter of fact," she answered, "we did meet on the Internet and have been chatting and sending each other e-mails every single day."

"Oh my God!" Scott exclaimed. "My grandmother is trolling cyberspace – and getting luckier at it than me. No, really, the guy's probably a serial killer in Montana. Please tell me you're kidding."

"Scott, you were the only person I decided to tell, please don't make me regret that decision," Eli said sternly. "Please try to understand."

"Understand what exactly?" He asked, a little calmer, but still somewhat incredulous about what he was hearing. "I mean, you don't even own a computer. Are you just messing with me?"

"No dear, I use the computer in the common area," she replied. "Scott, I am serious about this. Look at me. Look at this place. I admit when you and your sister brought me here three years ago, I wasn't doing well. I was very ill and needed the constant care and attention. But I feel better now. I feel better than I have in years and I refuse to just lie here and waste away what few remaining years I have left or else I may as well be dead already."

"I'm sorry," Scott said. "I didn't think that... I mean, I didn't know... oh hell, I'm just sorry. I can understand that. I really can. Some days I wake up and I look at myself and the place I'm at, and you know what, I feel the same way."

"Then come with me Scott," said Eli, getting up as if to emphasize that she was going somewhere.

"Whoa, slow down gramma," he said. "My brain is on overload. I thought I'd stop in and wish you well, exchange a few pleasantries, reminisce about my childhood and what a sweet young boy I was, and maybe, just maybe, if you weren't too tired from all of that excitement, watch a little 'Wheel of Fortune.'

"Now," he continued, "I'm in some kind of alternate reality where you have more ambition and energy than I do, you probably have a better long-distance relationship with someone you've never met than I will ever have with the woman I married, and, if I'm not mistaken, you've packed all your belongings and are planning to get your kicks on Route 69."

"It's 66, funny boy," Eli said, giggling.

"Oh, I think you know what I mean, you little cyber tease," Scott said, laughing himself.

"Scottie… just because we're on a first name basis doesn't mean that you will not show me the proper respect and courtesy. I know for a fact that your momma didn't raise you that way."

"Again, my apologies. But you are really freaking me out. Are you really planning to go see this Wendell guy? I don't think they'll let you out, you know."

"Of course they'll let you sign me out for a few hours Scott," she said, slowly sitting down on the bed again and reaching for the framed photo she had placed on the nightstand earlier. "Just a nice boy taking his dear grandmother for ice cream on her birthday."

"Oh, you're gooooood," he said, nodding his head. "I never had a chance, did I? You set me up perfectly. True love, missed opportunities and death. You hit me with all the heavy artillery. I suppose I could try to dissuade you, but somehow I'm thinking that I would just be prolonging the inevitable. So what's your plan and what part does your gullible grandson play?"

"You're such a good boy," Eli said with a smile. "I told you already. All you have to do is sign me out for ice cream at the front desk. Oh, and then drop me off at the bus station."

"I'm sorry, that's just too much effort on my part," Scott replied. "Sure, it sounds easy enough on the surface, but I'm too damn lazy to handle all of the second- and third-order effects. First, after you've disappeared, I'll have to make hundreds of flyers with your face on them and walk from neighborhood to neighborhood plastering them on telephone posts and public buildings. Then I'll have to spend countless hours driving around calling your name out of my car window and pretending that I'm looking for a lost dog, because it would just be too embarrassing for me and to traumatic for the school kids to tell them that I lost my grandmother. Finally, after they find your mutilated, bloody corpse, I'll be the one who has to go down to the morgue and make a positive identification.

"Now don't get me wrong," he continued, "I'm not saying you aren't worth that kind of time and effort, but frankly, I've got better things to do. My support group for older men who desire younger women meets three days a week and I feel like I'm just starting to make some progress, not to mention that the group facilitator is this hot college intern and I think she's a natural redhead…"

"Scott, I'll do it with your help or without," Eli said. "But I'd rather not have to set off a fire alarm to be evacuated and then slip away. I'm afraid I might give some of my friends here a heart attack."

"Jeez, you're serious, aren't you?" Scott replied rhetorically. "At least let me see that picture you're holding in your lap. Who's the guy worth all this trouble?"

He got up and crossed the room to sit down next to her and almost bounced right back up off the bed.

"You have to sit down slowly," said Eli. "The mattress is a little hard and springy."

"Hey, I could use a bed like this," said Scott, "it would hide the fact that Kate just… uh, never mind… where's your Romeo?"

Eli handed him the frame. He stared at the man in the photo for a good twenty seconds or more, then looked back at her. No change of expression on her face that he could tell. He wanted to laugh again, but he knew that would be the absolute worst thing he could do. Instead, he bit his lower lip and turned his eyes back to the suave, distinguished-looking gentleman in the picture. It was a close-up head and shoulders shot and there was no mistaking what he saw. He looked again at Eli, but she was just smiling and nodding as if to say, "See, what a catch."

He let out a small sigh. Damn, he had to say something. Better to do it now than before she actually meets this guy in person.

"Um, Eli, he's a pretty handsome older man," he started, "but, are you sure that this is… well, are you sure about this?"

"What are you trying to say Scott," she asked.

Shit, sometimes you just have to rip the Band-Aid off fast and hope for the best, he thought.

"Eli, this is a picture of Ricardo Montalban, the actor."

Her eyebrows perched a little bit as she met his gaze and seemed to consider her grandson's statement.

"Fantasy Island… Mr. Rourke…" he added by way of explanation. "You know, with the little guy, 'boss, de plane, de plane.' He also played a pretty good villain in "Star Trek – The Wrath of Khan."

Still nothing but that unwavering gaze.

"Fine Corinthian leather," Scott tried with an accent, mimicking the old automobile commercials he recalled which featured Montalban. "Come on, you've got to know who he is."

Eli started laughing at him. Great, he thought, she doesn't believe me.

"Of course I know who he is," she finally said. "I just didn't think that you would know. I'm impressed."

"Well, damn, if you know that, then you've got to realize this Wendell guy is lying to you," Scott said.

"No, he's not," she replied. "He didn't send me that. I cut it out of a magazine."

Seeing his confusion, she continued.

"I just wanted to have something tangible. Something to hold on to and make me think of him. You see, it doesn't matter what he looks like. It's how he makes me feel inside."

Scott considered that and then said, "Hard to argue with that kind of logic."

He passed the photo back to Eli, who gently stood it up on her nightstand, facing the bed. They both stared at it for a while, unsure what to say next.

Finally, Scott shook his head in resignation.

"So... you up for some ice cream?" He asked.

CHAPTER TWO

Even though it was a Sunday, the congestion on the
Martin Luther King Jr. Freeway seemed unusually heavy to Scott
as he weaved his little aquamarine, 1995 Saturn SC2 through the
early afternoon traffic. Were the Chargers playing at home today,
he wondered? That would explain it. Being a transplanted
Chicago native, he never really kept track of any of the San
Diego teams.

On the radio, Steve Perry's falsetto shrill brought a sense
of urgency to traveling down a dusty road as the wheel in the sky
kept on turnin'. Boy, you are oh so right Steve, it just keeps on
turning, thought Scott. The only difference was that he didn't
know what kind of road he was heading down anymore. He
joined in the chorus.

"Somewhere in New Mexico," his grandmother
interjected as Scott and Steve questioned where they'd be
tomorrow. Without flinching, he calmly guided the car into the

right lane and put on his turn signal for the next exit. He then calmly reached out his hand out to press the radio's power button off.

"Um, could you please repeat that?" he asked, beginning the sentence routinely but ending it a few octaves higher than normal, "because I'm not quite sure I heard you correctly over the music, my singing, the traffic, the wind, and the guy farting on the corner of 6th and Maple Streets!"

"That's what I thought you said," he sighed, when she repeated New Mexico.

Now what, dumbass? You just legally signed your grandmother out of a nursing home and promised the attendant you'd have her back before lights out, he chided himself.

"Let me get this clear," he said, veering the car onto the off ramp. "Is this my fault for neglecting to ask you where this Wendell lived because I just assumed he was somewhere in the local area and I trusted you, or is it your fault for purposefully keeping this little bit of information from me until it was too late?"

"Scott, I'm 85. I can't be expected to remember everything, you know. My memory isn't as sharp as it used to be," she said.

"Well, you certainly remember how to get your way," he replied.

"That's just a woman thing, sweetie, it has nothing to do with age," she answered.

TKO in the fifth round, he thought. Stop the fight; it's over.

"Good thing we were going to my house first anyway," he said, turning left at the top of the ramp and crossing over the freeway. "Guess I better call the home and tell them we're keeping you a little longer, and then pack an overnight bag."

"Hey," said Eli, "maybe Kate will come with us. It'll be quality time for the two of you to reconnect."

"I don't think so," Scott said. "Not unless they have an empty room at the Glendale Retirement Center, cuz after a few hours of us being together in a car, I'll be moving in with you."

"Why aren't you two in love anymore, Scott?"

He briefly thought about swerving his car head-on into the UPS truck in the oncoming lane to avoid the question. In fact, he didn't say anything in response through three stoplights. It was a question the shrink hadn't been able to answer for him, other than to blame Scott's lack of forgiveness -- "So your wife cheated on you with an old boyfriend a few months after you first got married," he could hear Dr. Ramos repeat in his mind. "That was 15 years ago and you've never moved past it. She did you an injustice for one day, but you've made her suffer for it emotionally for an eternity in comparison. Perhaps it's time to forgive her?"

But, damn, it's not like he hadn't tried so many times to forgive and forget. He had even gone for months and years at a time thinking he had finally gotten over it, at least in his mind, only to realize he had just blocked it out temporarily.

But ultimately his heart just wouldn't accept it.

"Because," he finally replied, turning his head to look at Eli, "I don't want to be."

"You see," she smiled, "sometimes all you need to look for is the simple answer."

He couldn't believe he was actually nervous as he guided the little sports coupe into the driveway of the two-story, brick townhouse he was now a mortgage payment behind on. Why the hell was his heart racing like this? Would Kate be able to tell? Would she see it on his face or in his eyes?

His grandmother had just casually extracted the long repressed reason for his crumbling marriage – the numbingly plain fact that he just didn't love his wife enough to even try to save their relationship. But he had been content to continue on indefinitely in his blissful ignorance for a certain level of comfort and security that had developed -- and now what?

He stopped the engine and stared straight ahead at the garage door. Chipping quite a bit, he thought absently, could use a fresh coat of paint. Deep down, he supposed he always knew, but it was just easier not to face it. But it was out there now and he'd have to deal with it and that scared the hell out of him, because now everything would change. He let out a huge sigh.

"Would you like me to come in with you Scott?" Eli asked.

"Only if you want to," he said. "If you need to use the bathroom or get something to eat or drink before we hit the road, you're more than welcome to. Otherwise, I think I'll just run in, throw a change of clothes in a bag and be right back out."

Hey, he thought, just because he had to deal with it, didn't mean he had to do it right then.

"I can wait here, it seems like a fairly good neighborhood," Eli said, patting his knee. "You just do what you need to."

He turned the key in the ignition switch a notch, enough to juice the electric system and slid the AC level to low.

"Five minutes," he told her and opened his door. He got out, but then leaned back in to face her. "Thanks... I think..."

My God, he thought walking toward the door, all I wanted to do today was watch a little football.

He found Kate in the kitchen, making herself a cup of tea.

"Well, good, there you are," she said as he walked in. "I was just trying to decide on dinner. What would you like?"

"Um, can't stay," he said.

"And why not?" She asked, playfully raising her eyebrows, as if she thought he was kidding.

Because I don't love you and I'm not even sure that I ever really did, his brain answered, although his mouth formed the words "Taking Grandma Eli out for her birthday."

"What? You're taking her out of the home for dinner?" Kate responded. "That's so sweet of you Scott. Do you want me to come along? I can be ready in a few minutes."

"Weeeeell," he hesitated, "It's a little complicated."

But as soon as he said it, he couldn't help but laugh. Life just didn't seem as complicated as it used to anymore.

"No," he corrected himself. "Actually, it's quite simple. She's slowly dying in that place and needs to get out in the real world – to live a little. I'm driving her to New Mexico to meet a man she's developed an online relationship with so she can feel alive again for a little while."

"Oh my God," said Kate, "You're pimping your grandmother? I know we're having money problems Scott, but really…"

"Hey, hey, they're old folks," he said, somewhat disturbed at the sudden vision that popped into his head. "They'll just talk, or cuddle, or maybe kiss each other on the cheek, come on…"

"I was kidding Scott, but are you serious? You're actually going to drive your grandmother to New Mexico to see some guy?"

"It's not like I have anything better to do, and how could I say no," he replied. "You weren't there. You don't know how much this means to her. I mean, it's like the last thing she wants in life, you know?"

"I can understand that," she answered. "I'd go to New Mexico too if I thought there was a chance I could get laid."

"Very funny," Scott said sarcastically. He absolutely hated it when she did that. They rarely made love anymore – maybe once a month, but oftentimes it was more like once every other month. It had been that way for years now. It's not that he didn't find her attractive, because she was – a small, brunette who looked like she was in her mid-20's instead of ten years older than that. But it all went back to that deeply buried resentment of her infidelity so long ago. His aversion to doing it with her now was mental, not physical, and he knew that. It's not that he was withholding sex to punish her, as she sometimes claimed. He just honestly had no desire to be with her in that way. Or any other way now, a little voice in the back of his head reminded him.

"I need to go pack an overnight bag," he said and walked out.

"Well, you're in a solemn mood," Kate replied, following him out of the kitchen and up the stairs. "Usually you come right back with the smart remarks. This visit with your grandmother really got to you, didn't it?"

"Grandma's downstairs waiting in the car," he answered, not turning around. He grabbed his gym bag from the top shelf of the closet and then went to the dresser. He started to throw some clothes in it.

"Goodness, you could have brought her inside Scott," Kate said as she went over to the window to look down into the driveway.

"She's in kind of a hurry," he replied. And so am I, he thought, before I wind up saying something that I don't have time to think all the way through.

"Well, you can't just leave her sitting out there like that," Kate said. "I'm going to run down and wish her a happy birthday."

"You do that. Tell her I'll be right there," Scott said, debating internally on whether he should take one pair of clean underwear or two. He decided on the latter.

After he had filled the bag with enough clothes for two days, he crossed over to the adjoining bathroom. There he scooped up a few essentials – toothpaste, toothbrush, deodorant, electric shaver – and added them, before zipping the bag and slinging it over his shoulder by the strap. He paused and looked at his reflection in the mirror above the sink. He didn't look old, but he sure felt tired.

He ran a hand over the stubble on his head. He had started losing his hair just out of high school. It had bothered him at first, to inherit his father's receding hairline, but then he started shaving what was left to make it look uniform. At least he had a good-shaped head for the bald look. Because of the large Navy and Marine Corps presence in town, most folks he met immediately stereotyped him as being in the military.

He shook his head at his reflection as if to say "I don't know what the hell is going on here," but was met with a look of helpless confusion by his mirror image.

"You're actually lucky, you know," he told himself. "At least you have a day or two on the road to clear your thoughts and figure out exactly how you're gonna deal with this when you get back."

Already, however, he knew there could be no middle ground on the issue. It would be one extreme or the other… either he told Kate he didn't love her and didn't want to be married to her anymore or he didn't tell her anything at all. Anything else would get too damn complicated and as Eli had put it, simplicity is key. But that thought caused another, more well-known colloquialism to pop into his mind – honesty is the best policy.

"Shut up," he muttered to his reflection. "Who asked you anyways?"

As he came back out the front door of the house, he saw that his wife had seated herself in the driver's seat and was talking with Eli. He used the trunk button on his keys to pop it open and deposited his gym bag on top of Eli's small suitcase.

He then approached the driver's side and bent down by the open door to find Kate and Eli both staring at him. Neither one said anything, or even moved. Their blank expressions made them look like they had been momentarily frozen in time.

"Okay, you're freakin' me out a little, ladies," Scott joked.

But whatever was going on obviously wasn't a joking matter, because neither even cracked a smile.

"Eli just told me," Kate whispered, and then placed both hands over her mouth in the traditional, clichéd pose signifying shock or disbelief.

Scott's eyes widened. No fucking way, he thought. She couldn't have. He glanced at Eli, but she continued to stare at him with that far-off gaze. Why would she say something like that? Be cool, he told himself, this is obviously one of those amusing little misunderstandings and she's talking about something else entirely...

"You really don't love me anymore?" Kate asked in a muffled hush from behind the hands still clasped over her mouth.

...or not.

Holy shit. He looked over at Eli and his eyes seemed to plead "Why? Why, Why, Why?"

"Oh my God, it's true," he heard Kate say and the next thing he knew he was spread-eagled on his back on the carport as his wife had pushed him out of the way and ran toward the house.

He didn't move. He heard the front door slam and the bolt lock into place. Could be worse, he thought, as he lay there and tried to make out patterns in the clouds. The sun felt warm on his face and he could almost imagine he was 10 years old and without a care in the world as he visualized the shape of a cuddly, cotton teddy bear above him. As if on cue, a large airliner appeared from out of the clouds – it's wing shearing off the teddy bear's head. He could almost hear the anguished screams of the billowy, severed head as it drifted away from the main cloud. But instead of fading away, the screams just seemed to grow louder until he realized they were coming from his house.

Slowly he sat up and looked toward the living room's bay window. He could still hear Kate screaming from somewhere inside, but all he saw was his comfortable leather recliner angled in front of the TV. He wondered how his fantasy football team was doing today… he had dropped the last two games in his league and Cam Newton was on another one of his inconsistent streaks… although, he mused, since he has them so often, would it actually be considered consistent… consistently inconsistent? Maybe he should offer a trade for…

"Scott!" His grandmother yelled. "Snap out of it. Let's go."

He collected himself off the hard concrete and looked at her in amazement.

"Geez, you are something else," he said. "I mean, you look all grandmotherly, harmless and sweet on the outside, but you are some kind of evil, withered hellspawn sent from the netherworlds to dismantle the very fabric of my being.

"Is it because I don't go to church?!" He yelled up at the sky.

"Quit being so dramatic," Eli said. "I did you a favor."

"You what?" He gasped. "You… you… huh?"

"Oh come on," she said. "You know you didn't have the guts to ever tell her how you really felt. And it's not fair to her."

"Not… fair… to… her?" He managed to repeat.

"She has a right to know Scott," Eli answered. "What if she wants more out of life? You can't just decide what you want to tell her and when you want to tell her. Sure, it would be nice if you could figure it all out to your advantage and how it would be best for you, but that's pretty darn selfish. What about her? At least now she can use the next few days as well to come to terms with this and make some decisions of her own. Who knows, maybe you'll both come to the same decision and you can work together to resolve things."

"I know you've been out of circulation for a while, but…" he said, again finishing his sentence by yelling, "try to come back to the real world!"

Eli turned her head back to face the windshield and folded her arms across her chest, as if to signal that the conversation was finished. Scott just looked at her incredulously.

He realized he had one of two options now. He had the keys to the house on his key ring and could go back in and try to talk to Kate, or he could get in the car and take Eli to New Mexico. No wait, he smiled, make that three options… he could get in the car, take Eli for some ice cream and then drop her back off at the home.

At this rate, if he went on a road trip with her, he'd probably wind up in jail for transporting some illegal substance across state lines, he thought, because something was making her act crazy. Either that or he'd be arrested for strangling her at a deserted rest area.

"I know you're mad right now, Scott, but trust me," he heard her say. "Get in the car, leave Kate to sort things out for herself, and let's get on the highway. The worst thing you could do right now is try to talk to her while her emotions are still raw. Besides, what could you possibly say that would change anything?"

"You know, you sure talk a helluva good game, grandma," he said. "But I am tired of being manipulated by your little designs. You don't want me to talk to her, well then, I think I will."

He turned to head toward the door and made it two full steps in that direction when he heard Kate's voice from their upstairs bedroom window.

"Don't you even fucking think about coming back here, bastard!"

As his right foot was coming down on the walkway, he turned it in mid-air and did a mini pirouette to turn himself back toward the car without missing a step.

"You know," he said, as he slid into the seat next to Eli. "I think her emotions are still a little raw and the worst thing I could probably do right now is to try and talk to her. Why don't we just get on the highway?"

"Why, I think you're absolutely right and that's a wonderful idea," Eli said.

CHAPTER THREE

Less than 15 minutes later, Scott had them eastbound on I-8 and cruising at 65 mph. He hadn't spoken to Eli since they pulled out of his driveway. Instead, he had put on the noisiest CD he could find in his carrying case as a sort of psychological warfare to keep her quiet. It also worked to take his own mind off of everything that had just transpired, until he actually heard the lyrics of the song "In The End" that he was singing along with by Linkin Park.

He turned the volume down a little and then glanced at both the fuel gauge and the in-dash clock. The needle was over half a tank and it was 1:45 p.m. He knew there was no way they could make New Mexico tonight. Maybe, if he didn't get too tired, they could get across most of Arizona and find a cheap motel; then make it to wherever they were headed in New Mexico by mid-morning tomorrow.

Every few minutes he noticed that Eli would turn and look back. He had ignored her until curiosity got the better of him and he glanced at the backseat. There, strapped loosely into one of the seatbelts was the framed picture of Ricardo Montalban. It was keeping time to the music by bouncing up and down and side to side from the vibrations of the road. His gleaming paper smile seemed to say he liked this generation's rock/rap stylings.

Scott was lost in his thoughts as they continued past the never-ending chain of off-ramp gas stations and fast food restaurants. Did he really have to make a decision at all, he wondered? Maybe he could just give it a few days, then go back and he and Kate could go on as they had been all these years. It was a mutually beneficial relationship. Heck, he mused, it's not like the situation between them is going to change that much because of this. He would go back to doing his thing, she would do hers and they could just as easily stay together – like roommates. At least they had never had any children, so whatever happened, that wasn't a complication.

His stress level subsided a little as he convinced himself that was the most rational course of action, and surely Kate would see it that way too. Then he turned the music back up a notch and watched the scenery go by, at least until shortly after the California-Arizona border … then the fuel stops and eateries thinned out considerably.

The sun was already below the horizon behind them, with its last water-color tendrils of red streaking across the darkening blue desert sky, when Scott saw the sign for Gila Bend, Arizona, and the exit for state highway 85.

They had been on the road for almost four hours now and not only did Scott need to put some gas in the car, but his butt was getting numb. He was happy to see the 50-foot high, illuminated "Triple J" truck stop sign ahead and slowed to get into the right lane. He glanced in his rear view mirror and didn't even bother putting on his turn signal as there were no other vehicles in sight.

Traffic on the highway had been relatively sparse since they passed Yuma, and consisted mostly of pick-up trucks and 18-wheelers. His sleek little SC2 had drawn a few unimpressed stares from the slower-moving trucks he'd passed, with the looks on most of those driver's weather-beaten faces seeming to say "Whatcha' doin' out here city boy?"

He had been so bored after Eli fell asleep that he had imagined them on their radios – monitoring his location and plotting some kind of redneck trucker's welcome: "I got aquamarine city boy at mile marker 270, still heading east, looking smug in his little girly car, over." "I hear you hoss, he gonna have to tank up some time and we be a waitin' for him then."

Okay, maybe that was overly paranoid, he thought -- the result of one too many road-trip-gone-bad movies. Besides, any truckers stupid enough to mess with him would find themselves mercilessly struck down by his crafty, demon-tongued grandmother.

He slowed to a stop in front of one of the well-lit, covered gas pumps. As soon as he cut the engine, Eli sat upright and reached for the door handle.

"Whoa," said Scott, giving her a look that said 'don't even tell me you've been awake this whole time.'

Seeing his non-verbalized reaction, Eli responded, "Sorry. I just didn't want to talk to you. You were being a … oh, how do they say it nowadays… a bonerhead."

"Close enough," Scott replied as Eli eased herself out of the low front seat on a pair of unsteady legs. She creaked upright, squinted and placed a hand over her brow as the bright fluorescents overhead temporarily blinded her.

"I have to take some of my feel-better pills," she said, heading toward the truck stop's 24-hour convenience store. "I'll be back in a few minutes."

Scott nodded and proceeded to fill the car. After putting the nozzle handle on automatic, he dug out the crisp, never used 1995 Rand McNally road atlas from under the passenger's seat. He had bought it a few days after getting the Saturn, with full expectations of getting the most out of his new car. Almost 20 years later, he realized this would be the longest trip he'd taken it on.

He flipped it open to the map of Arizona and laid it across the top of his roof. It looked like highway 85 would connect him with I-10 toward Phoenix – or he could continue on I-8. It all depended on where exactly in New Mexico good old Wendell resided.

He looked toward the store, but didn't see Eli. Must be in the bathroom, he thought. Scott glanced toward the right, behind the store, where a huge parking lot offered temporary refuge to weary overland truckers. It was still early – just a little after 6 p.m. – and there were only four large rigs resting there. A sudden flash near the closest truck caught his attention. Just a match, or a lighter, he thought, as he saw two burly Cowboys sharing a smoke. Was it his imagination or were they looking at him and laughing? Hopefully they weren't discussing how they planned to dispose of his hacked up body parts after forcibly sodomizing him and…

The click of the nozzle shutting off snapped his attention back. He looked at the pump. It said $41.58. He squeezed the handle and it went up to $41.73 before cutting off again. A few more squeezes took it to $41.92. Come on, he thought, you can make it to an even $42.00. It was something that usually annoyed the hell out of Kate – she said he was anal to try and round up to an even dollar amount when… crap! His thoughts were interrupted by the gas flowing out over the top of the gas tank and splashing onto the ground. Yep – that was why it usually annoyed her. He groaned as he read the numbers on the pump: $42.01.

Once inside the store, he noticed it was strangely empty. He grabbed a pack of gum near the front counter and dropped it next to the register along with his credit card. Man, what he could really use was a good cup of French vanilla cappuccino like he got down at his neighborhood gas station.

"Do you have a cappuccino machine in here?" He asked the abnormally skinny 50-something cashier.

"A what?" she asked in return.

"You know," he said, "one of those flavored coffees that…"

"I know what a cappuccino is, honey," she drawled. "But we sure ain't got none of that here. You want a regular coffee?"

"No thanks, tears my stomach up," he said, adding, "I guess it'd be too much to ask if you carried any mineral water – the carbonated kind."

"What pump are you on?" She asked Scott, completely ignoring his question.
Taken aback, he looked out at his car. While he hadn't noted the exact pump he had used, it shouldn't be too hard for her to figure it out … his was the only car out there.

"Whatever pump is next to that car," he answered, trying hard not to sound like a smart ass, but realizing from the sound of his own words that he hadn't quite succeeded.
To his surprise the woman merely backed up to her stool, climbed on it to have a seat, folded her arms and waited.

He knew he wasn't going to win this one. She'd probably been working here since fresh out of high school when she thought she'd lucked into a nice temporary position to get a little money before she started her "real" career. Now she was a bitter, disillusioned cashier who'd seen it all, wasn't going anywhere and just didn't care.

For some reason though, her smug demeanor really got to him. Perhaps it was the culmination of having lost every single argument with the women in his life since he got up that morning – his sister, his grandmother, his wife… He'd just had enough.

"Look here 'hon,'" he started, "I happen to be a secret shopper. Do you know what that is? It means the Triple J corporate office hires me to drive around the southwest and report back to them about the service, cleanliness and conditions of their facilities, to include employee attitudes. Now I already came through here a few days ago on my way out and gave this particular location some high marks, which is why I wasn't going to rate you again this evening, however…"

Without a word, the cashier got off her stool, punched a few keys on her register, swiped his credit card and presented him the receipt.

"Thank you," Scott said, unable to believe that spiel actually worked. He quickly signed the receipt and left the store. At least Eli was back in the front seat waiting for him, although it didn't look like she was planning to speak to him anytime soon. She had tilted her seat back so far that he could barely see the top of her head. He looked toward the two truckers and saw they were still out there smoking, but not paying him any attention.

He walked around the back end of the car thinking that he should have gotten a Mountain Dew or something caffeinated to keep him going a few more hours in the quiet darkness, but he certainly wasn't going back in the store now.

He opened his door, got in, turned to Eli and felt his breath literally catch in his throat.

Reclining in the chair next to him was a beautiful young Hispanic woman. Her thin face was framed by shoulder-length black hair, and the eyes looking directly at him were a Crayola burnt sienna shade of brown. She was fairly young, he thought, mid 20's maybe. He was at a complete loss for words and could only stare back at her. She was bundled up in a small caramel-colored blanket with tasseled fringe on the ends, and oh my God, thought Scott, as his eyes finally broke the magnetic lock between hers and he saw that she had one of the tassles in her mouth and was wistfully rolling it across her tongue.

Okay, get control of yourself, he thought. The whole experience had only taken three or four seconds, but it seemed like an eternity before he finally managed to speak.

"Um, I don't know what kind of pills you're taking granny, but they are definitely working for you," he said.

The woman next to him gave a shy smile and sunk a little lower into the chair.

He heard Eli giggle from the back seat and then she said, "It took you forever in there, let's go already."

Scott looked back at her, and then at their new passenger. Wow. Okay, that's dangerous, he thought, don't look directly at her again or you'll be agreeing to anything.

"What's going on?" he asked, turning back to Eli.

"She needs a ride, so let's go … now!" Eli answered.

"Oh shit," Scott sighed, shaking his head. "She's on the run. Who's after her? Is she illegal? Where's the border patrol?"

"Scott, please, just go," Eli implored, now peeking nervously out of the back window.

He was about to tell his grandmother that she'd finally gone too far and that they were all getting out of the car to figure out what was going on, but then he looked at the woman next to him again. She didn't look nervous or scared at all – it seemed that she was simply content to wait and see what Scott would decide. No, he thought, looking a little more closely, content was too noncommittal a description. More like resigned to whatever was going to transpire. It's not like she's given up, he thought, but more like she just didn't care and would accept and adapt no matter how the situation unfolded.

He briefly wondered if she weren't so damn beautiful if he'd just tell her to get out. If she were a fat, old Mexican woman who needed a ride under suspicious circumstances, would he dump her unceremoniously at the curb?

He realized that he wouldn't, and that brought a small smile to his lips. If somebody needed help, he'd try to do what he could and sort the rest out later. Why should it be different just because this woman had made his heart lock up in his chest – wouldn't that be some kind of reverse discrimination because of her good looks?

No, don't kid yourself, that tiny voice way in the back of his mind seemed to say, you're scared that if you leave with her now, you might not want to let her get back out of the car later...

He had already made up his mind to start the car and leave, but before he could act to put the key in the ignition, the mystery woman finally spoke.

"Geez Louise, I can see why it took you so long in the store – you really have a hard time making decisions, don't you?"

She hadn't said it in a mean way, but it caught him off guard.

"Okay, wait, you're actually insulting the guy who's trying to decide whether or not to help you out?" He asked, shaking his head in bewilderment. "It must be a language barrier. You just don't know English very well and what you really meant to say was 'Please, kind stranger, save me and I'll be forever in your debt.'"

She muttered something in Spanish, which he didn't understand, and pulled the blanket completely over her head.

Scott took a look around the truck stop for anything that might give an indication of what he was getting involved in, but the place was still deserted. Even the two Marlboro men had disappeared.

"Scoooott," Eli said.

"Yeah, yeah, going now," he replied, starting the car and wondering if this day could get any weirder. It didn't take him long to find out.

"Eli, we have a junction coming up, where exactly does Wendell live?" he asked.

"Just south of Wichita, in a small town called Salinas Point," his grandmother replied, cradling the picture of Ricardo Montalban against her chest.

Scott's fingers tightened on the steering wheel.

"Okay, I've heard of a Las Vegas in New Mexico," he said slowly, as if wanting to choose just the right words. "So I'm gonna give you the benefit of the doubt and trust that Wichita is another common town name and there's one somewhere in the tumbleweed overrun state we're driving toward."

"No, silly, it's in Kansas," Eli said cheerily.

"Um, nooooo," Scott replied, the impatience in his tone clearly evident. "Dorothy is in fuckin' Kansas. Wendell is in New Mexico."

Almost instantly, he felt the sharp pain of the photo frame's edge smack him on the right side of his head, just above the ear.

"Ow! Jesus Christ!" He yelled, automatically swerving the car over a lane as the sting spread outward along his temple.

"You watch your language Scott Allan Miles," his grandmother said in a hushed tone. "There's a young lady in the car."

He heard a soft giggle from under the blanket next to him.

"Look, grandma, this afternoon you said he lived in New Mexico," Scott said, trying to gently massage the rising welt on his head, but finding that too painful in itself. "I think I've been more than understanding and accommodating, but if I can't believe anything you say then…"

"You're right Scott. I apologize," Eli said as she dug through her worn handbag and brought out a small tube of generic pain relief cream. "While I didn't exactly lie to you, I'm afraid that I did mislead you, and that's no better."

She carefully applied some of the cream to Scott's temple, causing him to flinch.

"What I said," she continued, "was that by tomorrow we'd be somewhere in New Mexico, which is technically correct. I never said that was our final destination or that it's where Wendell lives."

"No wonder you never got remarried in fifty years," Scott muttered just under his breath.

The sharp stab of pain on his right leg wasn't quite as bad as the hit to the head, but it was still enough to be discomforting. He glanced at the covered figure next to him just in time to see a hand disappear beneath the blanket and a muffled voice say "That wasn't nice Scott Allan Miles."

"Unbelievable," Scott said. "First you insult me, then you hit me. Good thing I was nice to you. I can only imagine what you would have done if I'd refused to give you a ride – probably slit my throat with a straight razor."

"Too messy," she answered, pulling the blanket down and looking up at him. "How would I ever be able to drink all your blood? Most of it would spill in the car and go to waste."

"Oh that's funny," Scott said sarcastically. "But you're the one who got into a car with a man you don't know. That's not very safe or smart."

"It's a calculated risk," she said with a shrug. "But I'm betting that most serial killers don't use their grandmothers to help pick up victims."

"Maybe she likes to watch," Scott replied.

"I'm enjoying watching this," Eli chimed in.

"Also," their new passenger added, trying to stifle another giggle, "most serial killers don't ask for French vanilla cappuccinos or bubble water at redneck truck stops. I think I'm pretty safe with you."

"Hey… I didn't see… where… yeah, well, enough small talk," Scott replied, wondering how long she had watched him in the store without him even noticing. "What's your name? Where are you going? Who are you running from? Are you carrying anything illegal – drugs, weapons, yourself?"

"Now how am I supposed to be the alluring, mysterious stranger if you take all that away from me?" She asked, her eyes widening with fake innocence. "Isn't it more fun and exciting to just imagine the possibilities?"

"No, it's scary and disturbing to imagine the possibilities," Scott said. "Okay then, let's at least start with a name since you already know mine completely."

"Fair enough. It's Destini," came her soft response.

"Really, it is," she said, noting the look in Scott's eyes. "With an 'i.'"

"That's beautiful," Eli said from the backseat.

"Sounds like the name of a ... oh, um, this is our exit," Scott said, thankful he saw the sign so he could change the subject before he compared her to a stripper. He slowed as he approached the off ramp for highway 85.

"Anything else you want to share?" He asked as he guided the car around the gradual arc to the adjoining road.

"A piece of that gum would be nice," Destini said, pointing at the pack Scott had purchased back at the Triple J and thrown between the seats.

"Not exactly what I meant, but help yourself," he said.

"Wow," he heard Destini say a few seconds later. He looked over after straightening the Saturn out on state highway 85 and saw her looking at the sales receipt she had picked up along with the gum.

"You spent one hundred and forty two dollars and one cent on gas," she said.

"What!?" He yelled, a vein in the temple that Eli had just smacked straining against his skin.

"Oh no, I'm sorry, I read that wrong," Destini corrected herself. "You really only spent forty two dollars and one cent on gas. You spent one hundred dollars on the pack of gum."

"I... I... I give up. I just can't believe this," Scott replied.

"Me either," said Destini, "couldn't you have rounded the tank to an even forty two dollars?"

CHAPTER FOUR

No more than 15 minutes after Scott had taken the exit onto 85 it became obvious to him that they were being followed. The headlights of the lone car behind them kept an exact distance, no matter how much Scott slowed down or sped up. And the fact that those headlights were set on high beams and slightly irritating in Scott's rear-view mirror just seemed to say that whoever was behind them wanted them to know he was there.

Hell, maybe it's just that open-road paranoia again, he tried to tell himself. But if somebody was tailing them, it certainly wouldn't be because they were interested in an out-of-work slacker and his hipster grandma.

He looked over at Destini, who had balled her blanket up and placed it against her window to use as a pillow. He was a little surprised to see that she was leaned with her back against the door and looking at him as well. Scott was even more surprised when she gave him what appeared to be a genuine smile.

Don't get sucked in, he thought, turning back to face the road. She knows she's got the looks and she's gonna use them to use you.

"So seriously," he said. "Where do you need a lift to?"

"Kansas?" She asked, and although it was said playfully, there was just enough hint of hopefulness in her voice to let Scott know that she was serious, even though she quickly added, "Just however far you're going tonight will be fine. I really appreciate it."

"Well, I figure if I don't get too tired I'll just drive until either my car or the car behind me runs out of gas," Scott replied casually, looking over at her for some reaction.
She frowned slightly and then said more to herself than to him, "I shouldn't have gotten anybody else involved in this."

"I don't mind that so much as not knowing exactly what's going on," said Scott. "Now that we are involved, maybe you can let us in on the big adventure?"

"It's okay, honey," said Eli, reaching a hand out from the back and patting Destini's shoulder. "You don't have to tell us anything that you don't want to or aren't comfortable with."

"It's not that. I just don't want to cause you any problems or put you in danger," said Destini.

"Put us in danger?!" Scott exclaimed. "What kind of calamity have we gotten in the middle of here?"

"Wow," commented Destini, "I don't think I've ever met anybody who actually used the word 'calamity' in a sentence."

"He says strange things sometimes," Eli volunteered from the backseat. "But he's a pretty decent guy with a good heart. He won't just dump you on the side of the road if you're in trouble."

"Well, if I do," Scott said, looking back at his grandmother, "she'll have company..."

Destini sat up and then turned toward Scott and leaned between the front seats to look out of the rear window at the headlights behind them. Oh boy, she smells good, thought Scott as he caught the scent of her perfume. He had no idea what it was, but the aroma was sweet and mild. He couldn't help but sneak a quick, sideways glance at her, since he hadn't wanted to take a good look at her earlier and be obvious about it.

She was wearing a tight, dark sweater – maybe blue, but he couldn't be sure in the dim light of the dashboard – and underneath that she had on a cream-colored turtleneck. Jeans and tennis shoes completed the outfit. Casual and comfortable, thought Scott – and perfect for a girl on the run...

His eyes moved up the back of her jeans, pausing slightly at her butt, then continuing up her back, shoulders, neck and … damn, busted… those dark eyes were looking right at him again, but this time she wasn't smiling.

He could feel his face flush immediately with embarrassment and he quickly turned his head back to the front. Good going dumbass, he told himself. "Sorry," he mumbled and then realized that was a pretty weak apology.

"Let me try that again," he said, this time turning back to look her directly in the eyes. "I'm sorry."

"That's okay, I understand," Destini said. "You're just trying to figure out what you're getting into."

What the hell did she mean by that, he thought. Was that some kind of double entendre? Was she teasing him now for looking at her?

"You're awful red," she giggled. "You're almost glowing in the dark there."

"It's not your fault Scott, you're just a man," his grandmother added.

"Thanks, Eli. You're not helping," he told her.

Destini cleared her throat and then bit her lower lip, as if trying to figure out the best way to explain things.

"I won't bore you with the details," she began, "but that's probably my husband Jerry back there. He's a real asshole, which is why I left him three days ago. He owns a few guns, but isn't a very good shot, so if he points one at you from a ways off, don't panic. I don't think he's going to try and stop us, so that's good. He just wants to keep me in his sights. I thought I'd lost him at the truck stop, but I guess not. We'll just have to look for an opportunity where I can jump out of the car while you keep going, then maybe he'll continue to follow you."

"Here's an idea," Scott interrupted. "Why don't we just go tell the police? They can lock him up for the night and work on getting you a restraining order."

"It's not that simple..." she started to say, but Scott broke in again.

"Oh, if there's one thing I've learned today from my wise and worldly grandmother, it's that everything – no matter how complicated on the surface – can be broken down into its most simplest form."

"I'm glad you think so, then maybe you can help break this down for me," Destini replied. "I came to this country six years ago to get away from my father. You see, he's the head of one of the biggest drug cartels in South America. He's a murderer and I don't want to be near that kind of lifestyle. I grew up in it and watched a lot of family members die. My sister and I were even kidnapped once when I was little. That's when I found out that business comes before family and paying ransoms wasn't an option. After the rapes and torture, she was killed and I was left for dead."

"Oh my Lord in heaven," Eli gasped.

Scott didn't say anything, but the look on his face must have betrayed his thoughts as he was trying to determine if the woman next to him was telling the truth or was just some psychotic drifter who was playing them – and maybe the guy behind them was even in on it somehow. Perhaps they were working some kind of set up…

Those thoughts were dispelled when Destini used her hands to pull the top of the turtle neck down. Across the entire stretch of her neck was a deep, faded scar, visible even in the low light – it stood out as a pale, jagged necklace against the bronze of her skin.

"Fuck…" Scott whispered reflexively before he could stop himself. To his surprise, she laughed.

"Oh, I'm just fine, that was a long time ago," she said. "And you know what they say, what doesn't kill you only makes you stronger. But, it doesn't necessarily make you smarter, so I went to school at the University of Arizona studying criminal law, funny, huh? Anyways, given all that I'd been through, I was a very private person. I didn't want or need friends, or so I thought. I never realized how lonely I was until I met Jerry.

"Let's just say I made a huge mistake," she continued, "and when I finally tried to correct it, he didn't take it well. It's not that he even loves me, but it's an ego thing. Nobody does that kind of thing to Jerry Rawlins. Unfortunately, I had told him about my past, and he used that information to sell me out."

"What do you mean, sell you out?" Asked Scott.

"Well Jerry's a lot of things – a liar, a cheat, a crooked lawyer, a wife beater – but he's not stupid," she said. "Although I can't prove it, I'm sure he's taken money to help some of the mules who smuggle the stuff across the border -- gotten them off on mistrials and technicalities, and in turn made contacts with a few of the bigger players. He managed to get in touch with some of my father's enemies who had put a price on my head because it was an embarrassment that they hadn't been able to kill a little 12-year-old girl. Plus, I'm the only child of his who's left alive – three brothers and a sister, all dead."

The steady rush of the desert wind off the windshield was the only sound as Destini fell silent. Scott looked at the headlights of the car behind them through the rear view mirror, and to his surprise, it wasn't fear, paranoia or apprehension that he felt. It was anger.

"You know something," Destini said after a few minutes. "Your grandmother's right. It is quite simple really. My husband's following me until the hired killers arrive so he can tell them where to find me and collect the reward."

It wasn't long before the small stretch of Arizona 85 intersected with I-10.

Scott was driving on mental autopilot as he merged back onto the interstate and barely registered the sign that showed Phoenix was only 34 miles east. He had been trying to grasp the enormity of everything Destini had revealed, but was having difficulty coming to terms with it all. It had definitely put his personal problems in a different perspective. Still, the whole story seemed so damn improbable to him, that he couldn't help but harbor some doubts.

He didn't know what she would have to gain by lying to them, but at the same time, he wasn't just going to buy into such a grandiose Hollywood B-movie script from a total stranger. Heck, she might actually be a complete nutjob. Anyhow, he thought, it really wasn't his concern either way. They would let her off somewhere up ahead and she could continue on her way – criminally insane husbands and third-world, drug dealing assassins notwithstanding.

Meanwhile, Eli and Destini had been chatting about clothing stores as if they were old friends on a country drive. The headlights behind them didn't seem to be as much an issue as finding a place that carried just the right dress in which Eli could meet Wendell for the first time. Scott marveled at how they could just completely block out the implications of Destini's little story and discuss such mundane matters.

Scott, however, wasn't afraid to admit to himself that he was pretty nervous about the possible gun-toting, spurned lover following them. He had decided to press the gas pedal to the floor and see if his little, faux sports car could outrun their shadow. If he happened to get pulled over by a cop along the way, well, that would be okay too at this point, he thought. But before he could tell his passengers to hold on, the sound of his own name brought him out of his confused self-reverie.

"Huh, what was that?" He asked.

"I said that I'm really sorry Scott," came the reply from the seat next to him.

"Sorry? About what? I didn't catch that," he said, turning his head toward her. She did look contemplative, almost downright remorseful, he thought. At least it was nice of her to apologize for getting them into a bad situation.

"I said I'm sorry to hear that your marriage is falling apart and that your wife kicked you out of the house," Destini said. "Guess you're kinda on the run like me."

Scott let out an exasperated sigh and looked back at Eli. He was met instead by the smiling countenance of Ricardo Montalban, as Eli hid her face behind the framed photo.

He turned back to Destini and said "It's actually not that bad. Just a little spat. Everything will work out fine, but, uh, thanks for your concern."

Eli spoke up from in back with a forced accent as she moved the picture to simulate it talking, "Somebody is living on fantasy island, and it is not me."

Destini started to laugh, but saw Scott's unamused reaction and quickly put a hand over her mouth to stop.

"It's funny, really," Scott said, "to think that when I woke up this morning just 12 hours ago, my whole world was completely normal."

"Normal, or routine?" Eli asked, putting Ricardo back into his seatbelt. "Can't you feel the difference? Don't you feel exhilarated and more alive now?"

"Sure, I understand people usually feel that way right before they die," Scott answered.

"You're back in the real world again Scott," Eli replied. "Enjoy the magic and mystery of it all. I may have been cooped up in an old nursing home, but you've been just as much a prisoner in your own house. Destini is the only one here who's living a real life..."

"With all due respect," Destini interrupted, "I have to disagree with you on that. I know what you're trying to say, but in reality, I would much rather be a prisoner in my own little world, in a safe, quiet house, with a loving family, and minus all this lively exhilaration. Trust me, it gets tired real fast."

"Thank you," Scott chimed in, nodding. "Give me a cold beer and an old Seinfeld rerun, and I'll be happy."

"No," Eli said, "you'll be temporarily satisfied, but you won't ever be happy."

"Damn, woman, can't you ever be wrong?" Scott asked with a smile, the frustration in his tone not quite genuine.

"I think you're both right," Destini said. "This one doesn't have a simple answer. It's not one way or the other. I think it needs to be a little combination of the secure and comfortable mixed with the exciting and unexpected. It all depends on the individual, doesn't it? Some people might truly believe they are happy in either situation, so who's to say that their feelings aren't real? If they believe it, despite what others on the outside looking in may think, then that's all that matters."

"That's pretty ambiguous, coming from a lawyer," Scott said. "I thought you could only argue one side of a case. Black or white, with no shades of gray."

"Depends if you're the prosecution or the defense," she quickly replied. "It's that 'reasonable doubt' clause that opens up the possibilities for a variety of beliefs."

"Damn!" Scott suddenly yelled, causing Destini to involuntarily raise her hands in front of her in a protective posture and shrink away from him.

"I'm sorry," he said, reflexively reaching a hand in her direction, but pulling it back when he realized he was about to touch her. "I've just been so preoccupied with this little conversation, that I don't know which of the headlights behind us now are the ones that were following us. There's a little more traffic around here. But maybe we can use that to our advantage and try to lose him. In any case, once I speed up, we'll see who comes after us."

"If you don't mind, I think I have a better idea," Destini offered. "Just let me look at the map real quick."

Scott waited as she turned on the dome light and flipped to the page for Arizona.

"Okay," she continued after a minute, "in about five miles we'll come up on Loop 101 North, which will take us around the city and connect with I-17. Put on your turn signal for the exit and slow down, but instead of turning off, just pull over into the median between the exit ramp and the highway. Then we'll sit and wait."

"So whoever's behind us won't know exactly which way we're going and will have to make the decision on one or the other," Scott said. "I'm impressed. And also a little frightened – that just seemed to come too naturally for you."

"Or," Eli broke in, "he could just pull in right behind us."

Destini laughed. "You're good. You think outside of the box. But Jerry won't have the balls for a direct confrontation right now. If he doesn't think that we already realize he's following us, then I think he'll take the exit because he won't want to be spotted."

"There's a flaw in your plan, though," Scott said. "All he'll have to do is pull over at the top of the ramp and wait. If we continue straight on the highway, he can just get right back on again."

"I've already thought of that. If he takes the exit, then you'll begin driving straight, but stop under the bridge. If he bites and comes back down the ramp on the other side, then we can slowly back up and take the exit. If he doesn't, then I'll get out of the car under the bridge where he can't see, and then you'll take off and he'll take the ramp down and follow you again."

"You're something else," Scott said, shaking his head as he looked at her. "But what will you do then? Where are you going?"

Destini only shrugged in return, as if she either didn't know the answer or felt it best not to divulge that information to him.

The sound of a cell phone ringing startled all of them. It was coming from Destini's waistband. She reached down, unclipped the phone and read the illuminated display, then put it back on the clip without answering. It continued to ring. Scott counted 14 rings in all before the caller finally gave up. It was a little unnerving on top of everything else. Why wouldn't she answer her phone? Either she didn't want to talk with whoever it might be, or she didn't want anybody overhearing what she might have to say. Either way, he thought, it's not a good sign. For all he knew it could be Jerry calling to ask her to have him slow down because he was losing them in the traffic.

He was just about to say something, but Eli beat him to it.

"It's none of our business Scott."

He thought about arguing that fact, since she had made it their business by getting in the car, but then he saw the sign for Exit 133B and the loop. He started braking, keeping a close eye on the rearview.

"Hey, what kind of car does he drive?" Scott asked.

"We've got three – but he's probably in the Ford 150 or the King Cab; he likes his trucks."

Another thought flashed through Scott's mind, if they had three cars, why was she on foot?

He put on his turn signal and eased the Saturn over into the far right lane, slowing down a lot more than he normally would. There weren't any cars exiting behind him, so he could afford to take it almost to a crawl. At the last second, he turned the steering wheel to the left and smoothly brought the car to a stop in the median between the interstate and the off ramp.

It didn't even take a full minute before Destini said, "There he goes. He's such a dumbass."

Scott only caught a momentary glimpse of a large pickup speeding past them. He couldn't even make out the driver's features. The truck kept going and Scott found it awkward that the driver didn't even make an attempt to brake once he realized that he was passing them.

"Go ahead and take the exit here," Destini instructed him.

"Wouldn't that be too obvious?" Scott asked in return. "Why don't we wait a few minutes for him to turn around on the next exit, while we continue straight? He wouldn't expect that. Or, we could even take this exit and get back on I-10 westbound."

"You're driving," she said with a shrug. "Whichever way you want to go."

"Well," said Eli, "Wendell and I aren't getting any younger, so whichever way will get us to Kansas the fastest is fine with me. It's not like Destini's husband knows where we're headed."

Scott reached over towards Destini's lap and was met with a cold glare.

"The map," he explained, allowing her to pick it up and hand it to him. He studied it, handed it back to her and then swung the car over to the ramp.

"We'll jump on the loop here and take it to I-17. From there, we'll get on 40."

Receiving no objections from either of his passengers, he turned onto the loop and kept going.

They drove in silence again, each lost in their own thoughts. Scott occasionally checked the mirrors, but gave up when he realized that he wouldn't be able to tell if anybody was after them or not.

"How long have you been married?"

The question caught him off guard. He gave Destini a short glance, but no answer.

"Fifteen years," volunteered Eli. "No children. One dog. And a parakeet."

"The bird died this summer," Scott said dryly.

"I think I've overstayed my welcome," Destini said, changing the subject. "I can't thank you enough for the ride and for losing that jackass of a husband. You can go ahead and let me out at the next gas station."

Scott and Eli both answered at the same exact time, their words tripping over each other's.

"If that's what you want," Scott replied.

"Oh no, don't be silly," Eli said.

After a brief pause, Scott added, "You don't have to get out. We're going this way anyhow and … well, you can just stay with us instead of trying to find a new ride."

"I think I'm making you uncomfortable Scott, and you've been so kind. I don't want to do that."

"As I recall," he replied, "somebody once said that you have to get out of your comfort zone a little and mix the secure and comfortable with the exciting and unexpected."

"I can't believe you're using my own words against me now Scott Allan Miles," said Destini. "Maybe you should have been a lawyer."

They looked at each other and smiled.

In the backseat, Eli and Ricardo were smiling as well.

CHAPTER FIVE

The loop around Phoenix was roughly 20 miles, and then they were northbound on I-17, but their progress was slowed shortly after getting on the interstate. The flashing barriers signaling road construction forced all traffic into one lane at a greatly reduced speed.

Destini, apparently weary of conversation, had turned her back and was leaning on the door with her face pressed against her window and upturned to the stars. Eli was also leaning against the side of the car behind Scott, and he thought he could hear her faintly snoring. It was only approaching 8 p.m., but Scott also felt worn out from the day's events.

He yawned and turned the radio on low, but was greeted by static. He punched the scan button and let it cycle through three country stations before he stopped it on an 80's new wave classic by Duran Duran.

Traffic had now slowed to about 15 mph and he was stuck in between two large semis and choking on exhaust fumes.

"Man," he muttered to himself.

"Not the patient type?" Destini asked without looking around.

"Just getting tired. Sucking down carbon monoxide will do that. How about you? You tired or hungry?"

"A little of both," she replied.

"I saw a billboard for some restaurants up ahead in Black Canyon City, about 20 miles – or an hour at this rate," Scott said.

"That would be nice, if you don't mind," Destini said. "Maybe we can hit a drive through or something."

"Wow, I think we just had a normal conversation," said Scott. "No mention of guns, drugs, mafia, the meaning of happiness or anything out of the ordinary."

"Very funny," she replied. "I guess this is all just a little too much for you."

"Are you kidding? My grandmother is a little too much for me. The rest of this stuff is just way over my head."

"Boy, she is something alright. Do you mind me asking how old she is?"

"She's 85 and it just so happens to be her birthday today, which is why I'm out here in the middle of the freakin' desert fulfilling her crazy wish to meet with her internet boyfriend."

"That's sweet," Destini remarked in a hushed tone. "And I thought it was because your wife had kicked your ass out of the house."

"Well, that's part of it too…"

They both laughed and Scott couldn't help but think what a beautiful smile she had. Damn, watch it, he told himself. There you go again. Sure, she's attractive, but this is no time for a full-blown midlife crisis. It's been a confusing day – no need to make it worse.

"So…" he started, wanting to get the subject onto something harmless and neutral, but not quite sure what he was going to say, "um, what kind of music do you like?"

Geez, that was lame, he thought. Might as well ask her what her favorite color is. He suddenly felt like a dopey schoolboy with a crush.

"I like early Eminem," she answered. "Do you have any of his stuff?"

"Oh my God, you like that crap?" He said before he could stop himself. Way to go, insult her taste in music while you're sitting there in your little black AC/DC T-Shirt. "Uh, I mean, that's surprising, I thought he appealed mostly to… um, I think I better just shut up now…"

"Oh come on," she said, "he's actually very talented and he's using that whole image for marketing, just like Elvis did back when you were growing up."

He looked over at her and she was staring at him with a huge grin on her face.

"Good one," he said. "I deserved that."

His own smile disappeared rapidly, however.

"Um, can I ask you something?"

"Sure," she replied. "Anything you want."

"The only thing I want to know is what this Jerry looks like."

He saw her bewildered expression, so he continued, "Is he tall, with short, black hair and a beard?"

"Oh my God!" She yelled and spun around to see what Scott was looking at. There, driving slowly on the shoulder of the road next to them, was the man in the pickup that had gone past them half an hour earlier on the other highway. He smiled and waved at Scott and Destini, then sped up out of their sight.

"He was kind of cute, I don't know why you would have left him," Scott remarked.

Destini, who was biting her lower lip, gave him a look as if he were crazy – her eyes widening.

"Sorry," Scott said. "I tend to make stupid comments when I'm extremely nervous."

"Stop the car, Scott."

"What? There's a big truck behind me."

"We're only going ten miles per hour," she said and reached over to press the hazard lights button. "Slow down all the way and stop."

He gradually braked to a standstill and Destini opened her door and got out. She reached behind her seat and grabbed a small traveling bag that Scott hadn't noticed, then stood and looked at him with an expression he couldn't quite make out.

"Thank you," she said. "You'll be better off this way."

Before he could think of anything to say, she turned and started walking down the long line of cars behind them. A blast from the horn of the semi on his bumper got his attention and he turned off his hazards and started rolling again.

"What was that? Where are we?" Eli said as she straightened up and rubbed her eyes. As she gained a clearer focus, she noticed the now empty passenger seat.

"What the heck did you do with her Scott?" She demanded.

He looked in the rearview and met her eyes. "She got out. She's gone."

The resignation in his voice persuaded Eli not to push the issue and neither one said anything until they reached the Black Canyon City exit almost forty minutes later. As Scott turned off the interstate he saw the maroon-colored truck that had pulled alongside them. It was sitting at a Texaco, its driver standing in a pay phone booth watching the cars at the off-ramp intersection. Scott felt a momentary urge to drive over there and confront the guy, but held back. If he thought Destini was still traveling with them, then that might give her a better chance to put some more distance between herself and her stalking husband.

He drove past the gas station in search of a place he and Eli could have dinner. There were a few popular fast food eateries in the area, but he opted for one that looked like an old-style American diner with the silver trailer façade. His mind was still on Destini, however, and he was running through a number of possible scenarios in which they could go back and try to find her, even though he knew it was too late. It bothered him though that he couldn't stop thinking about her and wishing he had said or done something different…something that might have made her stay.

This is so unbelievable, he thought, telling himself that he should be thinking about his wife and saving his marriage. Yet instead, he was more upset about the fact that this woman he just met and barely even knew was gone. Why should it matter so much? There really wasn't much he could have done to help her, and like she said, it was probably for the best as far as he and Eli were concerned.

"I don't think they have car hops here, Scott," he heard Eli say and he realized he had been parked in front of the diner and staring off vacantly.

"Oh, does that mean if a woman comes up to my window and asks me what I would like, she's not talking about food?"

"Well at least you've got your sense of humor back," Eli said. "I'll tell you what I would like – a big, greasy cheeseburger on a toasted bun. I haven't had one of those in years."

Scott got out of the car and then tilted his seat forward to help Eli out. It sure hadn't taken him long to develop a new paranoid habit, he thought, as he scanned the parking lot and surrounding area for anybody or anything suspicious. He noted a man and a woman in a dark sedan parked in an adjacent lot on the side of a Burger King. It looked like they were both talking into cell phones. Ordinarily he wouldn't have thought twice about seeing such a thing, but after today, it struck him as a bit odd.

Maybe it's a new kind of phone sex, he thought and chuckled, then took Eli's arm and helped her into the diner.

The overpowering smell of sizzling fat hit them full force as they entered. A shiny, aluminum-topped counter stretched across the front and then down both sides of the diner in the shape of a horseshoe. A few folks were sitting on the stools along the counter, but most were packed into the booths that formed the outer ring of the eatery.

A "Please Wait to be Seated" sign on a thin metal stand blocked their way. Scott found it amusing that somebody, who had obviously waited a little too long, had written "don't" just over and between the first two words. He didn't see a waitress anywhere, so he guided Eli to an open booth to their right. He felt that was a good choice so he could keep an eye on the car as well.

They sat down and waited … and waited … and waited. Just as Scott was about to get up and grab the nearest employee, their server rushed over with two complimentary glasses of ice water. The man placed the drinks in front of them, offered the customary "hello my name is" Waiter 101 training spiel and handed them menus. Another oddity, thought Scott, as he noticed the little lapel pin on the man's red vest said "Bob," yet he had introduced himself as "Ben."

Okay, now you're losing it, he told himself. Before you sit here for the next twenty minutes and start having more paranoid delusions there's a quick and easy way to clear this up.

"Um, I'm sorry, what did you say your name was again?" He asked the waiter.

The response he got certainly didn't make him feel any better as the man actually looked down at his name tag before answering.

"It's Ben," he replied, "but I did it again and grabbed my brother's vest. He works here too. Well, unless you need anything else for now, I'll be right back."

"Did that seem just a little weird to you," he asked Eli after their apparently absent-minded server had wandered back toward the kitchen area.

"Oh good, you noticed his shoes too," she replied. "I didn't want to say anything and have you think I'm some old biddy who's seeing things that don't make sense."

"Yeah... his shoes," Scott muttered, sipping the cold water. "Um, what exactly do you think about them?"

"Oh, they're very nice, but why would somebody working for tips in a diner be wearing a three hundred dollar pair of Tanino Criscis and expensive slacks? Plus, he had on a class ring from some college. Did you also notice he didn't even have a pad and pencil to take our order?"

Scott's eyes literally widened as he listened to her. He was at a momentary loss for words as he tried to digest all of her observations.

"You watch a lot of Crime TV, don't you?" He finally asked. "Okay, how's this sound – it's Sunday, he just came from Church, so that's why he's dressed up. He hadn't been scheduled to work, but his brother got sick, so he's pulling the shift for him. And as for the ring… heck, maybe he's the manager here and just filling in at the tables because they're a little short of help."

Eli raised her eyebrows and replied, "Pretty good, but don't tell me what you think. Tell me what you feel."

Scott didn't hesitate.

"I think I'm pretty damn hungry, but I feel like we should get the hell out of here."

Eli nodded and they got up to leave. He looked around the diner but didn't see the waiter. For that matter, he thought, there was no staff to be seen anywhere – no grill cook, no cashier, nobody… only the customers, a few of whom also appeared to be looking around for some service.

Screw being casual and inconspicuous, he thought, as he took his grandmother's elbow and hurried her out of the diner as if they were running in a three-legged race. At the car, he helped her get back into the passenger seat and then took a quick look back at the diner. The dual-named waiter was watching them from the window at their booth with a confused look on his face. I know how you feel buddy, Scott thought as he walked around the front of the Saturn and got in.

He backed the car out and almost hit a small Honda that was driving past. The other vehicle swerved out of the way and the driver blared his horn at Scott.

"Yeah, yeah, yeah," Scott muttered as he righted the Saturn and headed back toward the interstate. The light at the only intersection between them and the highway had just turned red, but he floored the gas pedal and ran it anyway.

"Wooo, this is fun," Eli said, giggling as she looked out of her window.

Scott merely kept going, slowing only a fraction as he made the turn for the on ramp, then speeding up again. The road construction had ended just before Black Canyon City, so he was able to let the engine out and soon they were cruising at 85 mph, a good twenty miles above the legal speed limit.

He maintained that speed for about 10 minutes and then began to brake rapidly, making sure there were no cars anywhere close behind.

"Hang on little miss excitement," he told Eli as he slowed the Saturn down on the open road and turned the headlights off. Eli gasped at how dark it became. When Scott had slowed enough to turn, he veered from the left lane into the dry, desert strip separating the east and westbound lanes. With only a distant set of headlights coming from the opposite direction, Scott kept his lights off and crossed both westbound lanes and then turned the Saturn around on the opposite shoulder. He was about to cut the engine, when he decided to move off the shoulder completely for good measure. Without lights, he didn't want someone coming up from behind and sideswiping them.

He eased the car off the hardtop and onto the coarse ground, then turned the ignition off.

Eli started to say something, but was silenced by a quick "shhhhh" from Scott.

They sat and waited, neither really sure for what. Within two minutes, an 18-wheeler and a pickup passed them in the westbound lane. Shortly after that they saw a pair of high beams rapidly approaching from the direction they had just come. The car had to be going at least 90 mph, if not more, Scott calculated. In fact, it flew by so fast that they couldn't even tell what kind of vehicle it was. He thought it was probably a truck, because the headlights were higher off the ground than a regular passenger car, but it could have been an SUV or a jeep.

"And I thought you were the only crazy driver on the road," Eli said. "He sure was in a hurry."

"Hmmm, think maybe he lost something?" Scott asked.

He waited until the other vehicle's taillights were completely out of sight, which didn't take long, then started up his SC2 and pulled back onto the interstate.

"I think we'll get a hotel room back in Black Canyon City for the night and order in some pizza," Scott said.

"You want to go look for her, don't you?" Eli asked.

"Yes," he answered, "but there's no point. Let's just get a good night's sleep. We've got some serious driving ahead of us tomorrow."

He drove the speed limit back to Black Canyon City and couldn't help but check his mirrors every few minutes, but it didn't appear that they were being followed. At the same exit they had left a short while before, he scanned what hotels he could see on both sides of the interstate, and settled on a little, nondescript locally-owned establishment on his right, rather than one of the bigger, major chains.

He also didn't want to cross the bridge and get near the diner again, even though he realized that was silly – he had let his imagination get the better of him on that one, although he still couldn't quite explain the speeding car well enough to satisfy himself. But, it could have been nothing more than somebody in a hurry to get home taking advantage of the desolate highway, he tried again to convince himself.

He parked in front of the L-shaped motel's office, which looked no bigger than a converted room itself at the bottom tip of the L. Two neon signs whose luminance had long ago dissipated into the desert dust hung crookedly from the window. The formerly-red-but-now-diffused pink looking one said "Office" and the once-green-turned-grayish- lime one said "Vacancy."

Scott smiled at the nostalgia it evoked in him and made him think of the few trips his parents had taken him and his sister on during their childhood, when they had stayed in places like this. The motels were bigger and brighter in his memories, but he realized they were probably just as run-down and dirty as this one, only they had been seen through the wondrous eyes of a child.

"Scott," Eli said hesitatingly, "I wanted to get out of the nursing home so I wouldn't have to sleep another night in a small, crappy room."

That made him laugh.

"But Ricardo likes it … look at him, all happy and excited to be here," Scott said, nodding back at the photo still propped up behind them. "Wait here and I'll go get us a room with a Jacuzzi."

"That's not funny," Eli said as Scott got out of the car and went to the office door. Assuming it was unlocked, he grabbed the knob and pushed inward on the door as he kept walking. He managed to slightly turn his shoulder when it dawned on him that the door wasn't opening and so he wound up only hitting the side of his face against the wood. The loud thud of his body banging against the door made the collision sound more serious than it really was.

"Now that's funny," Eli yelled from the car.

Scott backed up with a pissed-off look on his face, half of which was stinging from the collision. He looked at the window and that's when he noticed the one non-illuminated sign taped to the lower left corner – "Please ring bell for manager."

He pressed the buzzer next to the door and shook his head slowly from side-to-side as if to wonder, "What else could possibly happen today?"

"Hang on!" A woman's voice called out from inside. "I heard you the first time, no need to break down the goddamn door!" This was followed by a barely audible "fuckin' idiot…" as her footsteps approached.

Just smile, be polite and get a room, Scott told himself, trying to remember if he had packed the Tums in his bathroom kit.

He heard the sound of the lock clicking and then a large blue-haired woman in a faded, yellow flowery dress yanked the door wide open. Scott guessed she was in her mid-60s at least, but then decided she could be ten years either way, give or take – it was hard to tell as she looked about as washed out as everything else. However, the utter surprise and embarrassment on her face when she saw him made Scott feel a little better – at least he wasn't the only one feeling stupid.

"Oh my," she stammered, "I'm sorry, I thought you were that lousy, drunken husband of mine come back to ask for more money. Please come in, we'll get you a nice room right away."

Scott was on the verge of one of his trademark smartass comments -- "Oh, are you going to make me a reservation at the Sheraton across the street?" -- but decided to keep his mouth shut for a change. He just wanted to crash -- to close his eyes and try to forget the day's craziness.

"Hey," the woman said with a pause as she went behind the counter, "you don't drink do you?"

Oh well, he had tried…

"Of course not," Scott answered, unable to stop himself. "That takes too long and then you smell bad. I just ride the white horse."

She looked at him suspiciously.

"Oh, okay, you got me," he added. "Sometimes I do a little crack too."

"Well, just as long as you don't drink," the older lady said absently, shuffling through some papers under the counter.

He quickly and quietly filled out the guest registration form, paid with his credit card and was handed the key to room 27 -- because, he thought, obviously one through 26 were full. With a tired smile he thanked the blue-haired lady and stepped back out to the car.

It was empty.

He stood in the still open doorway a moment, then looked side to side at the deserted parking lot. He turned back to the car, placed a hand on each side of his temple and started slowly rubbing them with his two forefingers.

"No, no, no, no, no…" Scott repeated.

"Are you having a nervous breakdown?" He heard Eli ask from behind him.

"Yes, yes, yes, yes, yes…" He answered, eyes still on the Saturn.

"I'm Sorry. I followed you in and got a soda from the vending machine in the office. I can't believe you didn't notice. Thanks a lot. Somebody could have kidnapped me and you'd have never known."

"Yeah," he sighed, "but all I'd have to do is wait right here and they'd bring you back within five minutes."

He helped her back in the passenger seat, not that she really needed it, but more because it was just the proper thing to do. Then he got in and drove to the other end of the hotel and stopped in front of their room. He had a brief impulse to park five or six spaces away as he conjured up a vision of some South American mafia heavies kicking in their door in the middle of the night and spraying machine gun fire around the room.

"God, I have got to get to bed, my head is going to explode," he said.

"No way, you promised me dinner," Eli said.

"Don't worry, I'll get you something," he replied, turning the engine off and pulling the lever under the dash to pop the trunk.

He went to the motel door first, unlocked it and turned the lights on for Eli. It was about what he expected -- cramped; with two single beds, a small stand between them with a lamp and phone, and a dresser with a TV on the opposite wall. It was the basic architecture of hotel design -- simple but effective. He was impressed however to find it all very clean, almost immaculate.

After he had carried their bags in, he told Eli he was going back out real quick to find a drive through and bring her back that greasy cheeseburger.

"I hope you find her," Eli said.

Scott merely nodded, grabbed the room key and instructed Eli not to open the door for anyone or for any reason.

He stepped back out and noticed for the first time how chilly it had gotten. Damn, that's what he had forgotten -- a jacket. He hurried to the car and got it started, then turned the heater on high. He hesitated before backing out and wondered if he shouldn't just bring Eli with him, but then decided she would be safer here in case spurned Jerry with the gun was still around.

CHAPTER SIX

He drove slowly up one side of the street and then down the other. It wasn't quite as busy as before. There were several fast food places he could have easily turned into, but he was looking for something entirely different. However, there was no sign of either a maroon truck or a diminutive hitchhiker. He was so focused on his search that he didn't realize he had subconsciously driven right back to the diner they had fled earlier. He pulled into the same parking spot up front, killed the engine and lights, and then sat there watching the windows. It was hard to really see anything though, because the diner sat up on a higher level.

What the hell, he thought, let's take another look inside. He could always tell Ben that his grandmother had become ill and he had taken her home.

He entered the diner again and his eyes scanned the interior: a few customers here and there, but not even half as many as before. That's what you get for poor service, he thought, still unable to see anybody that looked like they actually worked there. He shrugged and made his way back to the same booth and slid down onto the black leather seats.

He was absently playing with the salt and pepper shakers on the red-and-black checkered tablecloth when he sensed someone standing off to the side. He turned and looked up. It was a young waitress and she was smiling at him.

"Sorry to bring you back to the real world," she said. "You looked like you were in a much better place."

"I was," Scott nodded. "I was in a land full of dancing cheeseburgers and singing French fries."

"Delirious with hunger, huh? Okay I get it -- sorry to make you wait, how many cheeseburgers and fries would you like?"

"Two orders of each, to go, along with two cokes, please," he said, then casually added, "Oh, and is Bob still here?"

The waitress gave him a funny look and then answered, "Bob hasn't been here in weeks, the little jerk. I'm not even sure if he works here anymore."

"Oh," Scott said. "Well, how about Ben? Is he still here?"

"Um, no… I, uh, don't think so," she said, putting the eraser end of her pencil in her mouth and chewing on it as she glanced around.

That touched a nerve, thought Scott. Better do something fast or she'll bolt for the back and maybe call Ben and… hey… that's an idea…

Scott motioned for the waitress to come closer to the table and he said in a low, secretive voice.

"Did our mutual friend leave his business card by any chance? I have some pretty important information for him and I need to get in touch with him."

"I think he did," the waitress whispered back conspiratorially. "Let me go check."

She started for the counter, but paused and then turned around and came back to the booth.

"Did you really want the burgers and fries, sir? Or should I just get you the phone number?"

Scott laughed. "Oh yeah, I definitely want the burgers and fries. Thanks."

That seemed to put her at ease a little more as she smiled again and hurried off.

As he watched her go back to the kitchen area, Scott couldn't help but wonder yet again just what the hell he was doing. This could really turn out bad because he didn't know who or what he was dealing with. Perhaps he should just forget about it and go. He was taking a huge risk now that he knew this Ben guy really wasn't a waiter but someone who was actually keeping tabs on them. There's some serious stuff going on around here and if you're smart you'll walk now and not look back, that little voice inside his head was urging.

For the first time, as he sat there waiting and watching each second tick by on the big clock above the counter, he felt afraid. Truly afraid. It wasn't just paranoia anymore. As the minutes passed, that feeling grew more intense. First five minutes. Then six. Then seven gone by and no sign of the waitress. He knew he could still just get up and walk out, but maybe she was trying to find the number Ben had left behind and having the cook slap his burgers on the grill. He would wait and give her the benefit of the doubt, but he also knew that wasn't the real reason he wasn't going to skip out.

It was Destini. Plain and simple.

Other than looking for Jerry, this might be his only possible link to find her somehow. It was all he had to go on considering that her husband was probably a hundred miles out of Black Canyon City by now.

So, even though his palms were getting sweaty and he had a nauseous feeling rising in his stomach, he could not make himself get up and leave. My God, he thought, do I want to see her again so damn bad that I'm willing to get involved in whatever's going on and maybe even put myself and Eli at risk?

He didn't even have to think about the answer to that question. He just smiled and picked up the salt and pepper shakers again. Hmmm… now there was a kind of symbolism, he thought.

Eleven minutes had passed on the clock when his waitress came back out of the kitchen. It looked like she had neither his food nor the information he had asked for. Even her smile was gone.

She came over carrying an icy water pitcher and a glass, and took the seat in the booth opposite him.

"Your burgers are almost done, but I've looked everywhere and I can't find that business card," she said. "I'm so sorry. My manager must have taken it and he's on break and won't be back for a little while."

"How long?" Scott asked.

"Maybe 15 or 20 minutes," she answered, her fingers tracing abstract patterns through the condensation on the pitcher.

"I'll wait."

That brought the smile back, and a look that was undeniably pure relief. It was that look that told Scott all he needed to know, and the fact that her hand was still a little unsteady as she poured him a glass of water. She gave him another smile as she left to attend the other customers, but Scott felt that second one was a bit forced.

He smiled to himself because he was sure he already knew how this was going to play out, and that gave him a small sense of satisfaction. He was tired of being the mouse. Although he still wasn't the cat, he was … well, kind of like the cheese in the mousetrap, he thought. And someone was coming to take the bait.

If he had it figured correctly, the waitress and the manager – who was no doubt hiding in the back – did indeed have "Ben's" business card. Only, instead of giving it to him, they had called Ben themselves, as instructed, to tell him that Scott had come back. Of course, Ben had told them to go slow on the burgers and stall until he could get there – in 15 or 20 minutes. It all seemed pretty obvious to Scott. The only thing that even mildly surprised him was the fact that although he felt positive about this, he was still going to sit there and wait for the guy. It even seemed crazy to him when he started to think about it, but he was determined to see it through. All he had to do was picture Destini's big, brown eyes. Nope, he wasn't going anywhere.

He was in the middle of a huge yawn about ten minutes later when the overhead fluorescent lights behind him were suddenly blocked out and a large shadow fell across his table.

"Wow, you made some pretty good time getting here," Scott said, not bothering to turn around. "Of course you really didn't have to rush. But I'm awful glad to see you."

"Why is that?" came the curious reply.

"Because maybe now that you're here, they'll bring out my damn cheeseburger. I'm starving."

No laugh. Not even a chuckle. Great – one of the all-business rockhead types, thought Scott. Probably going to try and be all intimidating and threatening too.

Ben walked slowly to the opposite booth and sat down, never once taking his eyes off of Scott. The fake-waiter smile from earlier was gone. He was taller than Scott remembered; sitting evenly across from each other he was at least a good six inches above Scott's 5'8 frame. His face was relatively young, late 20's maybe, but hardened and leathery looking – like he spent too much time in the sun. His short-cropped hair was a streaky brownish-blonde. He looked to Scott like a body-building, surfer dude in a tight, white button-down shirt that was making him uncomfortable.

They stared at each other for a while in silence. Buddy, I've been married too many damn years to crack like this, Scott felt like saying. Instead, he let out a sigh, which halfway through turned into another yawn. Perfect, he thought – that'll send the message that I'm getting bored.

Surfer Ben frowned.

"This is a waste of my time," Ben finally said. "You can't help me."

And with that, he got up and left.

That took Scott by surprise. The man has got to be joking; just another tactic to try and make him start volunteering information. But no, he was actually walking to the door.

Opening the door.

Leaving the diner now.

Holy shit, he was starting his car.

Fuck, fuck, fuck, Scott repeated in his head. Should he run after him or is that exactly what he's wanting? He heard the car pull out and then drive away. Son of a bitch. Well this certainly wasn't the way he had hoped their meeting would go – although the beach boy was probably right: now that Destini was no longer with him, he probably wouldn't be of much help to him.

Scott was suddenly mad at himself. What the hell just happened? He had tried playing a game he didn't know the rules to and got his ass handed to him. Apparently Ben made the first move by showing up and Scott had failed to make a move and thereby lost his turn.

Cue the waitress, he thought, as he saw her approach with a large bag and two drinks.

"That'll be $12.75," she said, placing the items on his table.

"Excellent," Scott replied with a big smile and made a point of searching his pants pockets for his wallet. All is not lost, he told himself, she might still have Ben's number. He stalled, wondering how he was going to ask for it again, or maybe he should just ask her to call him again? He was too damn tired and hungry to think of anything clever to say to try and get any more information, but fortunately he didn't have to as the waitress had obviously never played this game before either and felt she had to make some conversation to fill the silence with the customer.

"You and the FBI guy sure didn't have much to say," she offered unwittingly.

"Just enough to get the point across," Scott answered, then quickly added, "And he did say for you to go ahead and give me his card now."

"Yes, I know, he already told me that on the phone earlier," she said, and then leaned down to whisper, "it's in the bag."

Scott couldn't help but smile for real. That tricky bastard. No wonder he carried out his dramatic little exit all the way to the end. He pulled the wallet from his back pocket, handed her a twenty and asked for five back. Then he took his change, the big white sack and the cardboard tray holding the two drinks and left.

Man, Eli is going to be pissed, he thought as he drove back to the motel. As he turned into the parking area, he noticed a big RV and two motorcycles had now pulled up digs in front of some of the other rooms. This time he actually did park two doors down from his own room. Not like the FBI couldn't find him if they really wanted to, he thought. That's when the enormity of it slapped him in the face. The freakin' F-B-I. Damn. Are they after Destini? Are they after Jerry? Are they hoping to catch the cartel killers? Tune in tomorrow, Scott thought, as we take another exciting journey with… ah fuck it, even the jokes in his head didn't sound funny anymore.

He walked down to door 27, let himself in and quickly proceeded to drop the tray holding the plastic cups filled with Coke on the worn, green carpet. The lids popped off both tops and sprayed crushed ice and liquid all over the floor.

"I have that effect on men," Destini said, flashing a brilliantly white smile as she looked up at him from the bed closest to the door where she was casually reading a magazine. She was wearing only a tight, black halter top and gray gym shorts, laying on her stomach with her legs crossed up behind her.

"Wow," was all Scott could manage to say. "Woooow."

Trying to recover after the door slammed shut behind him, he added, "Well, I will say this -- a lot of men want you."

He walked over to her and handed her the business card from out of the sack as Eli emerged from the bathroom.

"Thank God," Eli said, "I was about to eat my toothpaste."

He handed Eli the food and then grabbed a towel from the rack. While Destini stared at the FBI agent's card with a look of concern and Eli unwrapped her burger and set her fries on the night stand, he picked up the spilled cups and put the towel over the wet spot on the carpet.

He heard Eli trying to say something, but it came out garbled because of the food she was eating. He looked over and she had her hand out to him with something in it. Confused, he went over and put his out. She dropped two quarters in his open palm.

"Not much of a tipper, eh?" Scott joked.

"Need soda… vending machine… go now…" Eli replied between chewing as she motioned toward the door.

"Grandma, you can't even get a bag of Cheetos for 50 cents anymore, but I'll spot you this time."

He looked back over at Destini. She was still there. He wasn't dreaming it.

"What are you doing here?" He asked, unable to suppress his smile.

"Why'd you come back for me?" She asked in return with a grin.

"I… I don't know," Scott said hesitantly, looking into those eyes again and suddenly knowing exactly why.

"Ah, so you admit that you did come back for me," Destini said.

It took him a moment to regain his composure from the out-of-control thoughts suddenly filling his head. He just looked at her in disbelief – not of the fact that she was there, but of the way he felt just looking at her. He didn't want her to disappear again … ever.

Finally, he sighed and then said in a very somber tone: "Of course I came back for you. There's a big reward out for you, so can I have that card back? I need to make a quick phone call…"

Destini shrugged and held it out to him. He took it from her and headed to the door.

"Should I be worried," Destini called after him.

"Only if I don't come back with a soda," he answered.

"If you don't come back with a soda," said Eli, "you better be worried."

Scott didn't look back or say anything else. He just had to get the hell out of there … fast. He needed some air. He needed some time to think. As soon as the door shut behind him, he leaned back against it and looked up at the sky.

"Oh my God, I love her," he whispered.

But as soon as the words were spoken aloud, he started trying to convince himself otherwise. No way, he thought, it's impossible. You don't just fall in love like that. It doesn't work that way. Hell, you don't even know her. Besides, you're fuckin' married, you idiot.

He shook his head as if to snap out of his self-imposed daze and then walked the short distance left to the last room, number 30. Next to it, under a small tarp overhang was an ice machine and a vending machine. The soda machine was so old that it wouldn't accept dollar bills. He dug through some change in his pocket and came up with enough for two sodas and realized that he hadn't even asked Destini what she would like.

He stood in front of the machine staring at the selections. But the lit buttons blurred indistinguishably as his focus drifted back to Destini. He hadn't quite expected this, but then that voice in the back of his head told him that was bullshit. He had felt something from the very first moment he laid eyes on her.

She was pretty; but so what? There were plenty of pretty girls everywhere.

Maybe he was subconsciously trying to create a distraction for himself to get his mind off of the trouble with Kate earlier that day.

Maybe he was confusing what was simply a physical attraction with something else because he didn't want to admit he was just a typical guy lusting after a beautiful woman.

Maybe he really was going through some kind of a mid-life crisis spurred on by his grandmother's birthday and her desire for one last adventure.

Or maybe – just maybe – he was falling in love.

That thought scared and excited him at the same time. This isn't something I was looking for, he thought, it just happened. So maybe it is real. But, he decided, the best thing to do right now was absolutely nothing. Just wait and let things sort themselves out naturally. As long as she was here, he wouldn't spend a lot of time psychoanalyzing himself. Just enjoy it, he told himself, because let's face it, she's got a lot of issues she's dealing with herself – she's married too and she's on the run. Chances are that after tomorrow he'd never see her again. Besides, and he couldn't help but laugh out loud at this thought, what the hell makes you think that she even feels remotely attracted to you?

His body shook with an involuntary chill from the cold and he felt goose bumps raise on his arms. Brrrrr… get the soda and get back inside.

He decided to get a Coke and a Diet Coke, figuring he could share the first one with Eli.

He felt more goose bumps tingling on the back of his neck and suddenly had the strange sensation that it wasn't from the cold air. He slowly turned around, a soda can in each hand, but there was nothing behind him. Great, I'm starting to spook myself now, he thought. He was about to turn back toward the room when a dim light caught his attention.

There was a pickup truck parked in the gravel just off the main road, angled with the front of the cab pointed in his direction. It must have been sitting there the whole time because he hadn't heard it pull in. Then again, he probably wouldn't have heard a swarm of angry wasps over his head just now.

The lone driver had flicked on the dome light and it looked like he was motioning for Scott to come over. Well, it had to be one of the ice cream men, he thought – either Ben or Jerry. Not that it mattered much; both carried guns and neither were on his list of people he really wanted to chat with at this point. He didn't feel like he had much of a choice however – if he went back to the room, the guy may actually come knocking on the door and that would risk exposing Destini, if he didn't already know she was there.

He started toward the truck and realized his legs were shaking a little. His heart was pounding a little faster too. It pissed him off to think that the guy in the truck could probably tell by his unsteady walk that he was nervous and afraid.

About halfway there, Scott could tell that it wasn't Ben in the truck, although the man seemed just as tall, he was a lot skinnier. He had almost hoped it would be the FBI agent, because the alternative seemed like the more unstable option – a crooked, spurned lawyer. Instinctively he walked to the passenger side and got in. Although the engine wasn't running, Jerry had the key turned enough so that the heater was on and Scott welcomed the steady flow of warmth.

He looked over at Jerry, but the man was staring straight out the windshield, seemingly transfixed on the front door of Room 27, or maybe it only appeared that way to Scott.

Not this quiet, manly bravado shit again, he thought. Fine… I'll say something.

"You're the guy who passed me and waved from the shoulder of the road, and then Vicky jumped out of the car," he said, hoping Jerry didn't notice the slight pause before he came up with that fake name. He didn't want Jerry to know that he knew anything at all about him – his name, his occupation, the reason he was here… the less he thinks Destini told them, the less he'll hopefully think that she's still around. Or the less he may feel inclined to mop up loose ends in the form of innocent bystanders who knew too much…

But Jerry surprised him.

"Her name is not Vicky. It's Destini. She's…." before he continued, he turned to look directly at Scott, "She's a wanted felon and if you have any information at all about where she is or where she might be going, you need to tell me."

As Jerry spoke, Scott played out two options in his mind. One, he could be the unknowing and frightened civilian and agree to cooperate, or two, he could be the indignant and angry vacationer who wants to be left alone. He realized that he was actually a little of both, so he just opted to be himself. Easier that way, plus he wouldn't have to worry about Jerry seeing through him and then thinking he's hiding something.

"Look," he started with the tone of a man who was on the verge of losing his patience, "I don't know anything about any of that. I certainly don't know anything about you either – how do I know you're even a cop? She's gone, she didn't say anything about where, and she obviously didn't even tell me her real name, so I can't help you even if I wanted to. Sorry."

"Oh yeah," said Jerry, a small strand of tobacco bobbing over his lower lip from the chew in his mouth. "Then why is she in your motel room?"

Scott's eyes widened and his own mouth fell open.

"Wha… what?" he said, glancing quickly at the motel and reaching a hand back for the truck's door handle.

Even more shocking was the fact that Jerry started laughing.

"Hey pardner, calm down, I'm just kidding. I was just testing you to see your reaction and make sure that you weren't hiding her."

Oh my God, thought Scott, he mistook my reaction as surprise that Destini would be in my room. Not as surprise that he knew she was actually there.

"Anyways," Jerry continued, nodding at the sodas in Scott's clenched hands, "If you'd have gotten three Cokes, then I would have been suspicious. Or if you'd have gotten a Coke and a 7-Up, which is what she likes to drink."

"Yeah, whatever, can I go now?" Scott asked, not wanting to get into a long conversation where he could possibly trip himself up and give something away.

"Well..." Jerry said slowly, as if considering it, "I suppose. Odds are slim that you'll be crossing paths with her again. But let me just say this, if you do – don't pick her up. In fact, if you see her, call me."

With that, he pulled a business card from his shirt pocket and handed it to Scott, who placed one of the cold sodas between his legs and immediately regretted doing so.

Scott squinted in the semi-darkness and read it: "Misner, Mendel and Williams, attorneys at law, 778-2255."

Before it struck him what he said, the words were out: "I don't see your name on here."

Oh you stupid fuck, he chided himself. How would he know that since the man hadn't introduced himself yet?

"It's on the back," Jerry replied casually, but there was an underlying smugness in his tone.

Scott flipped the card over and saw Jerry Rawlins embossed in gold on the other side.

"That still doesn't make sense," Scott said, attempting to cover up his gaffe. "What I mean is, why would your name be on a card for a law office if you're a cop?"

"Never said I was. You did. You know what doesn't make sense to me," Jerry drawled in a two good-old boys just having a neighborly conversation kind of way, "why in tarnation would you peel outta here like Mario Andretti and turn the road into your own personal race track, only to turn around and come right back? See, that's abnormal behavior for a normal person. I don't get it. It tells me that there's maybe a little something more than meets the eye going on here.

"Now, you don't have to say anything, cuz I can see that you're involved in things you don't understand and you're a little scared," he continued. "But I'd hate to see you and your granny get hurt because of poor judgment. Excuse me…"

He opened his door and spit a huge wad of tobacco juice onto the gravel, then shut it again.

"Nasty habit," he said with a shrug. "Probably one of the reasons my wife left me."

Scott tried not change his facial features at that comment. This guy was good. Hell, of course he was good – he's a freakin' lawyer and he's cross examining you right now, dumbass.

"Now, as much as it pains me to think badly of you, because you really do seem like a nice guy," Jerry went on, "I have to assume that just maybe you and Destini had worked out some kind of plan to meet back here later and continue on your little road trip. Kind of throw me off the trail, so to speak. That's why I'm sitting out here uncomfortable as hell and popping no-doze."

Scott had picked up the other soda again and was now tapping his fingers against both cans trying to digest everything Jerry was saying. Okay, he thinks I'm clueless and inept … oh yeah, wait a minute, I am. Might as well let him reel me in a little more.

"So, um, why are you after her … especially since you're not a cop?" Scott asked.

"Well, believe it or not, I'm trying to help her," Jerry replied. "She's done some bad stuff and there are some other folks after her that won't be as kind if they get to her first. I'm hoping to bring her in safely. You might say that I've got kind of a personal interest in the situation."

"What kind of bad stuff," Scott asked, ignoring his last remark.

"You ask a lot of questions for an 'uninvolved' party," Jerry said, "but I'll be straight up with you because I expect you to be straight up with me as well. She's an accessory to the murder of three federal agents."

112

Scott managed to look at him for a good three or four seconds with a straight face, but couldn't keep it any longer than that. His laughter started out almost like a little cough he was trying to hold back, followed by a couple more intermittent laughs, until he couldn't contain it anymore and was just flat out laughing his ass off to the point that tears were forming in his eyes. After a minute, he managed to calm down enough to speak.

"Oh man, that's a good one," Scott said. "You're trying to tell me that she killed three FBI agents?"

"First of all," answered Jerry, "Again, I never said they were FBI. You sure do make a lot of assumptions. In fact, they were DEA. And secondly, I didn't say that she killed them, but she was there and she's an accomplice."

Sorry Eli, Scott thought as he popped the Coke open. His throat hurt from the laughing and he needed to do something with his hands. He drank long from the can, emptying almost half of it at once.

"Okay, I'm listening," Scott said.

"First you tell me something Scott," Jerry replied. "Oh don't look so surprised. It wasn't hard to run your plates and get your name and address and particulars. Grandma on board and wife at home, right?"

"Whoa, hold on, why are you talking about my family? What the hell are you doing… are you threatening me with them?"

"Calm down pardner, I'm the good guy, remember? I'm just saying that I know you're a solid citizen and family man. You've got no criminal record of any kind. You're totally clean. You're just an ordinary guy who got caught up in a bad situation and that's why I'm taking a big chance talking to you like this. I don't want to see you or anyone else get hurt."

"Another threat?" Scott asked.

"Not from me, but I'll tell you this…" he stopped, opened the door and spit another long brown glob on the ground, closed the door and continued, "you and your grandma are more than just a free ride if Destini comes back. You're also potential hostages that she will use if it comes down to that. Now I'm asking you for everyone's sake – what do you know? Where is she heading?"

As Scott looked at him and noted the seriousness lined on his long face, he had his first flash of doubt. What if this guy was telling the truth? What if Destini was deceiving them and he just couldn't see it because of his own emotions?

Jerry must have sensed him wavering in indecision and prodded him again.

"Please, talk to me before it gets out of control," he repeated.

"She said something about going to Kan… ada…," Scott answered, making his choice on the fly. He couldn't do it. He couldn't sell her out, even if she was a lying accessory to murder. He just hoped he wouldn't regret it later.

"Canada?" Jerry answered. "No way. I mean she is doing the opposite of what we thought, which would be running for the Mexican border – but to think she could get all the way up north from here. No… she must have planted that info with you to throw us off if we talked to you. There's no way."

Oh yeah, thought Scott, I am not the only dumbass in town, thank you very much. Good old country Jerry just said "us" and "we." Us and we. Scott didn't think he meant Misner, Mendel or Williams. He just couldn't picture a whole posse of old attorneys scouring the Arizona highways in custom-built pickups. Maybe he meant Surfer Ben with the FBI, but Scott had already talked to him – well, so to speak – and Jerry had also said "if we talked to you" as if implying "they" hadn't yet.

That lent some credence to Destini's outrageous claim of Jerry having called in some South American muscleheads.

"Your turn," Scott said.

"I hope you have some idea of the serious nature of what you're doing if you're trying to toy with me," Jerry stated. He gave Scott a long, hard stare and then continued.

"Two days ago we had set up a sting operation with the DEA," Jerry said. "Unfortunately, one of our bright, young attorneys – I think we both know who I'm talking about – had been getting what seemed like airtight cases thrown out and dismissed on a regular basis, allowing small-time pushers to walk clean. But that was okay. We sacrificed the small fish in hopes that she would lead us to the big ones, and she did. You see, she wasn't selling out or taking bribes – she was doing this out of pure loyalty to family. This was her job in the organization. She went through years of college and law school, paid for by daddy, just to get into a position where she could facilitate the family business.

"We planned this raid for a long time, but she set us up. She's anything but stupid. She led us to a rundown trailer in an abandoned trailer park and when our men approached it, they were gunned down in the open ... from the trailer on the other side of the road. There was a lot of gunfire, a lot of blood and in the end we lost three of our top men and two more are still in serious condition."

Jerry sounded choked up and stopped a moment and Scott could swear that he was sincerely shaken by the retelling of events. Scott also remembered seeing something about this bust gone wrong on the news a few days ago and footage of police tape around a trailer. Again, the doubt crept in.

"Anyways," Jerry finally went on, "during the shootout, Destini got away."

Scott didn't say anything for a while. When he did, it was déjà vu.

"Wow. Wooooow."

CHAPTER SEVEN

He didn't know if Jerry expected him to say anything else, such as maybe "Okay, I know where she is, take her away!" But Scott sat there quietly and considered the new information.

Both Jerry's and Destini's stories had some common elements, but somebody was definitely playing mind games with him. The only thing Jerry didn't mention, for whatever reason, was that he and Destini were married. Not having anything else to say, Scott thanked Jerry for the information in a cordial manner that suggested they could have been talking about stock tips and investment options, and told him he would most definitely call if he saw Destini again, then he got out and walked back to the motel.

Halfway back he heard the truck door open behind him and had a fleeting thought that he was about to take a bullet in the back, but then he heard Jerry cough up another wad of chew. Yuch, she kissed that mouth?

He let himself in and immediately turned off the overhead light, leaving only the small lamp on the stand to cast a low light across the room. Eli was where he had left her, just finishing the last of her French fries and giving him a look that said she didn't appreciate having to eat her whole meal without a drink.

The bathroom door was shut and he heard the water running in the tub. That was good -- he needed a little time to think about everything before seeing Destini again. He didn't want to think the worst, but he'd be crazy to ignore the possibilities and right now she might be able to sense his uneasiness.

"Sorry," he said, handing Eli the Diet Coke.

"Oh, that's okay. You know, I'm worried about you Scott," she said. "You seem so tense and bothered. I know you have a lot on your mind. Would you like to talk about it?"

"I appreciate that," he said, giving her a smile, "but I don't feel like talking right now. My head feels like it's going to explode. I just need some mindless entertainment."

He found the remote, switched the TV on and started channel surfing. He found ESPN's Sports Center, which was recapping all the football games he had missed that day, but instead of stopping there, as he usually would have, he continued until he found a local news program. Might as well see if there's an update on this trailer park raid, he thought.

He stared blankly at the screen, his own thoughts far away as the newscasters bantered about some gambling restrictions being lifted at a nearby Indian casino and then segued into a "touching tale" of a homeless man with amnesia being reunited with his family. Scott was still lost in his own little world recapping every scrap of information he'd been fed and wishing that he had talked with FBI Ben when Eli suddenly grabbed his arm and shouted something.

"Huh? What?" He said, drifting back to reality.

"I forgot all about filling the tub with water for my bath, I hope it's not overflowing – can you go turn it off for me Scott."

"Wait a minute... what? Your bath? Isn't Destini in there?"

"Oh no, goodness she went out looking for you," Eli replied. "She was worried because you hadn't come back. Isn't that sweet? She sure has been gone awhile herself now though."

Scott ran for the door. He yanked it open and sprinted halfway across the parking lot before it registered that the truck he was running toward was no longer there. Oh shit. He got her. He took her. Oh shit. He had to...

His thoughts were interrupted as his foot struck something hard in the dark and sent him falling forward. He put his right arm out in front of his face and hit the ground hard, with his elbow absorbing the brunt of the impact.

"Fuck!" He yelled in a mixture of frustration and pain as he managed to roll the rest of his body over using the weight of his right arm. He heard a loud cracking sound from his elbow and felt a sharp pain. Oh man, this could be bad, he thought, as he wound up flat on his back looking up at the clear night sky and the half moon and the bright stars and Destini's worried face…

"Geez Louise, that had to hurt," she said, dropping to her knees behind him and gently lifting his head and resting it on her legs. "Are you okay Scott?"

"Yeah," he lied. "I'm fine. Just a little sore."

"Oh good, then I hope you don't mind, but…," she started giggling, "I gotta laugh my ass off now."

And she did.

Soon, he was laughing along with her – despite the throbbing ache from his elbow.

"Goddamnit!" They heard a woman's voice yell from the manager's office. "You told me you didn't drink! You sonuvabitch!"

Scott had tears coming out of his eyes at that point, but he couldn't tell if it was from all the laughter or the excruciating pain he was in.

"Just what the hell were you running around like that for?" Destini asked.

"Well," Scott started, "I, uh, heard they closed the pool at 10, and it's five 'til."

"It's a damn good thing you fell here then," she said, "cuz there ain't no water in that pool."

They both started laughing again. Meanwhile Eli had wandered up behind them. She stood there smiling for a few seconds and then turned to go back to the room.

Destini slid her legs underneath her and Scott's head was now in her lap. He could feel a trickle of blood dripping off his elbow but couldn't care less.

"It's a beautiful night," he said, not wanting to get up just yet.

"Hey," she said, smiling, "you're supposed to be looking at the stars when you say that – not me."

For the first time that entire day, Scott had no thoughts racing through his mind. Nothing. He didn't have anything to say either for a change. He felt a strange calmness, and was content to just lie there and look up at her. Her eyes met his gaze and neither moved for a long time.

"What are you thinking about," she whispered after some time.

"Fate," he said simply.

"Boy, I'm so glad you didn't say destiny – you don't know how many times I've heard that line."

"I've never really thought much about," he said, "but I can't help but wonder why things are suddenly all happening like this. I mean, it's so unbelievable to think I woke up in my own comfortable bed this morning, expecting to have a leisurely day and then go to sleep in my own comfortable bed tonight, just like every other day. But then I go to the store this morning to get some beer to watch a football game, I get a call, I go see my grandmother at the nursing home, we get into a discussion about true love and I realize I don't have a frame of reference for debate, which makes me doubt my marriage even more. It doesn't help when Eli tells my wife this, suddenly we're driving cross country, pick up a damsel in distress, start getting chased by a jilted husband and the FBI with underworld assassins en route, and then I wind up on my back under the stars, hurt and bleeding, but with the most beautiful woman I've ever seen and somehow none of the rest of it matters. Nothing else matters but this brief moment in time – right here, right now."

There was another long pause as they just looked at each other.

"That's incredible," Destini said after a moment, running her hand softly across his forehead.

"Yeah, it's just amazing. I mean, what higher power designed this intricate sequence of events to get to this point in time?"

"No, I meant it's incredible that you think I'm the most beautiful woman you've ever seen," she said. "I don't believe it, but it's nice of you to say."

"Oh man," Scott said quickly. "Maybe I shouldn't have said that. I'm sorry, I don't want to make you feel uncomfortable."

"Sure, because that kind of talk just upsets a girl – don't ever tell her how pretty she is," Destini said with obvious sarcasm.

"My God, wait a minute," she added, "did you say you were bleeding?"

"Um, yeah, can I blame the loss of blood and lightheadedness for my inappropriate comments."

"Geez, let's get you inside and take a look," she said, lifting his head up gently and then helping him up all the way. He tried to straighten his elbow, but the pain was too much, so he left it bent and cradled against his stomach as he walked back to the room beside her. He did look around, hopefully inconspicuously enough not to arouse Destini's curiosity, but Jerry's truck was nowhere to be seen.

If luck and timing were on his side, then maybe Jerry hadn't seen Destini leave their room while they were engrossed in their conversation – after all, Scott certainly hadn't noticed her come out. Surely he would have said something at that point. And if he had believed Scott about not knowing where she was, then perhaps he had left right afterwards to look for her elsewhere. However, if Destini had come out of the room while they were still talking in the truck, how could she not have seen them, or heard the supposedly familiar sound of his oral excretions?

And if she was wandering around out here…?

"Hey, where the heck have you been?" He asked her.

"Oh, I came out to find you, but you weren't by the soda machine, so I went to the office and you weren't in there either, but that was a mistake."

"Why?" He asked as they reached the door and went back into the room.

"Well, it's not exactly like I was a registered guest, you know," Destini said. "That weird old lady gave me the third degree and then I wound up having to get my own room." She took a key out of the waistband of her shorts and held it up – number 28. Scott took it from her with his left hand, since he still didn't want to move the right arm.

"I'll stay next door," he said. "You sleep here with Eli."

"What? Are you afraid I'm gonna run off again?" She said with a wink.

"Please don't," he replied seriously. "I'll do whatever I can to help you."

"I believe you," she said, "but for right now, let me help you."

She put a hand on his back and led him over to the sink.

"You okay in there Eli?" Scott called through the adjacent bathroom door where his grandmother was presumably taking a bath. Eli replied that she was just fine.

Meanwhile, Destini had turned on the cold water and was soaking a small washcloth. She then gingerly ran it over Scott's elbow, but he flinched anyway.

"Ow, shit," he said. "Not very manly of me, huh?"

"That's okay, I'm tired of men anyways," Destini said. "They're all assholes."

"Hey, don't look at me to argue with you," Scott said. "I can vouch for that as a fact. Men suck. If I were a girl, I'd be gay."

"Ha, easy for you to say, since you're a guy," Destini replied, dabbing the washcloth around a huge swollen bruise directly above Scott's elbow bone. He gritted his teeth.

"Isn't it every guy's fantasy to watch two chicks doing each other? You'd just be living the dream."

"No – every guy's fantasy is to have two chicks doing him," Scott replied. "Two chicks on each other would be like placing a T-Bone steak and a cold Heineken in front of a guy, but telling him he couldn't have either."

"Hey!" Eli yelled from the other side of the door. "I'm no prude, but I can hear every word you two are saying! In my day, foreplay didn't involve a lot of dirty talk!"

Scott's face turned red and Destini laughed.

"Well, I don't think it's broken, but it's going to hurt pretty darn good for the next few days," Destini said. "I'll go back outside real quick and get some ice in the bucket and then wrap it on your elbow."

"No... I'll get it," Scott said, grabbing the little motel ice bucket off the sink before she could reach for it. "I like the fresh air. You stay here and I'll be right back."

"See what I mean about men," she said. "I hardly know you and already you're trying to boss me around."

"No, no," said Scott. "That's not it, really. I just... I... well, to be honest, we don't know who might be out there looking for you, that's all."

"Okay," she said with a little pout, "I don't mind a little over protectiveness, I guess. But hurry back."

"No worries there," he said, leaving the room yet again. He was back in less than a minute with a bucket full of ice, which Destini dumped into a small towel and then wrapped around his elbow. It took a moment for the cold to seep through, but soon it was effectively numbing the pain.

He had laid down on Eli's bed while she was still in the bathroom and was looking at Destini, who had taken up reading her magazine again on the opposite bed.

"How's it feeling?" She asked without looking over.

"Better, thanks. So what do you plan to do? I mean where are you going, really?"

"Look at this," she said shaking her head. "Michael Douglas and Catherine Zeta Jones are still together. I mean, the guy's like 25 years older than she is. What do you think of that?"

"I think he'll die happy," Scott replied, "so, where did you say you needed a ride to?"

"One thing's for sure, he'll die a lot sooner than he would have," Destini said. "That woman's in shape. And here's

Harrison Ford with Calista Flockhart – another good 20-plus years difference. What's the attraction?"

"You're saying you wouldn't have a relationship with Indiana Jones if he asked you out because he's twice your age?" Scott asked.

"No, I didn't say that. I don't think age matters. Heck, I'd go out with that guy," she said, motioning toward the ever-present shot of Ricardo Montalban, which Eli had set up next to the phone.

"But you were just saying that…"

"I was asking what you thought about it. That's all. How old are you anyways?"

"Doesn't matter," Scott said, "Because I wouldn't go out with Harrison Ford no matter what our age difference is."

"Funny," Destini replied. "I'm guessing 35 or 36."

"And I'm guessing that you're not going to tell me what your plans are or where you're going," Scott replied.

"Told you already," she said, suggestively fixing those dark brown eyes on him. "However far you're willing to take me."

Jesus, he thought, now she's teasing him. He'd already told her that he found her attractive, so now it looked like she was going to have some fun with it. But, if she's willing to flirt with him, it must be a good sign, he thought. People usually don't say suggestive things like that to someone they aren't attracted to, well, he paused… unless they're just playing with you because they're an accomplice to murder and using you and don't want you to realize that…

Just then Eli came out of the bathroom in a long robe, humming "Strangers in the Night."

"This Wendell sure is a lucky guy, I hope he can handle you," said Destini.

"He's in trouble all right," said Eli, looking in the mirror. "I haven't felt this alive and full of energy in years."

"I think that's so romantic," Destini went on. "To build a long-distance relationship and then finally meet each other. Don't you think Scott?"

"Oh yeah," he said, "it happens all the time nowadays. Flowers, candlelight and 40-year-old pedofiles soliciting 14-year-old girls in chat rooms for sex. Very romantic."

"Okay, now that's an age difference I would have a problem with," Destini said. "But, really, I think it's wonderful that you are following a dream Eli."

"Oh, sweetie, this isn't a dream I'm following, it's just a pleasant diversion and a chance to get out into the real world," Eli replied. "I already lived my dream a long time ago. It was all too short, more like a heavenly nap than a dream I guess, but like they say, memories last forever. They really do."

"I'm sorry," Destini said. "Did you lose your husband early?"

Nooooooo! Scott groaned inwardly. He had almost made it through the entire day without having to hear his grandmother's woeful epic of lost love. It always depressed the hell out of him to hear it, and of course he couldn't be rude and not listen. The thing that tore at him the most – and he hadn't realized it for many years – was the fact that it wasn't just the life of the grandfather he never knew that ended on that snowy battlefield in Europe. Two lives ended that day. Two people had died from that one bullet.

The only difference was that one of them had kept on breathing, kept on walking and talking and going through the motions. Eli had never really seemed to be living completely in the present because she had never let go of the past. He didn't understand it though. Growing up, he had always felt sorry for his grandmother because she was alone. But that was her choice, and he supposed she made it because she was happier that way than she would have been otherwise.

"Yes. Yes I did," Eli simply said in response to Destini's question.

Scott was amazed that she didn't elaborate, but his own thoughts were now centered on Eli's life and he remembered overhearing her say something once at a family gathering when he was just kid. He had never forgotten it for some reason. He had only been seven or eight years old, but it remained one of the earliest memories he could recall. His mother had asked Eli why she had never remarried or even shown any interest in another man and his grandmother had replied "It wouldn't be fair."

Perhaps he hadn't forgotten it, because it had never made any sense to him.

"Grandma," he suddenly asked, surprising himself, but what the hell… "A long time ago you said that you never remarried because it wouldn't be fair. What did you mean by that? Did you mean that it wouldn't be right to take away from your husband's memory or that you would feel guilty for finding someone to take his place?"

Before she answered, Eli walked over and sat down on the bed next to Scott and took his hand in both of hers.

"Actually, it has less to do with either me or Robert, but more to do with any other man that I may have met," she said.

When she didn't continue, Scott prodded her.

"I'm sorry, but I don't suppose you want to dumb that down a little -- maybe give it to me at the 6th-grade level?"

"I understand," Destini interjected, sitting up and facing them. "It wouldn't have been fair to any other man, because they would have never been able to compare, no matter how wonderful they might have been in their own right."

"That's right," said Eli. "Once you've met your true love, the love of your life, how can anybody else even come close? I would have never been able to love like that again, to give my heart and soul so completely to anybody else, and because I couldn't do that, it wouldn't have been fair to be with anybody else."

"But how can you know all that for sure? I mean, you've been alone for the last 50 years because of that belief," Scott said. "My God, how do you know it's right? How can you possibly know that you wouldn't have met someone and fallen completely in love again? How can you believe there's only one true love for you, or for anybody, in this world? You can't know that. Nobody can know that."

"All anybody has to know is what feels right for them in their own hearts," Eli said. "If it's what you believe and feel to be true, then it is true for you and that's all you need. I'm not saying it can't be different for somebody else. Everybody defines and feels love differently. No one way is necessarily right or wrong. But this is my belief and how I feel, and so that's the way it is for me."

"You know, that almost makes sense," Scott said.

"Well maybe someday you'll understand, Scott," Eli said, not in a condescending way, but in a manner which implied that she actually hoped that he would.

"Hey, I've got a question for you Destini," Scott said. "It's one that somebody asked me earlier today and things have been pretty much downhill since then, but have you ever been in love? And before you tell me that you're married, I want you to take a minute and think about it.

"Have you," he continued, using the words his grandmother had spoken to him that morning, "ever truly been...

out of control… nothing else matters… completely heart and soul… you'd do anything and give up everything… in love?"

"No," she said, without hesitation.

"See, I told you it was a simple yes or no answer," Eli said.

Destini stood up and stretched her arms over her head and arched her back, her firm breasts pushing against the fabric of her halter top.

Oh man, I can't take this, Scott thought as he purposely looked away toward the clock radio on the table – 10:27. Time to go take a nice cold shower. He couldn't help but sneak one quick glance as Destini walked around the edge of her bed and toward the bathroom.

"Is it stiff?" Eli asked.

"Jesus! What?!" Scott replied.

"Your elbow – is it getting stiff?" Eli said with a just enough hint of a smile that he could tell she knew exactly what she was saying.

"Good night grandma, I'm going to bed," he said getting up.

"Where are you sleeping?" She asked.

"Next door. Destini got another room, but I think it's best if the two of you slept here together. If you need me, just scream real loud."

He was going to say goodnight to Destini, but she had already shut the bathroom door and once again he could hear the bathtub filling with water. He could just imagine her slipping off those shorts and that little top and then getting into the water. The little droplets shimmering off that perfect, tan body and… whoa, that's enough, he caught himself. He grabbed his gym bag from the foot of the bed, made sure to leave the room key for 27 on top of the TV set and then started for the door.

But then he thought about it and turned back around and walked over to Eli. He gave her a big hug.

"Happy birthday grandma, I hope you're having a good one. Oh, and lock the door behind me. Maybe put a chair in front of it too."

CHAPTER EIGHT

Scott was more mentally exhausted than physically tired when he finally laid down, but he was unable to fall asleep for a long time. Partly because he could only lay on one side – anytime he rolled to his right, the pain in his elbow jolted him fully awake again – and partly because of the thoughts he couldn't get out of his mind. Most involved Destini in some way or another. He had to figure out what was going on and fast… she could be gone tomorrow or the next day. Could he live with that? Could he just go back to his wife and suburban home, knowing that she was out there somewhere?

Let's face it buddy, he thought, you've got it bad. He'd always been a romantic at heart and the thought of falling in love at first sight had a certain, undeniable appeal. But was it love or lust or something in between?

It was after midnight when he finally drifted off, but he slept lightly and every little noise in the unfamiliar surroundings woke him. By the time he was staring at the little flip digits reading 5:52 on the white 70's-era AM radio clock, he decided he might as well get up and take a shower, even though he felt more tired than when he had actually laid down.

By 6:30 he was sitting on his bed fully dressed and once again staring at the TV in hopes that the local news might have an update on the shoot-out that Destini was somehow involved in, according to Jerry.

This time, there was indeed a short piece about the police raid, noting that one of the two hospitalized DEA agents had died the previous night from gunshot wounds and the other was still in serious condition. Spliced into the story were file shots of the scene itself with covered bodies laying in the dirt outside a bullet-ridden trailer. As the announcer came back on at the end of the story, Scott was about to shut it off, but then a picture of Destini appeared in the background. He quickly turned it up: "Police now say this woman, Destini Rawlins, a Phoenix attorney, is wanted for questioning in connection with Friday's shooting. Anyone with knowledge of her whereabouts should immediately call the police. Law enforcement officials warn that she could be armed and dangerous."

He pressed the power button on the remote and the screen went black.

Scott sat there staring at his reflection in the gray screen. A quick phone call and it would all be over and he wouldn't have to worry about it. If he'd been faced with this dilemma as a hypothetical situation a few days ago, he had no doubt that's exactly what his response would have been. After all, it was the logical and sensible thing to do. In fact, if she were in police custody, she might also be out of any potential danger from her husband and her father's enemies, so in a way, he'd be doing her a favor by getting her to the relative safety of a jail cell.

He knew he could rationalize it to death and every indicator would point to calling the police. But he couldn't do it. It wasn't even an option anymore as far as he was concerned. Whatever she did or was possibly guilty of didn't matter to him. He knew he was making his choice based solely on his feelings, but it sure as hell felt right.

The first thing he had to do was wake Destini and Eli and get out of there. He'd feel a lot better if they were on the road and heading out of state as soon as possible.

He threw his bathroom kit in his bag and left the room. The sun was glowing orange just above the horizon and the sky was a clear blue as he opened the Saturn's trunk and dropped his bag inside. He winced a little as he closed the trunk with his right arm, but he wanted to test his range of motion. It had bruised and swollen, but didn't hurt too badly overall. He looked around. The few other cars that had pulled in for the evening were still sitting undisturbed in the lot. Apparently nobody else was in much of hurry to start traveling this early.

He wondered if either Destini or Eli might already be up. He got his answer in the form of his repeated, and increasingly louder, knocking on the door of 27 before it finally opened. Destini was in mid-yawn when she let him in and her hair was stuck out all over the place. God, she's beautiful, Scott couldn't help but think, even catching her in a less than flattering circumstance.

"Are you nuts?" Destini whispered as he stood there smiling at her. "It's not even 7 a.m. Checkout time is noon. Go away. Vaminos. Beat it. And quit looking so damn cheerful."

She returned to her bed and crawled back under the sheets, leaving Scott standing in the semi-darkness.

"Oh, and how's your arm feeling?" He heard her ask from under the covers.

"Amazingly, a lot better than it looks," Scott answered in a hushed tone as he walked over to her bed and sat down on the edge. "Listen, I hate to get you up so early, but we really need to get going."

"Nooooooo," he heard her moan, her head beneath the pillow. "Just one more hour of sleep, that's all I need. Maybe two, but no more than three, I promise."

"Sorry, we really, really have to get out of here. Now."

She pushed the pillow away from her head and looked at him with raised eyebrows.

"Tell you what," she whispered, pulling the sheet back "you can crawl in here with me and hold me for as long as you want if you let me stay in bed. Just don't take it personally if I start snoring. Deal?"

"As tempting as that is," Scott said, making no effort to conceal the fact that he was taking a good, long look at her semi-naked body, "I don't think it'd be in your best interests. Or my grandmother's. How about a compromise? I'll grab this pillow and blanket and put it in the car for you and you can snore all you want."

She propped her elbow up and rested her head on her hand, giving him a puzzled look.

"I can't believe you just turned down a chance to get in bed with, how did you say it, 'the most beautiful woman' you've ever seen? I knew that was just a line. You were just overcome by the moon, the stars and the stinging tears in your eyes last night. I could have been the old bitch from the front desk and you'd have been declaring your undying love."

"Baby, if you were that hot, wrinkled, fleshy bag of sex, I wouldn't have been wasting my time with lines," Scott said. "I would have just carried you to the deep end of the empty pool and made you scream for a lifeguard."

"Eeeeeew, that's disturbing," Destini said, looking over at Eli as if making sure she was still asleep and had been spared that description. "I'm not sure I can get back to sleep now after that visual. Thanks a lot."

"Well, good. Let's go then. Come on … please," Scott said.

"You know, must guys say that when they want to get a girl into bed, not out of it," Destini replied. "What's your big hurry anyways?"

"Oh, just the fact that I saw your picture on the news a few minutes ago and how the police are asking people to call them if they see you. That's all."

"Okay, that's a good one," she said, getting up. "Give me a few minutes and I'll be ready."

"That's fine. Can you wake Eli and get her ready too? I'm gonna go top off the gas tank before we leave. I'll be back in about 15 minutes."

"Can you bring a large coffee back with you?"

"Sure, cream or sugar?"

"Neither, just black," she said.

"And how about a biscuit or maybe some donuts?"

"Oooh, yeah, that would be…" she paused. "You're being sarcastic, aren't you?"

"Wow, you're beautiful and smart," Scott said, giving her a playful wink as he went out the door. Closing it behind him, however, caused the pain in his elbow to flare up again and he went back into his room to grab a small towel and the ice bucket to put together another wrap.

It'll take them a good 15 or 20 minutes to get ready anyways, he thought, as he walked to the ice machine looking down at his misshapen and discolored elbow. In examining the injury, he wound up walking right past the vending machines and off the edge of the sidewalk beyond the motel. As he was about to turn around, shaking his head at being so absorbed in his thoughts, he noticed something unusual. Tire tracks.

The tread marks were clearly visible coming off the pavement of the parking lot in the mix of soft sand and a sparse, grassy patch that grew in the wake of the ice machine's run-off. The tracks faded about ten feet into the rock-strewn, empty desert that stretched out behind the motel, but he didn't have to squint too hard to make out the shape of a truck about a hundred yards in the distance where the tracks led.

He wouldn't have even considered investigating something as common as an old pickup rusting under the desert sun, except that the tire tracks originated from the motel parking lot and had to be recent. He had an uneasy feeling it was Jerry's truck and couldn't think of a good reason as to why he would have abandoned it like that.

"Fuck," he sighed, knowing he'd have to go check it out or it'd be on his mind the rest of the day. He started walking in that direction, keeping a close eye on the ground around him. He was paranoid about snakes and could just imagine being bitten by a rattler and dying out there on the hard desert floor before he'd even had the chance to sleep with Destini.

Damn, did he really just have that thought? What a typical guy thing to come to mind, you deserve to get bitten by a snake for that one, he thought.

As he got halfway to the truck he could tell it was Jerry's and that it was empty.

"Now that's pretty freakin' weird on top of everything else," he muttered to himself.

He slowed as he got to within 50 feet and then stopped completely 10 feet from the back end of the truck. He stood there in the surreal quiet of the landscape as the rising sun behind him cast his shadow out toward the vehicle.

What if the bastard was laying in there dead? Or worse, what if he was in there alive? No wait, the first one would be the bad option, he corrected himself. Hell, it was actually kind of hard to say at this point.

Instead of approaching straight on, he decided to take a wide arc around the driver's side and slowly walked far to the left of the truck as he made his way closer, trying to angle his view at the window. Suddenly he stopped again and started laughing. Jesus, what the fuck am I doing, like I'm some damned secret agent or something, he thought and then just walked directly to the truck's door at a normal pace. Screw these little games and stuff. He came upon the window and looked in.

Yep, okay, there he was alright, just lying there with his eyes wide open and staring vacantly at the roof, a neat little trail of blood dried around the bullet hole square in the center of his forehead. Well then, that answers that question.

Hey, he suddenly realized, that means Destini is a single woman now – that's cool… God, he thought, it's just amazing the thoughts that pop into a person's head when they see a dead body for the first time. Get a grip. Holy shit. Just get away from there before you're seen. He turned quickly and started walking back to the motel. He got maybe 15 feet, then turned around and went back to the truck. He looked inside again.

He had to capture this he told himself, because there was a definite point not too far off in his future where he could see himself sitting in a hard chair in a little room trying to describe this scene to the police or the FBI. And they probably wouldn't let him have a glass of water if he didn't give them specifics.

He made several mental notes as he took pictures with his phone – both doors were locked, the car keys were in the ignition, a small gun was on the passenger floorboard, just under Jerry's open right hand. There were also some scattered pills on the seat and floorboard, perhaps the No-Doze he was taking to stay awake. It sure looked like he shot himself, or somebody went to the trouble to make it look that way. After talking with Jerry last night, he didn't believe the guy would get the urge to drive out here and put a bullet through his brain. It made no sense at all. He was on a mission and pretty determined to find Destini and exact his revenge. Somebody found him first. The FBI? The South American hit squad? Oh my God… Destini?

He saw something else too and quickly looked away. Nah
– he was imagining things. There was no way that...

He looked again. Nope, he wasn't imagining things. The
man had a bulge the size of a grapefruit in his pants. Can
someone die with a hard-on? He didn't think that was medically
or physically possible. Unless... oh man, he didn't even want to
consider that option, but maybe the pills weren't No-Doze.

Okay, here's what he could imagine the crime scene
investigator piecing together – subject is despondent because
wife has left him and is on the run, subject takes too many Viagra
pills and goes off road to relieve some of the pressure, but
decides instead to kill himself because he's so depressed. Case
closed. No wait, he thought, it gets better... fingerprints of
unidentified man found all over the inside passenger area of the
vehicle suggest a homosexual tryst gone bad. And who the fuck
uses the word 'tryst' anyways, he thought, that's pretty gay in
itself. Oh man, if they dust the cab for prints, and they will, his
face will be on tomorrow morning's newscast next to Destini's.

Somebody must be setting him up. The authorities will no
doubt check the hotel's guest register from last night, of which
there weren't too many, get his name, run the prints, put an all-
points out on his car. Shit. They wouldn't make it halfway across
New Mexico before they were pulled over.

His only advantage right now was that they probably
hadn't expected him to find the truck. Then again, they could be
watching him right now from a distance – laughing their asses off

at his total bewilderment. And why did he keep thinking in terms of "they?" He had to consider the real possibility that Destini might have done this. She was outside last night, right before or while Jerry disappeared. The lady on TV said she was "armed and dangerous." Jesus, that might even explain the hard-on if she was in the truck, led him out here, distracted him… oh man, this shit was just getting to be way too much. He'd always considered himself cool under pressure. Nothing ever stressed him out. But now his head felt like it was going to explode.

"Don't panic, don't panic," he repeated aloud, and then he made a fist and smashed it into the driver's side window.

"Oh you motherfucker!" He screamed as he fell to the ground. He didn't know what hurt worse – his hand or his elbow, as his eyes teared up again. He rolled on his back, cupping his elbow in his left hand and tucking his right hand under his left armpit as if that would make the pain go away. He could see the window still intact, mocking him with his own writhing reflection. Those things always shattered in the fucking movies, he thought. At least he was pretty sure now that he wasn't being watched or he'd have heard the laughter echoing across the vast expanse of desert.

No time for this, he told himself, get up. Do something. He used his left elbow to help him get to his knees and then shakily stood up.

"Fuckin' piece of shit goddamn truck… shit… fuckin'… whatever…"

He steadied himself and then began to run back to the motel, cradling his right arm against his body. Thank God his legs were still okay … for now… Fortunately there was still not a soul to be seen. He did hear some traffic on the freeway, but that was out of sight.

He didn't have much time now. He'd been gone at least 10 minutes. He rounded the corner of the motel, went straight to his car and got in. He cussed some more as he pinched a muscle in his left shoulder reaching around the ignition to start the car with his left hand because the knuckles on his right one were throbbing. He backed the Saturn up, turned a sharp right and then a quick left over the curb at the end of the motel and sped toward Jerry's truck.

His CD player had automatically started and he couldn't help but laugh as Joey Ramone's punk remake of Louie Armstrong's "Wonderful World" blared through his speakers as he bounced over the desert. He made up some lyrics of his own as he looked at his sweaty, tear-stained face in the rearview mirror.

"I see skies of blue, clouds of white,

a man in a truck, someone killed last night

And I think to myself… what a fucked up world…"

"Okay, that's it," he said, slamming on the brakes and sending a huge cloud of dust in the air as he skidded to a stop next to Jerry's truck. "I am now officially crazy. I've lost my freakin' mind. I cannot believe that I'm doing this."

Scott popped the trunk open and almost fell out of the car in his haste to get out.

He dug under the spare tire with his good arm and frowned because he saw there wasn't much available space in the back. Kate had bugged him to get a bigger car, a sedan – it sure would be handy now. Finally he came up with the tire iron and a smile that he figured probably looked like Jack Nicholson's in "The Shining" when he busted the axe through the door.

He stumbled back to the pickup, and sent the tire iron against the same driver's side window. This time it did shatter, punctuating Joey's continuing, determined exclamations that it was indeed a wonderful world.

Quickly, he unlocked the truck and opened the door. Then he grabbed the pants around the ankles of Jerry's left leg with his own left hand and pulled with all his weight. Amazingly enough, Jerry came gliding across the leather seat, bounced out of the cab, banged his head loudly against the metal step-up below the door, and landed awkwardly on the ground as the music drifted languidly across the sand.

Scott kept a firm grip on the pants leg and dragged the body to the back of his car. This is the hard part, he thought. Jerry had a good 40 or 50 pounds on him. He propped Jerry into a sitting position with his back against the Saturn. Then he put his head underneath Jerry's right arm and draped it over his shoulder. Scott knew he'd have to use his back to lift Jerry up and into the trunk. He stood up and guided Jerry's body with his right shoulder over the trunk ledge, but he had sat him up too straight. Jerry's head hit the top of the raised trunk and he momentarily sat there like some wide-eyed ventriloquist's dummy awaiting instructions. Scott caught his breath and then realized his gasping mouth was inches away from the man's enlarged penis. That was all the motivation he needed.

"Aaaaaarrrgh!" he yelled as he used his right arm to force Jerry all the way into the trunk, again making his own eyes water from the effort.

Scott ran back over to the truck and leaned across the seat to pick up the small revolver. What bullshit, he thought. A big, tough guy like Jerry with a girlie gun like this. Come on, Destini, who's gonna believe that...

No, no, don't make those kinds of assumptions, he told himself.

He returned to his car and was about to tuck the gun in the front of Jerry's waistband.

"Oops, you're already packing, dude," he said, and instead just slid it underneath the body.

Okay, what else? Think, you won't get a second chance here, so think. What else do you need to do? At most, if anybody found the truck and was curious, they'd get a missing person's report after a trace of the plates. No body. No murder weapon. God, it scared him to think that he was actually trying to analyze the situation from a criminal perspective... and doing a halfway decent job. He pushed Jerry's legs off of his bag and as far back in the trunk as they would go. He then unzipped his bag and pulled the T-Shirt out that he had worn yesterday and went over to the truck.

He climbed into the cab and slid into the passenger seat he had occupied the night before. He didn't know what, if anything, he had actually touched, but he used the shirt to wipe down the interior around him. As he wiped around the glove compartment, he popped it open and took a quick look through the papers inside. It was just ordinary junk – owner's manual, maintenance papers, a small map. He then opened the passenger door and ran the shirt along it, inside and out, especially around the door handles. He did the same on the driver's side door and then stood there again staring at the empty vehicle.

He picked up the ice bucket and towel he had dropped in the sand earlier during his failed attempt to bust the window and threw them in his front seat, but he still felt like he was missing something. He didn't know what and didn't have the time to try and figure it out. He had to get going. He hoped his actions would at least slow down anybody trying to come after them and that's when it fully struck him as to what he had done – completely disturbed a crime scene and helped out whoever it was that had shot Jerry. If there was a point of no return in this situation, he had just reached it.

As a last measure, he took the truck keys out of the ignition and put them in his pocket. Then, after he closed his trunk with a strange sense of accomplishment, he got back into his car and drove toward the motel. They'll of course see his tire tracks and realize there was another car out there, but he couldn't worry about all the minor details now. He'd done the best he could, even though he still wasn't completely sure why.

Scott eased the Saturn down the curb by the motel and then swung into his original parking spot. He grabbed the bucket and towel and went straight to the ice machine, but as soon as he lifted the lid, he dropped them both on the sidewalk and instead stuck his whole head into the small, cubed blocks of ice.

"Oh my God," he sighed, closing his eyes with relief, as the coldness momentarily numbed everything. He remained that way until he heard a door open. Great, he thought, that's no doubt Destini and Eli and I'm standing here looking like a moron once again. I'm not even gonna look. Maybe they'll just ignore me and go away.

He was starting to shiver when he heard Destini's voice from directly beside him.

"You're not having an orgasm, are you?" She asked.

"Actually, right now, this feels better than sex," he replied, keeping his eyes closed.

"It's a good thing we haven't slept together yet or I'd be offended," she said.

He stood up, opened his eyes and looked at her.

"You know, that's the second time I believe that you said 'yet'," Scott pointed out, raising his eyebrows in question of her word choice.

"Is it?" she asked innocently. "Hmmmmm… I didn't notice."

Then she turned and walked over to the car where Eli was standing, trying to get the trunk open. "Noooo!" Scott yelled, running over to her.

"Here, here," he said, taking her small suitcase, setting it down at the back of the car and then guiding her to the passenger door. "I'll take care of that, let's just get you in the car. How are you doing today?"

"A lot better than you from the looks of it," she said. "What happened now?"

He looked at where her eyes were fixed – the swollen, blue knuckles scraped with dried blood.

"I, uh, well… never mind, it's embarrassing, you don't want to know."

He helped her in the back seat, noticing that Ricardo was firmly tucked under her arm and ready for another day on the road.

"You look nice today," Destini said as he took her bag and held the door for her to get in the car as well. "I like that glittery shirt, it's kinda styling and bold. It says that you don't care what others think about you." He looked down at his dark blue, short-sleeved Polo and grimaced at the sight of the sunlight reflecting off dozens of tiny slivers of glass all over the front of his shirt.

He shut the door and then went back to the trunk. After squeezing the two bags in around Jerry's bent form, he shook his shirt off with the intent to shake out the shards, but then decided a second-day wearing of Angus atop the late Bon Scott's shoulders was the better option. He was about to close the trunk again after changing when he gave Jerry a serious look.

"Damn, I think I love that girl," he said softly. "But don't tell anyone, okay?"

Scott promised his passengers that as soon as they put Black Canyon City a reasonable distance behind them, he'd go through the first drive-through he saw and buy some coffee and breakfast. He noticed his gas gauge was under half a tank and hoped that Destini wouldn't see it and wonder just what he'd been doing when he was supposedly filling it up.

But she apparently wasn't much of a morning person, he noted, and was already curled up against the door with her eyes closed. He chuckled to see that she had taken his earlier suggestion literally and was resting her head comfortably on one of the pillows she'd carried out of the motel room. Hey, what's a little minor theft when you're looking at 60 years to life for homicide anyways, he thought?

As he made his way back onto I-17 North, he kept looking over at her and wondering if she was really capable of such a cold-blooded act. He wasn't a detective or anything, but she seemed the most likely suspect in his mind, given the circumstances. But why would she just leave the evidence out in the open like that?

"Interesting girl, don't you think?" His grandmother interrupted his thoughts.

"She's something," Scott answered, aware that Destini was probably still wide awake and listening. "I just wish she'd tell us a little more about what she's involved in. I'd hate to run into that husband of hers without having all the facts and knowing what's going on, especially if he's got a gun."

He saw that she didn't flinch at the mention of Jerry, but that didn't mean anything. She could be resting peacefully knowing that there was no chance of them running into Jerry anytime soon. Well, that's not quite true, considering the guy was following them more closely now than he had been the previous day. He laughed.

"What's so funny?" Eli asked.

"Oh, just this whole crazy situation," Scott said. "I feel like I'm in some kind of disjointed Tarantino movie. And those never end well."

"Well, I'm having a great time and I think things are going very nicely on this little adventure," Eli said. "Do you think it's just coincidence that on the very day you split up with Kate you should happen to meet Destini?"

"Okay Eli," he said, meeting her eyes in the rearview. "First of all, Kate and I haven't technically split up. We're going through some … issues … I don't know what's going to happen between us right now. And secondly, I know you're on this romantic quest and talking about the meaning of love and stuff, but don't let your ideals cloud reality. Real life and real relationships aren't some knight-in-shining armor fantasy about rescuing damsels in distress, finding true love and living happily ever after."

"Scott? I didn't say anything about any of that. What are you talking about?"

Yeah, he paused, what the hell are you talking about? That's what you get for vocalizing your thoughts and rambling out loud. Fortunately, Destini came to his rescue by filling the awkward silence.

"Ooh, don't forget the part about fighting the fire-breathing dragon," she said, "that's my favorite."

"Scott..." his grandmother intoned. He looked back, waiting for her to continue.

"Love ... is what you feel. Life ... is what you make it."

She emphasized the "you" in both sentences.

"Eli, do you have some kind of subscription to Harlequin quotes of the month?" He asked, shaking his head.

"I do," she replied, "but that wasn't one. Those are usually like 'He inserted his throbbing organ into her dripping ...'"

"Hey! Hey! Hey!!!" Scott yelled. "Whoa. No need to go there. Jesus!"

Eli and Destini both laughed.

"I'm too tired to look, but is he turning red again?" Destini asked.

"Blushing like a beet," Eli replied.

"That's sooooo darn cute," Destini said.

Scott was about to defend himself, but felt a lump rise in his throat with the unexpected sound of a cell phone ringing.

It was loud, and it was coming from the trunk.

Destini sat up straight with a shocked look on her face and started looking around as soon as she heard it.

"What's that? Where's that?" She asked – somewhat nervously thought Scott.

"Just my cell phone," he replied as casually as he could. "Must have dropped it in the trunk with my shirt. Can't think of anyone other than Kate who would be calling me, so I'll worry about it later."

"That's a unique ring," Destini prodded. "Very familiar. What tune is that?"

"Oh, one of my favorites," Scott said, thankful that he recognized it. "The opening strains of 'Sweet Home Alabama,' the classic by Lynyrd Skynyrd. I'm a big fan of 70's southern rock."

"That's just very, very weird," said Destini. "That's the same ring that Jerry's cell phone has programmed into it. Scared me a little just now."

"It's just annoying me. I think you should pull over and answer it," said Eli. "You know Kate's just going to let it ring until you do."

They all sat there quietly, expecting each electronic verse to be the last, but then it would start all over again.

"Please pull over and answer it," Destini said to him.

"Might as well," he mumbled, slowing down and drifting to the shoulder of the highway. As soon as he came to a stop, he and Destini both opened their doors at the same time.

"Uh, what are you doing?" He asked.

"I need something out of my bag while you're getting into the trunk."

"Oh, um, listen… I don't mean to be rude, but… well, can I take this in private? I don't really want anyone listening to my marital problems, you know?"

"I'm not trying to eavesdrop on your personal business," Destini said, clearly offended. "I just need to get my bag real quick if you don't mind."

"I didn't mean that," Scott apologized quickly. "It's okay. I'll get your bag for you."

He got out and hurried to the rear of the car. This time he hadn't popped the trunk open automatically, but took his keys to unlock it. The phone was still repeating its musical refrain from inside as he turned the key in the lock and lifted the trunk.

Well son of a bitch, he thought, Jerry hadn't died with a hard-on after all. Somebody had shoved his cell phone down the front of his pants. Had Destini done that? The thought disturbed him more than her putting a bullet through Jerry's brain did for some reason. Aw Christ, he didn't want to reach his hand in there and pull it out, but the damn thing was still ringing.

Just then Destini came around the end of the car. He hadn't seen her get out with the trunk lid raised up and his attention on Jerry's pulsating crotch.

He felt his breath catch and he froze. Too late now, he thought.

But Destini wasn't looking into the open compartment. Her eyes were peering directly into Scott's and they looked very intense. She walked over and positioned herself in front of him, only inches away, with her back to the body of her dead husband.

"Before you answer that," she started, "I just... I... damn, now I'm the one embarrassed and stuttering. I don't know exactly what I want to say right now. I only know that I may not get this chance again after you talk with your wife and I... I just wanted to... well... I know this is inappropriate, but time is not a luxury and..."

Suddenly her lips were on his and her tongue was furiously exploring his mouth. He had imagined this moment being soft and gentle, if it ever came, and was taken aback by the abrupt roughness. She had cupped both her hands on the side of his face and was pushing it closer to hers as she sucked, licked and even bit his tongue with a passion he'd never experienced before. He had just started to kiss her back with the same intensity when he opened his left eye and looked into the trunk.

Jerry's dead eyes seemed to glare at him accusingly while his pants continued to vibrate from the steady ringing.

"What's the matter?" Destini said, pulling back. "You just stopped. Oh God, I shouldn't have done that. I'm so sorry. Not a very romantic first kiss."

"It's... uh... a very memorable one, that's for sure," Scott said. "Probably not too many quite like that."

"Oh no, now you're making fun of me," she said. "What the hell was I thinking? What am I doing?"

She spun around, ran back to the car and got in, slamming the door.

Holy shit, how lucky was that, he thought? She never even looked into the trunk. Thank you God, thank you, thank you, thank you...

Just one thing left to do now. He gritted his teeth and bent over to retrieve the phone. He lifted the waistband of Jerry's jeans with his bruised right hand, closed his eyes and reached in with his left. Oh my fuckin' God, whoever did this had jammed the phone in his underwear too. This was so damn disgusting. The ringing was even louder now and he heard Eli yell from the backseat: "Would you answer it already, for heaven's sake!"

Just yank the goddamn thing out, he told himself. But the phone only came partway and then snapped back. Oh sweet Jesus, what the hell is it stuck on? No, I don't want to know, he thought, pulling again. But again it snapped back in as if tied to a rubber band.

Oh, I am not believing this, he thought, pulling it halfway out yet again. This time he kept his grip when it started back and gave an extra jerk. It came up a little more and then held fast. Frustrated, he yanked on it several more times in rapid motion, not realizing that he was talking out loud: "Come on, come on, come…"

When he realized what he was saying and doing, he let the phone go in horror. It shot back halfway into Jerry's pants and then flipped upright in the space Scott had created by lifting the jeans up. Now the phone was pointing upward under the pants, making it look like Jerry was enjoying the proceedings greatly.

"Shit!" Scott yelled and slammed the trunk lid back down. "Why does this fucking comedy of errors always happen to me?"

"That's it," he heard Eli yell. "I'm gonna get it myself!" And she started climbing out his side of the car.

Can this nightmare possibly get any worse, he thought? She's serious. She's working her way out the door. Come on, she's 85 years old, you can beat her, move, move, move! He fished the keys out of his pocket again, keeping an eye on Eli's progress as he tried to insert the key into the lock. It wouldn't go. Of course, he thought, why had he expected it to be that simple? He tried to force it in and then wound up fumbling with it and dropping the keys on the ground as Eli stepped clear of the driver's side door.

Oh shit, this is gonna be close. He bent down and scooped them up as fast as he could and realized they weren't his keys. Game over.

He stood there staring at Jerry's truck keys in his open palm as Eli walked up beside him.

"I've never had a problem with Kate," she said, "but I'm about to, how do you say it, go off on the bitch."

Scott shook his head in disbelief at his continuing misfortune and pocketed the keys.

Just then the phone stopped ringing. They looked at each other. Eli's expression was one of mild wonder, while Scott was smiling from ear to ear.

Halle-fuckin-lullah, he thought.

And that's when Destini yelled "I got it!" and pushed the trunk release button from under the dash inside the car. The lid sprang up and Eli and Scott gazed down on Jerry's lifeless form, fake erection and all.

Scott looked over at Eli, waiting for some kind of reaction. All the color had drained from her face and she looked like she was going to fall over. Please don't let her have a heart attack, please.

She didn't say anything, but looked back over at Scott. He mouthed the words "I didn't do it." Her eyes narrowed and she glanced toward Destini in the car. Scott shrugged as if to say "I don't know."

"Scott, please help me back to the car, I don't feel well."

"Don't worry," he said, motioning to Jerry, "I don't think it's contagious."

Eli fixed him with an incredulous look for his attempt at humor under the circumstances. He took her elbow and helped her into the back seat.

"Who was it?" Destini asked.

"I have no idea who he was…" Eli said, confusing the question.

"Um, wrong number," Scott said quickly. "Some guy. Don't know who he was. Dumbass."

"Listen," Destini said, touching Scott's left hand, which was resting on the steering wheel as he leaned into the car to help Eli get settled, "if you want me to get out here, I'll totally understand. I can walk or catch another ride or something. I'll be okay."

Before he could respond, the familiar tones of "Sweet Home Alabama" assaulted them like a horror-movie killer who wouldn't die.

"Don't move," he said, pointing at Destini. "Don't do anything. Give me a sec."

I've had enough of this shit, he thought, walking back to the open trunk. He looked around and spotted the tire iron. Casually, he picked it up and took a swing at the protruding object straining against Jerry's zipper. It was a direct hit and hurt his arm, but he didn't care. The phone was knocked flat again and the ringing tones changed to a slower, deeper and somewhat warped version of the same melody. But the phone had also come halfway out the top of Jerry's pants.

Scott reached for it with his left hand and this time had no problem freeing it. He punched the green send/receive button and placed the phone to his ear.

"…about time," he heard a distorted voice on the other end that sounded like it was coming from another dimension. "What is going on? Where are you? Have you made contact yet?"

"Hello?" Scott tried, "Can't hear you."

"What?" Came the reply. "Bad connection. Where are you? Do you have her?"

"Can't… over… repeat," Scott answered in broken speech, hoping that would further confuse the caller.

"Losing your signal," the voice said. "No time to play games. Bring her in now. The civilians are collateral damage if necessary. Copy that?"

Scott didn't know how to reply, so he didn't. He waited.

"You there? Hello?" The caller asked. "Did you receive last message? Your signal is weak. Where are you?"

"West… I-8… San Diego…" Scott said, thinking it was a long shot, but worth a try.

"Kind of makes sense," he heard the caller's voice echo. "That's where this Miles guy is from. Predictable. Won't get far."

Scott suddenly realized who was on the other end of the line – FBI Ben. He was working with Jerry. That didn't seem right. Wasn't Jerry the bad guy?

"Just keep your cell on, so we can try and track your signal," Ben shouted, but the words were faint.

You've got to be kidding me, he thought. They can track his cell phone to get his location? Crap. He hit the disconnect button and then flung the phone out into the desert. It didn't go very far, however, since he used his left hand. Damn, it's still on, he thought. He walked off the shoulder to the phone about 20 feet away, then started smashing it with the tire iron, using both hands. He was soon awash in a shower of little plastic pieces.

After he was satisfied that he had completely demolished the internal workings of the phone, he kicked some sand on top of it for good measure. He was sure Eli and Destini were probably both watching and realized that he must look like he's losing his mind. Hell, maybe he was.

He walked calmly back to the car, dropped the tire iron in the trunk without looking and without regard for where it landed on Jerry. He slammed the lid, then walked over to the passenger side of the Saturn. He opened the door and leaned down on the window.

"Can I see you for just a minute?" He asked Destini in a calm tone, and then walked back to the rear of the car before she could say anything.

Scott watched her get out a little tentatively with an unsure look on her face, but she came and stopped before him. I'd be worried too, he thought, if I just saw some guy killing and burying a cell phone in the desert.

"In reference to your earlier question about you getting out here…"

That's all he said. Then his mouth was on hers and he was the one aggressively kissing her.

CHAPTER NINE

The rest of the drive up I-17 was relatively quiet. Scott kept his promise and found a McDonald's drive-through a short while later off the Camp Verde exit. Despite his aversion to regular coffee, he ordered a large cup for himself in addition to Destini's and Eli's. It tasted bitter, but after the morning he'd had, it didn't seem to matter much. He was just happy to have the caffeine.

It took them about an hour and a half to reach Flagstaff, at which point they headed east on I-40 toward Albuquerque – a good 320 miles away. Destini had happily assumed the role of navigator and plotted their course.

"It's only 9:30 right now," she said as they left the green hills of Flagstaff behind and entered another stretch of dry, desert landscape. "We should reach Albuquerque by 3 p.m. After that, we just stay on 40 and it's another 290 miles to Amarillo, Texas. If we get there about 8 p.m., it might be a good place to get a room for the night."

Scott noticed how she emphasized the singular form of accommodation and when he glanced at her, she gave him a playful smile.

"That's a lot of driving," said Eli. "I sure hope things don't start to smell bad in here."

Again, Scott found himself trying to cover for Eli's directness.

"She's got some gas problems," he whispered to Destini and then spoke up, "Just take your pills Eli. You'll be fine."

"Like hell," she muttered.

"Are you okay Eli?" Destini asked, turning back to talk with her. "You haven't seemed your outgoing, cheerful self since that phone call. I hope it's nothing I've done."

"Well, I hope it's nothing you've done either dear," Eli replied.

Destini gave Scott a puzzled look, but he just shrugged.

"Sooooo," Scott said, trying to think of something – anything – to change the subject. "Who's your all-time favorite cartoon character?"

Eli and Destini both stared at him, but neither said a word.

"Okay then, I'll go first," Scott said, undaunted. "I think I would have to go with… SpongeBob SquarePants. How about you Destini?"

"Who's SpongeBob what pants?" She asked.

"SquarePants," Scott said laughing. "Don't tell me you've never heard of SpongeBob SquarePants? Come on…" He started singing the show's theme song a bit too loudly.

"You're scaring me very much Scott," Eli said. "Maybe you should take some of my pills?"

"Who's your favorite Eli? One of the Disney classics I bet. Mickey? Donald? Maybe a Warner Brothers Looney Tune, like Bugs or Daffy?"

"Cartman," Eli said.

"What? The foul-mouthed fat guy off of South Park? Are you kidding me?"

"Screw you, hippie," she replied, mimicking the voice of the character.

"Okay then, your turn," Scott said quickly, looking at Destini.

"I think my favorite is Tigger," she answered. "Because he thinks he's smart and makes it look funny because he really isn't smart. I also like the language twists he uses. But, I've always liked the Green Goblin too."

"The Green Goblin?" Scott asked, trying to comprehend the logic of that choice.

"You know who he is, don't you?" Destini asked in turn.

"Well, sure I do," Scott said. "But… well… it's just an odd character to pick. I mean, he's a psychopathic, murderous villain. What's the appeal?"

"Pain and suffering, I guess," Destini replied.

"So you feel sorry for him?" Scott asked.

"No, I can relate to him."

"Damn… that's pretty harsh," mused Scott.

He began humming the SpongeBob SquarePants theme, but the mood had turned solemn, and he let it trail off with a couple of coughs at the end.

"I just think that no matter how bad a person might be, they've always got some redeeming qualities," Destini continued on the same subject, as if she felt compelled to explain. "Nobody is completely without goodness or compassion. Sometimes bad people do good things, just like good people do bad things."

Scott sensed there was some definite personalization going on, but wasn't sure if Destini was referring to herself or maybe her father.

"What's the worst thing you've ever done?" Eli asked her.

"Hey, that's kind of personal," Scott interjected, assuming the role that Eli had taken as Destini's protector the previous day. "You don't have to answer that."

"I've done some pretty bad things in my life, mostly out of necessity – not because I wanted to," Destini said. "It's a long list, but I try to do good things to make up for all the bad."

"Everybody's done bad stuff, it's no big deal," Scott said.

But Eli pressed the issue.

"Well, out of all the bad things you've done, what's the worst?"

Destini turned around to look at Eli before she answered. "Everybody has secrets, and some of the things I've done are just that. I don't want to talk about them with anybody because they are so bad. Sometimes I don't like myself for the things I've done, so I certainly can't expect others to like me if they knew – and I wouldn't blame them for disliking me. I can't change the way my life has gone, I can only try to make it better with each day. I could give you some relatively plausible and seemingly horrible answer just to appease you, but I won't. I'm not going to tell you, but I'm not going to lie to you either."

The two women stared at each other in silence for what seemed an eternity to Scott.

"I respect that," Eli finally said, and Scott let out an audible sigh, but then rolled his eyes as Eli added, "but I don't completely agree with your logic if some of these secrets that you're not sharing could potentially endanger the lives of others – such as my grandson."

"I don't want that to happen," Destini said, looking now at Scott. "I've already thought about it and if the people that are after me find me, then I'll go to them quietly with my hands in the air."

"There are only two things complicating that scenario," said Eli. "First, the people who you said are after you seem to be the nasty type who shoot first and ask questions later. They probably won't care who happens to be in the way, and secondly, I don't think Scott will just let you give yourself up and go like that. He's falling in love with you."

Scott shook his head in disbelief and looked out the driver's side window to avoid any eye contact with Destini. "Man, I wish somebody would shoot me, no questions asked," he said. "This is the last road trip I'm taking you and your friend Ricardo on, and you can forget about an ice cream treat later."

"Ah, but do you see the difference from the last time I asked you if you had ever been in love Scott?" Eli posed, and then went on to answer her own question. "You didn't have to think about whether it was true or not, and you didn't deny it. You already know the answer."

Scott turned to Destini and was about to make a smartass comment to hide his embarrassment and change the subject, but she was smiling at him. Even her eyes seemed lighter and shinier. Wow, he thought, she looks happy. She actually looks happy at the thought of him being in love with her. He smiled back.

"I'll only say one more thing and then I'll shut up," Eli went on. "If you two want any kind of relationship, you can't start it with secrets between you."

"Oh fine," said Scott with some hesitance, "I'm a closet techno music freak. There, are you happy?"

"Look, there's a..." Eli started to say as she pointed out the front windshield.

"Hey," Scott cut her off, "you promised you'd shut up."

He looked at where she was pointing and saw a sign for several Winslow exits coming up, as well as the outskirts of civilization as marked by gas stations, truck stops and the another set of golden arches.

"That's good timing," he said. "Gas is getting a little low. I better fill up."

"Can you pull into a truck stop?" Destini asked. "They have bigger stores and I need to pick up a couple of things."

Scott saw a truck stop on the other side of the highway, so he took the appropriate exit and crossed over to it. After he had pulled alongside the gas pump, they all got out of the Saturn – with Eli and Destini heading toward the convenience store. Halfway across the lot, however, they stopped and turned around. Scott wondered what the heck they were discussing now, until Eli called "Destini needs her bag!"

Scott had just inserted the nozzle to start pumping the gas, but quickly jumped over the hose and used his keys to open the trunk. He grabbed the bag, slammed the trunk and ran the bag over to them.

"Honestly, I could have gotten it myself," Destini said. "But thank you. I'll go ahead and pay for the gas inside. It's the least I can do. We'll be back in a few minutes."

"No problem," Scott said and walked back to the car.

Aside from the dead body in the trunk and the FBI looking for them, he thought it had been a relatively good morning. It was all a matter of perspective, and that kiss made up for a lot...

Eli and Destini still hadn't emerged from the store after he finished filling the tank, so he pulled the car around to the front parking area to wait. He briefly toyed with the idea of dumping Jerry's body in one of the men's room stalls, but realized that once it was discovered it wouldn't take long for the FBI to start looking for them in this direction. Besides, it was broad daylight. He'd have to wait until night time to figure out how to dispose of their extra passenger.

He looked at the dashboard clock and started to get a little worried. It had been 15 minutes since they had gone in the store. He was just about to get out and look for them when Eli came out. She was motioning toward the trunk and walking toward it. Now what, he thought? He got out quickly and met her at the back of the car.

"What? What's wrong?" He asked.

"I just need to put this in the trunk," she said, lifting the little plastic bag in her hand.

Scott waited for a woman with a small child to walk past and made sure nobody else was around, then opened the trunk again. Eli seemed to have gotten over the initial shock of the body as she casually set the plastic bag in the trunk and started digging through it. Scott was about to ask what she was doing when she pulled out a handful of pine-scented air fresheners, ripped the seals and threw them haphazardly into the back.

He started laughing.

"Hey, you're not the one sitting in the back seat," she said. "Who is this guy anyways, why is he here, and better yet, when is he leaving?"

"His name is Jerry and he's Destini's husband – or was. I'm not exactly sure why he's in his present condition, but at least while he's here, he's not attracting any undue attention or causing any trouble, and I hope he'll be going bidding us adieu tonight."

"Do you think she killed him?" Eli whispered as she finished scattering the green, tree-shaped fresheners. Scott seriously considered the question as he closed the trunk.

"I think it's a possibility, which is why I'm hiding the evidence," he said.

"You shouldn't do that, Scott. We need to call the police."

"Now wait a minute," he replied, "not only were we trying to help Destini, but you've been not-so-subtly playing matchmaker between us ever since you, and I emphasize you, picked her up. Now you just want to turn her over to the police? I hate to say it Eli, but I'm a little disappointed in you. That all-knowing and wise-with-age sheen surrounding you is starting to burn off like morning haze in the sunlight. It's exposing you as somebody who wants to take the comfortable, easy way out of a bad situation instead of taking a risk for what you believe."

"Well, maybe what I believe is fundamentally different from what you believe Scott," she answered. "I know your judgment is clouded right now. You're the one in a haze. I like her too, I really do, but that doesn't change the fact that if she's involved in murder, then she can't be trusted. Anything she says to you -- or anything she does to you -- could all be part of a big fat lie to save herself. I think she's using you. I'm sorry."

"Well, that's just great Eli. Thanks for your opinion. Where is she anyways?"

"I don't know. I thought she came back out here with you," Eli replied.

Scott felt a momentary rush of panic and likened it to a bad dream where something's coming but you can't move. He wanted to run into the store, but his legs suddenly felt heavy and frozen in place. This can't be happening again, he thought. She's gotta be here somewhere.

He watched Eli get into the car. He saw the mother and child coming back out of the store and walking past, holding hands and laughing. He watched a pretty, young girl in cut-off jeans, ankle-high white boots, T-Shirt and baseball cap going into the store. All the activity was taking place at the same time and it all seemed to be transpiring in slow motion to Scott.

Damn, snap out of it, he told himself. He slowly began to walk in the direction of the store. As he entered the glass door, he could see a similar exit straight across on the other side of the facility, leading to the diesel fuel pumps and a truck parking area. He walked directly to the opposite door, scanning the inside of the convenience store as he went. The girl in the baseball cap was looking at him and smiling. His eyes quickly moved on to the next aisle – sure, he thought, have a little marital spat and suddenly it seems like all the girls are looking at you.

It took less than 10 seconds for him to reach the other door and then he was standing outside again. A couple of big rigs were being refueled, a couple more sat empty in the lot beyond, and another was slowly driving out of the truck stop to get back on the highway. Scott watched the 18-wheeler leaving and had a terrible feeling that if Destini had found a new ride, he'd never see her again. But would she really have run off for some reason or had she been taken against her will?

He looked to his left and saw a row of pay phones lining the wall, followed by the men's and women's restrooms, and then a restaurant/café of some kind. Ah ha, he nodded, she was probably hungry and had gone in there. He hurried down the sidewalk toward the café, but stopped as he reached the women's bathroom. He thought about getting Eli to go in and check, but didn't want to waste the time and really didn't care how it would look for him to do so. He placed a hand on the door and swung it open. He stuck his head inside and called her name, but the small room appeared empty. Not taking any chances, he went inside and pushed open the two stall doors. Nothing. He turned to leave and was shocked to see the girl from inside the store leaning up against one of the sinks watching him.

"You're a little bit of a freak, huh?" She asked him. "Into kinky stuff, I'll bet."

"Uh, no, just looking for something," he said. "I mean, my grandmother was in here and lost something. Sorry."

He tried to walk past her, but she stepped in front of him with her hands on her hips.

"I'm looking for something too," she said suggestively. "Can you guess what it is?"

"Boy, I am really in a hurry, if you don't mind," he answered and made a move to go around her, but again she placed herself in his path.

"Now you've hurt my feelings," she said. "You're all alone in a truck stop bathroom with a hot chick like me and all you want to do is leave. Damn. I don't get it. Do I have something stuck between my teeth?"

As she asked the question, more to herself than him, she leaned over to look in the mirror at her teeth. Scott took the opportunity to angle past her and made it to the door. He opened it to find two burly, Hispanic guys in black suits blocking the exit. God, how fucking cliché, he thought, just as each put a hand on Scott's chest and shoved him hard back into the bathroom. He lost his balance and wound up sliding halfway across the floor on his ass, coming to rest just past the girl, who had taken up her previous position of resting against the sink. She gave him a disappointed little pout and shook her head.

"Man," said Scott, "I'm just glad this isn't the men's room. The floors in here are a lot cleaner."

"You're the funny-boy type, aren't you? Get nervous or get into a jam and you start cracking jokes. Funny-boy types usually don't last long, not much of a challenge," she said. "In my experience I've found that over 90 percent of the funny boys start crying like little girls when things get tough – and trust me, funny boy, things will get tough if you don't tell me what I want to know."

"God, you are much too young and pretty to be doing this shit," Scott said, slowly getting up. "Don't you ever sometimes wake up in the morning and just ask yourself, 'What the fuck am I doing with my life?'"

Scott was hoping to throw her off her obviously scripted routine designed to instill fear, not that it was necessary – he was plenty afraid. But she ignored his comments and went on.

"The question you should be asking yourself is just how much of a life you have left," she said, getting off the sink and moving in front of him again. She stopped with her face just inches from his. She opened her mouth, and he thought she was going to threaten him again, but instead she leaned closer and ran her tongue from his chin slowly up to his lips. When she pulled away, he could feel the hardness pressing against his jeans. Too bad that's not me, he thought, glancing down and seeing the switchblade on his crotch. Damn, she was pretty good – distracted me like a pro and now has a knife to my balls.

"Is this the part where the other 90 percent start bawling?" He asked. "Um, no funny-boy pun intended there."

"I don't have a sense of humor – occupational shortcoming. Just tell me where the bitch is hiding and I'll only slice one off," she answered, poking the knife a little harder into his pants – enough so that he could feel the prick on his skin. He could feel her hand pushed up against the inside of his thigh as well.

He quickly considered his options and determined that there was no way he could move away from her fast enough to avoid the blade being shoved into his balls. The hard look in her eyes pretty much confirmed she wouldn't think twice about cutting him there and the fact that the two big dudes outside felt no concern about leaving her alone with him pretty much meant that she could take care of herself – especially when dealing with a harmless amateur like him.

The blade went in a little further and he flinched at the sting. Holy shit, she must have drawn some blood, he swore he could feel a small trickle – or maybe that was just the sweat building up. As long as he wasn't pissing himself, he thought.

"Running out of time," she said.

The idea popped into his mind and at first he was about to dismiss it as a matter of pride, but then he really didn't have time to think of anything else, did he? Oh geez, this has got to be the worst fuckin' plan in the history of bad plans, he thought, but right now it's better than the alternative. All he needed to do was distract her for a second and he didn't have any other options at his disposal.

"Um, I can't be sure," he said stalling, "but she might have been on that 18-wheeler that drove out of here a few minutes ago." He added some tremble to his voice for effect and then let his bladder go, thankful for the extra large cup of coffee he'd had earlier. He kept his eyes directly on hers as he felt the warmth of his urine spread across his groin. Her hand was still pressed against the inside of his thigh holding the knife, come on, she's gotta feel that…

When his brief chance came, he was ready. The tough girl dropped her eyes to his crotch with a disgusted look and reflexively pulled her hand back. He grabbed her wrist with his left hand, at the same time bringing his right forearm and elbow up and slamming it against the side of her face. To her credit, she didn't cry out in pain or yell; but he did – the elbow was still hurting from the previous evening's fall. Oh well, he thought, the big guys outside will just think she's doing a number on him.

He used the momentum of his assault to push her all the way to the wall and then managed to swing around behind her and force her hand and the knife up to her own throat. At least he had strength on his side.

"You are fuckin' sick," she said in a low voice, but with what actually sounded like admiration. "That's a helluva move. I underestimated you."

"It's not exactly what James Bond would have done, but it worked," he said, now feeling the discomfort of the wetness down his leg. Better than your own blood, he told himself.

178

He turned her toward the door and realized he was pressing the knife quite hard on her skin, and blood was running down the blade. He almost eased the pressure, but didn't – he didn't want to turn right around and give her an opening to take away his advantage. He was stronger physically, but he knew that she could probably kick his ass in a matter of seconds.

He pressed himself tight against her butt and led her toward the door. At least she'll cover his embarrassing situation somewhat, but he quickly noted that another one was coming up – literally. Damn, what a time to get a hard on.

"Bringing out the big gun now, huh?" She asked.

"I thought you didn't have a sense of humor," Scott replied. "Oh wait, I see, you're one of those funny girls. Get under a little pressure and start cracking jokes."

"Fuck you. Who are you with?" She asked.

"I'm just a pissed off family man trying to take his poor, old grandmother on a trip," he answered. "Tell them to open the door."

"It won't work," she said. "I just hooked up with these slugs. They don't give a fuck what happens to me. They'll shoot you through me if they have to."

"I don't have any other options," he said, trying to sound tougher than he felt. "Tell them to open the door now."

"Open the door! I'm bringing him out!" She yelled.

The door swung inward and Scott shoved himself and the girl out, yelling at the two men to back up. They did, their expressions not changing in the slightest.

Scott saw that they also gave each other a look and a slight nod as if agreeing nonverbally on some course of action, but they didn't try anything. He was walking backwards now, trying to guide the girl along with him, but it was hard to do while keeping her in front and an eye on the two big guys. The "slugs" began to take one step in their direction with every step that Scott and the girl took backwards, keeping an even distance of about 10 feet between them.

He reached the convenience store just as a trucker was coming out of the door.

"Thanks buddy," Scott said as he slipped in the opening. The girl was really slowing him down now by dragging her feet along. Scott had the feeling she was going to try something soon. He noticed a stand of motor oil right by the door and had another flash of inspiration. It wasn't very gracious of him, but he quickly pushed his temporary shield away and then actually kicked her in the ass and sent her flying out the door they'd just come in. He then used the knife to stab two of the oil containers and tipped the whole stand over in front of the door. The slick, brownish-colored oil spread across the floor and Scott turned and ran as fast he could for the opposite exit. He heard some commotion behind him as he bounded out the other door, but wasn't about to turn around and see if he had actually caused his pursuers to slip.

Just need to jump in the car and step on the gas and... where the fuck is the car?!

It was gone.

Naturally, he thought, nothing ever works as planned. Didn't he know that by now? Like a man who can't believe what his eyes are telling him, he wound up running all the way to the empty spot it had occupied anyways. He stopped and then doubled over, a little out of breath and a lot in pain. The moment he stopped moving is when he felt all of it – the pain in his elbow, his hand and between his legs.

Shit, I can't stand here in the open after all this, he thought, I gotta find someplace to hide. Just as things seemed to have happened in slow motion earlier, the next few seconds all happened so rapidly that he barely registered it in his mind.

The two Men-In-Black wannabes came barreling out of the convenience store and they did not look happy. Scott smiled as one of them raised a small handgun. At least he had the satisfaction of knowing he had pissed them off as he saw they were still sliding a bit from oil. It was some small measure of comfort, he thought.

That's when his little green SC2 came peeling around the corner from the other lot, tires screaming on the tight turn. His two pursuers turned to see the car coming right at them. The one still closest to the door managed to dive out of the way. The other, with the gun raised, got off a shot before the Saturn plowed into him and sent him flying up over the windshield and roof.

Although Scott didn't see the guy land, he heard the hard thud of the body hitting the ground even above the noise of the car's engine.

The Saturn came to a screeching stop beside him, about two feet away. Close enough that he didn't even have to move to reach his hand out and open the door. He smiled as he saw Destini behind the wheel. He got in and collapsed in the seat as she sped away.

CHAPTER TEN

"Don't worry, they won't be coming after us, at least not for a while," Destini said a few minutes after getting back on the highway as she saw Scott looking intently into his side view mirror. He gave her curious look.

"Let's just say their car will need a little repair work before it's roadworthy," she explained.

Scott was about to ask her what she'd done, and how she would even know to do such a thing, when he felt something drop in his lap. He looked down to see one of the Pine-scented air fresheners resting in the middle of his stained pants. Apparently Eli had decided he needed a little assistance.

He looked over at Destini, who was looking straight ahead while gripping the steering wheel with both hands, her jaw clenched and the muscles around her face tight.

"Oh go ahead and fucking laugh," he said. "But it's not what you think. I didn't just wet myself because…"

That's all he managed to get out before his voice was drowned out by her laughter.

Scott was glad to note that Eli hadn't joined in, and after a minute Destini calmed down enough to reassure him that it was okay – that it could happen to anybody in a traumatic situation like he had just experienced.

"I'm telling you, I meant to pee my pants so I could…"

Destini lost it again and this time even Eli couldn't help but laugh.

"Fuck it, never mind," Scott grumbled, but the absurdity of his own comments struck him and it wasn't long before he started to laugh himself.

"You know," he said, after they had quieted down again, "it would be really nice if you could pull over at the next gas station or rest stop so I can kind of clean myself up and change clothes."

"On one condition," Destini said. "As long as I still get to drive. I kind of don't want to sit over there right now."

"Yeah, I kind of gathered that you didn't want to sit over here anymore when you mysteriously vanished back at the truck stop," Scott said, smoothly changing the subject to her disappearance. "I honestly thought you had decided to take off."

"Weeeeeell…." She said, hesitating, "actually, you're right. I did decide to take off. I'm sorry. As much as I like you both, I just didn't want to endanger you like Eli mentioned earlier. It made me think about the risks I might be placing on you. So, for your own good, I was getting in a truck and leaving… but then I saw those guys and that girl pull in and just knew they were looking for me and were gonna cause you trouble. So, I guess I was a little too late in keeping you out of danger. But aren't you glad I at least decided to get out of the truck and come back and help you?"

"Did you know those people?" Eli asked.

"No, but I've seen their type," she replied. "A couple of imported knucklebusters paired with a local hire. You know, I think I should be insulted that's all they sent after me. They must have thought I'd be a soft target."

"I don't think that one guy you ran over will be thinking that anymore," Scott said.

"He may not be thinking anything," Eli cut in. "He may dead. What if you killed him? What if the people in that store are calling the police and we're now fugitives in a hit and run?"

"If he's dead, they'll remove him before any police get there," answered Destini. "They can't afford the scrutiny."

"So they'll just throw his body in the trunk and drive away? Makes you wonder how often that happens on the highways," Eli mused. "Boy I sure feel sorry for them, because I just bought all the air fresheners in that place."

"You know," Eli continued, just as Scott was about to try and change the subject again. "For having just run over

185

somebody and not even knowing if you killed him, you have a pretty cavalier attitude. Have you ever killed anybody before?"

"Eli!" Scott yelled. "If she hadn't come around that corner, I would be the one dead right now. It was like self defense. They were the ones with the guns. In fact, I heard him shoot at the car. You're lucky he missed … he could have put a slug through Ricardo's glossy little head."

There was a long silence after that, which made Scott wonder why Destini hadn't said anything in reply to Eli's question, and when she did finally speak again, he suddenly wasn't sure if she was making an honest observation or trying to cover up.

"You know what's really strange?" Destini asked. "If those muscle heads tracked us down, then why wasn't Jerry with them? I didn't see him anywhere and I would think he would have been the one to lead them to us."

"That's a good question," Scott answered quickly, not giving Eli a chance to intercede with some kind of accusatory remark. "Maybe he was in the area, or somewhere close by. Or maybe they just found us on their own, since Jerry saw last night what direction we were headed and what kind of car we were driving. He could have passed that info on to them."

"I suppose so," said Destini, sounding like she didn't quite believe herself. "I just thought he'd want to be there for the action and to collect his little reward. He's a cold- blooded bastard."

"Yes he is," agreed Eli, nodding. "Very cold... blooded."

Scott gave her a warning look and she added, "I mean, to do something like that to his own wife."

"Please, Destini," Scott said. "As soon as you can possibly find a place to pull over so that I can change."

"Well, I'm a little leery of stopping anytime soon," she said, "just because if Jerry was back there with them somewhere then they do have another vehicle and could be after us right now."

"Trust me, I am willing to take that risk," Scott said, shifting a little uncomfortably in his seat.

"Okay, look, the Petrified Forest National Park is about 45 miles ahead, how about we stop there? They probably have a gift shop and bathroom and we should be a safe distance away by then."

"Yeah, I think Bogey said the same thing before they caught up with him and shot him there," Scott replied.

"Ooooh! The Petrified Forest! I loved that movie. Can we go see the place?" Eli exclaimed.

"Sure," said Scott. "We're only being chased by the FBI, hunted by local law enforcement authorities, and running from the Cosa Nostra. I think we have time to visit the park for an hour or two and enjoy the scenic wonders of nature."

"Oh that's just fabulous," Eli replied, completely ignoring the sarcasm in Scott's statement. "Destini, that's a wonderful idea. I'd like to stop there and get some postcards and see where that movie was made. Did you know that Bette Davis was in that movie with Humphrey Bogart?"

"I'm sorry – never heard of it," Destini said. "Oh and by the way Scott, the Cosa Nostra is a conglomeration of Italian-led mafia groups – not South American. We're probably being chased by some independents in the Columbian or Bolivian trade, as most of the major cartels have splintered now. Although they might be part of the Cali 'Old Guard.'"

"It worries me that you know that stuff," Scott said. "I have no idea what you're talking about."

She laughed and looked at him. "I wish I lived in your world. Fenced in back yard, maybe a swimming pool, Sunday afternoon barbecues, throwing Frisbees to the dog."

"Are you saying I live a sheltered life?"

"No, I don't mean to imply that you're not living in the real world. We both are – just on different continents, so to speak. But they're equally real. I've just been trying to get away from mine and it always ends up finding me. Your lifestyle is a fantasy to me, because I'll never have it," she said.

"I believe that's a choice you can affect," replied Scott. "For example, if you'd gone to college for a degree in, oh, say geology or anthropology or something low key, and married a guy who actually loved you, you wouldn't be in this situation right now."

"Okay, mister optimistic, then tell me what I can do from this point right now to make that alternate reality happen," Destini said.

"Um, too much time and money to go back to college," he mused. "I'd say become a fry cook at Wendy's and marry a guy who loves you."

"I see what you're saying – it doesn't matter what you do in life as long as you share it with someone you love and you're happy."

"Did I say that?" Scott asked. "Damn, that's pretty good. Yeah, that's what I meant."

"You know there's an old Chinese proverb that applies to this situation as well," Eli chimed in. "Never take advice from man who soil his pants."

"I'm not sure that's a Chinese proverb," said Destini. "I think that's just a universally accepted rule."

"Just pull over somewhere, that's all I ask," Scott moaned.

"Okay, okay, you're in luck, there's a little rest area up ahead," Destini said, slowing down.

It was an old, dilapidated rest stop that consisted of half a dozen picnic tables, each covered by some flimsy, rusted metallic awnings. There were no bathrooms or enclosed facilities. He was about to complain, but thought better of it. Even the fact that there was a little white pickup truck parked there didn't matter –

he just wanted to clean himself up and change into some dry pants.

Destini was at least thoughtful to his needs as she pulled into the rest area. She drove past the pickup, then at the end of the row of picnic tables she swung a half U-turn and backed the Saturn up to the opposite curb by the table – which would shield Scott from passing traffic. As they drove in, they had noticed a lone man, his face covered by a straw cowboy hat, sitting on top of the first table with his feet on the bench – presumably the owner of the pickup. He had raised his head as they went past and continued to look in their direction as Destini brought the car to a stop.

"Old Indian guy," Destini said, noticing Scott's gaze. "There are three reservations right in this area – Hopi, Zuni and Apache. As well as a lot of Navajos scattered about here."

She saw his awed look and answered his unspoken question.

"Lot of the young ones want to get out of here, so they come to the big city. Most have few skills that translate to the job market and wind up getting into trouble with the law, so I've had to defend quite a few. Ninety percent wind up going right back here and making a small life for themselves the way their past generations have done."

"Man, that's kind of sad," Scott said. "I never really thought about it..."

Destini released the trunk latch and it popped open behind them.

"You better get out there before the buzzards do," Eli said.

Scott hurried to the back of the car. He peeked around the raised trunk and saw the old Indian man still looking in his direction. Oh well, the guy can't really see me back here, he thought, taking his tennis shoes off without untying them, then undoing his belt and pulling his pants and underwear off.

"What a scenic postcard this would make," he mumbled as he stood half naked in front of the body in the trunk.

Despite the cool breeze blowing unimpeded across the flat desert, he took time to examine his groin area. The bitch at the truck stop hadn't gotten him too bad – just a small nick, about half an inch long, on the inside left thigh. He reached for the half-full, gallon-size cartoon of windshield wiper wash at Jerry's feet.

Gotta clean off with something, he thought, as he twisted off the cap and then poured the pre-mixed light blue liquid all over his lower body.

"My God! Are you peeing again?" Eli called, as the windshield wash splashed loudly off the asphalt.

"Very funny," he yelled back. "Just washing myself off. Almost done."

After drying himself and putting on clean underwear, socks and jeans, he closed the trunk. The old Indian guy was still staring in his direction.

Scott wasn't sure why, but he started walking toward him.

"What are you doing Scott?" He heard Destini ask. "Just get back in the car and let's go."

He didn't answer, but kept walking. What was he doing? He had initially wanted to go over there and ask what the fuck the old guy was staring at and to mind his own business, but halfway there realized how idiotic that would sound. He had been under a lot of stress and was just looking for a release – but this wasn't it. There was no reason to get confrontational.

Instead of stopping in front of the man, whose eyes had followed him all the way, he climbed onto the bench and then sat down on top of the table right next to him.

"How you doin' today?" Scott asked pleasantly, as if they were old friends greeting each other on the street. He wasn't even looking at the man, but watching Destini and Eli in the car.

"Seen better days… but seen worse too. Take the day for what it brings," the man answered, not turning his head either.

"Why is it that when Native Americans say stuff like that it always sounds so wise and mystical, no offense," Scott asked, trying to be politically correct.

"None taken," he replied, rubbing his chin as if pondering the question. "It's how the media portrays us in movies and on TV. Young Indians are bitter, peyote-smoking alcoholics, but as they age they apparently become kindly and wise."

"That is pretty cliché," Scott agreed. "How close to the truth though?"

"Let's just say if it were true, this wise old Indian wouldn't be sitting here with a broken serpentine belt on his truck because he would have been smart enough to change it before it snapped."

Scott nodded empathetically.

"Well," he said, "no need to be stranded out here. We can give you a ride to the next gas station."

"I may not be wise," the man answered, lifting his left hand to reveal a small cell phone, "but I'm not dumb either. I've got Triple A – already called them."

Scott laughed and leaned his head back to enjoy the warmth of the sun on his face.

"Your kachina needs rest," the old man said. "Always listen to what it tells you."

"There's a fine line between wise and cryptic," Scott sighed, looking at his table partner.

"The kachina is your inner spirit force of life. It was not ready to continue the journey you are on," the man said. "That is why you came over here to rest."

"Well, that's not exactly why I came over here, but it sounds like a good idea. Every time I get back in that car, events seem to be out of my control."

"Sometimes you can not control events, but you always have control over your reactions to them – remember that," the man said, lifting the brim of his faded yellow hat to look into Scott's eyes.

"That's cross-cultural plagiarism. I think I read that on a fortune cookie once," Scott joked.

The man's lips turned up and the lines on his brown, leathery face seemingly stretched into dozens of tiny smiles.

"You do not believe in God or a higher power."

"Um, I'm not really religious, but yeah, I think I believe in God and…" Scott started.

"That was not a question. I was making an observation," the Indian interrupted.

Just then Destini honked the car horn and waved for Scott to come back. He held up his index finger to let her know he'd be there in a minute.

"I feel like you came to me for a reason," the old man said. "Destiny brought you here to this lonely, desert rest stop where I was meant to be waiting."

Scott laughed out loud.

"Buddy, you just earned your wise old Indian membership card. You got that one right on the nose. Destini did bring me here, I'm just worried about where she's taking me next."

"Wherever she takes you, I want to give you something to carry with you on your journey," the man said, getting off the table and walking toward his truck. Scott shrugged and followed.

The old man opened his passenger side door, reached toward a box on the floorboard and pulled out a figurine of some kind. He turned and handed it to Scott. It was a Native American in ceremonial costume with one leg raised as if doing a dance and each hand holding a lightning bolt. It stood on a small wooden base and the predominantly turquoise and white paint of the costume actually appealed to Scott.

"This is a Kachina doll," the man said. "Kachinas also represent spirit fathers or gods of nature, such as the clouds, the sky and the trees. This is a storm Kachina. I did not pick it for you, but closed my eyes and my hand was guided to it. I do not know the meaning it has for you, but it is yours."

"I like it," Scott said with genuine affection. "What is its purpose?"

"Kachinas are protective, supernatural beings who help humans," the old man replied. "They can be invoked to bring the elements, such as rain, and they can bestow good fortune."

"So it's kind of like an angel – only the Native American version," Scott wondered.

"In a manner of speaking, yes. It is a Hopi belief."

"Thank you, sir," Scott said. "I wish I had something to give you in return, but trust me, you wouldn't want what's in the trunk of my car."

To Scott's surprise, the old Indian simply turned his back and walked toward the bench again. No goodbye, no have a nice trip or be well and safe on your journey. The purpose of the conversation was apparently over and done, Scott mused, so why waste time with formalities?

Wow, what a trip, he thought, as he made his way back to the Saturn. He reflected again on how the last two days had turned into a surreal mix of cinematic events. Maybe Bruce Willis can play me in the movie version, he thought. Wait, doesn't he usually get shot and die? Maybe not such a good choice…

"How much did you pay for that hideous thing?" Eli asked as he got back in the car with his Kachina doll.

"Nothing, it was free."

"Well, you still got ripped off," she said.

"I like it Scott," Destini came to his aid. "I think it's cool. It'll bring you good luck."

"That's what he said," Scott replied.

"Sure, because he got lucky," said Eli. "He found some sucker to take that thing off his hands. If you'd have held out, he probably would have paid you to take it."

"Hey, you've got your little Ricardo and I've got my little Indian dude, and I think my guy can kick your one-dimensional friend's ass, so quit messing."

"I guess I just need to get me a little friend to play with now," Destini said, looking right at Scott's lap. He wasn't sure if she was looking at his new figurine or eyeing something else, but he smiled. Maybe it was bringing him luck already…

True to her earlier statement, Destini refused to relinquish the wheel, so Scott found himself thumbing through the road map as they merged back onto the highway.

"It looks like we can go either one of two ways to get to the Petrified Forest," he said. "If we stay on 40, we'll see an entrance about 30 miles down the highway, but if we get off of 40 just up ahead at Holbrook and jump on 180, we can catch another entryway into the park and take the park road all the way through and back up to 40 on the other side."

Destini shot him a look that seemed to question whether he was really sure he wanted to lose time and ground on their pursuers.

"It'd be the last thing they expect us to do, wouldn't it? Stop at a tourist attraction and relax – they certainly won't be pulling over to look for us there," Scott said.

"You do have a point," Destini said. "It'd be unbelievably stupid to just go visit a park while being chased."

"Then it's settled," Eli said. "I'm so excited. The Petrified Forest... there are fossils there that are millions of years old."

"Yeah, and maybe a million years from now somebody will find our fossils there after we get shot and dumped in the dirt, and they'll wonder what our story was," Scott said, bouncing his Kachina doll on his knee. As soon as he said it, however, the idea of dumping their extra baggage in some ravine in the middle of nowhere seemed like a good one.

Destini chose the southern route, turning onto Highway 180, and fifteen minutes later they were at the entrance station to the park. A serious-looking older woman in a park ranger outfit and cream-colored hat sitting in a little wooden booth in the center of the road told them it would be $14 for a vehicle pass. Eli quickly took the money out of her little change purse and passed it up front to Destini.

In return, the ranger lady handed them a small brochure and told them that the Rainbow Forest Museum was about one mile ahead on the right and that driving from one end of the park to the other, nonstop, would take about 30 minutes.

Lastly, she tapped the big brown sign below her window and instructed them to read the notice that removal of any petrified wood from the park was prohibited by law and would result in a fine. Scott felt like asking if they would be charged for making a deposit of a stiff artifact of their own.

Eli began enthusiastically rattling off information from the brochure as Destini drove them towards the museum.

"The park has 93,533 acres," she said. "That includes the multi-hued badlands of the Painted Desert, archeological sites and 225 million-year-old fossils."

"Any other time, that would actually sound pretty fascinating," said Destini. "But I'm afraid we won't have much time to see the sights."

"Why not?" Asked Eli. "You're not going anywhere particular, or if you are, you haven't told us. This is my birthday trip and we're in no rush. I'd like to take a look around."

"I agree," Scott said, causing Destini to look at him as if he'd lost his mind. "Think about it. Whoever's after us will just keep on going down the highway looking for us. We might as well let them get further away."

"Your decision," Destini said with a shrug, clearly not pleased.

"Hey, here's something interesting for you and your little lightning bolt doll, Scott," Eli said, still reading the guide. "It says that afternoon thunder and lightning storms are frequent. Avoid high observation areas, open areas, and rocky overhangs. If you are caught in the open, squat with your hands on your knees, keep your head low, and wait for the storm to pass."

"See, I have nothing to worry about," Scott said smugly. "I'm protected. I have the God of Lightning."

"Hey," he said, suddenly, as if the thought had just occurred to him, "when does this end?"

Both Destini and Eli gave him puzzled looks.

"I mean, when are we safe? When is it over? When do these people stop following us? If they lose us now on the highway, will they say 'Gosh darn, they tricked us and got away. They win. We might as well take our ugly asses back to Columbia.' Or will they get pissed and just keep looking – for weeks, months or years until they find us?"

"Don't you mean until they find me?" Destini asked.

"No, I meant 'us'," Scott answered. "It's my car. If I have to drive you around the country for the next 20 years, then I'll have to make that sacrifice in order to ensure your safety."

Destini laughed and looked over at him, but then bit her lower lip when she saw the look in his eyes. He may have been joking about driving around the country, but she sensed a certain seriousness in his gaze that implied he was willing to stay with her for a long time – and not just because some people were after her.

"Scott, you don't even know me. You don't know anything about me. I can take care of myself. I just can't afford to…" she let her thought trail off.

"What?" He prodded. "You can't afford to have to take care of me too? I'd be slowing you down?"

"No, Scott. That's not what I was going to say. Let's discuss this later."

"So you can try to run away again?"

"No," Eli cut in, "she means when you two can talk privately. Which you can do up here at the Rainbow Forest Museum because I need to find a bathroom."

Destini let out a long breath, as if welcoming the distraction, and pulled into the half-empty parking lot on her left. She stopped the car directly in front of the Rainbow Forest Curio Shop, which appeared to have a snack bar inside.

As soon as Destini turned the key in the ignition off, Eli was tapping on Scott's shoulder for him to get up and let her out – which he did. Noticing that Destini was staying in her seat, Scott got back in and shut the door.

"She must really have to go," Scott said.

"I'll bet you're good though," Destini said, smiling at him.

"Doesn't matter if I am or not," Scott replied. "I've suddenly developed a phobia about public restrooms, and it has nothing to do with dirty toilet seats. Besides, if you think I'm letting you out of my sight, think again."

"Oh stop already with the hurt feelings," Destini said. "Do you think this is easy for me? I don't know what to do or where to go. And I don't want to worry about you or these feelings I'm having... because, honestly, before you get any ideas, I don't know if I'm really falling for you or just falling -- and looking for something to grab onto in desperation. And how the hell can you possibly think that you're having feelings for me? This situation isn't fair to either of us. I like you, but... these aren't normal circumstances. We can't trust our feelings for each other right now."

They sat in the front seat staring at each other.

"So what the hell was with the big kiss and talk about getting a hotel room?" Scott asked.

Instead of answering, Destini looked down and shook her head apologetically. Then she opened her door, got out and walked off toward the open desert area away from the building.

"What the fuck..." Scott muttered to himself, totally confused by her reaction. He got out of the car and followed her.

She had stopped at the end of the parking lot and was looking out over the sandy horizon. He came up beside her, but she continued to stare blankly straight ahead and didn't acknowledge his presence. Scott moved directly in front of her and placed his hands on his hips as if to show that he wasn't going away until they finished their conversation. He looked into her eyes and they appeared a little glassy.

"Okay, you're absolutely right about all those things you said," Scott said quietly. "Maybe our feelings are being influenced by these events, but I don't think that means we should just ignore them completely. The feelings are there and maybe the danger and uncertainty is just speeding up the natural process. There's a little sense of urgency, but it's not like I just want to get laid because I might be dead tomorrow."

"But what if I do?" She asked.

They both started laughing.

"You sure as hell are persistent," Destini went on. "Look, I can't make you any promises Scott. I just don't know what's going to happen. I'm scared and I'm confused. I hate to admit that, but there you go. And I'm worried about you and your grandmother on top of that. Maybe I should tell you the truth. Maybe then you won't feel so obligated to rescue me and you can just leave me here. I don't deserve your help."

"Just be honest with me," he said.

She turned her eyes away from his and looked to the ground as she spoke.

"Well, first of all, those goons back at the truck stop that are trying to kill me, and who almost killed you, well… they aren't from some rival drug family and there is no reward out for me."

"What?!" Scott blurted out. "Then who the hell are they and why are they after you?"

"They work for my father. He wants me dead."

Scott studied her facial features for any sign that she was joking, but her expression didn't change.

"Why?" He finally managed to ask.

"The truth is that I'm not a good person, Scott. Usually when people are on the run, there's a reason they're being chased."

She paused, as if still debating on whether or not to continue. She looked back up into his eyes and spoke.

"First of all, I'm sorry I lied to you. I guess I was scared you'd call the cops or leave me on the side of the road."

"Do you really think I could do that Destini?" He asked, raising his left hand and gently brushing her hair away from her eyes. The act was useless in its intent, as the wind blew it right back across her face, but the intimacy of it got his point across.

Her smile answered his question, however brief it was before she started explaining.

"My father financed my education so I could work for him in the legal system of the city where he trafficked the majority of his drugs into the United States," she said. "It wasn't

Jerry, like I said, who helped get the drug runners and bad guys set free on technicalities. It was me."

She stopped and waited for his reaction.

"Hey, I'm not making any judgments," he said with a shrug. "I have no idea what your life was like."

"Don't be so goddamn naïve, Scott. Think about it – I was directly supporting those who brought illegal drugs into this country and getting school children hooked, which in turn leads to other crimes as these kids look for ways to get the money they need to buy the drugs. Robbery, prostitution, even murder. I just kept the whole system turning in a nice, smooth circular motion by putting the bad guys back on the streets. That makes me a bad guy, Scott."

"But you finally realized that and are getting away from it," he said. "It takes courage to break away from something like that and face the consequences you're dealing with now."

To his surprise she laughed even more, brushing her own hair back from her face and revealing her tears.

"God, you just don't get it, do you," she said. "I knew it was wrong all along, but I didn't have that courage you're talking about to break away from it or do anything about it. I just kept on doing it, Scott. I just kept... on... doing... it."

She took a deep breath, looking up toward the sky, before continuing.

"I'd still be sitting in my 20th floor luxury office pulling in more than $50,000 per month, and trust me that's not a regular starting attorney's salary, if it weren't for one minor detail. You see, even at being bad, I apparently wasn't very good. My sterling public defender's record obviously raised suspicions, and I'm sure it didn't take long for someone to piece together my own background – despite the fact that I changed my name and tried to hide my past.

"I didn't know it, but the FBI had tagged me and built up a pretty good file against me. By the time they confronted me with it, I had a choice – go to jail for the rest of my life or immunity from prosecution and witness protection if I helped them bring down my father's North American operations by supplying names."

"So you fled rather than betray your family?" Scott interrupted.

"That sounds like the noble, if somewhat misguided, thing to do," she answered with a slight chuckle. "Haven't you been paying attention here? Do you think I was raised with any morals or values? To hell with family loyalty. My dad was just using me. It worked for him while it lasted, but I'll be damned if I'll spend the rest of my life in prison for him – not that I don't deserve it."

"Okay, maybe I am naïve and sheltered – but I'm not making the connection. I don't understand how you got here," Scott said.

"That's easy," she said. "Apparently I wasn't the only one on my father's payroll. I was cooperating with the FBI, but my father was always one step ahead. The FBI began to think I was double crossing them with tips that didn't pan out, and as a result I thought they had a mole in their organization."

"Jerry…" Scott muttered.

"Hey, you finally got one right," Destini said. "Too bad I didn't figure that one out as quick. My father's business associates had gotten to my dear, sweet husband and he sold me out. They probably didn't even have to threaten him – just dangle a little cash in front of his nose. I didn't realize it until after the trailer park ambush, but Jerry set me up. Then again, I was trying to do the same to my father's contacts – it's an ugly, little world I live in, so I can't really complain. Everybody's expendable.

"So, now the FBI wants to put me away for life and my father just wants to end it. I'm not sure which option I would prefer at this point."

She finally brought her eyes back to his and waited for a response. Scott took a step back and looked her up and down, as if literally sizing up the situation.

"You're not expendable," he said flatly.

"Either you're very damn idealistic or you really do like me, and if that's the case then I'm worried about being with a foolish guy like you," she said, shaking her head in wonder. "Let me summarize for you … Destini is a lying, untrustworthy criminal with little conscience or morals and who's only out to save her own ass. Is that clear enough for you?"

"It's hard to argue that point," Scott said, "but your characterization is flawed. You saved my ass too. You could have left on that truck instead of coming back to help me when you saw I was in trouble, but you didn't. And that tells me something more than just what you want to have me believe. Even the Green Goblin has some redeeming qualities, remember?"

"Geez, and I'm talking to SquareBob SpongePants – you are porous. How can this not be sinking in?"

Scott laughed. "It's SpongeBob SquarePants. And don't forget, he's absorbent too, so I can soak up a lot of bullshit."

"Oh come on," she said, "how do you know I didn't have my own self interests in mind when I came back. They would have broken you in five minutes. That's not much of a head start. I came back to fuck up their car so they couldn't come after me."

"You know, you're right about one thing," Scott said, grinning. "You are a liar. I don't believe that, so fuck you. Why are you trying so hard to turn me away?"

"I just want you to see the truth," she said. "This is what I am. This is what I'll always be."

"Yeah, well I want you to see the truth too," Scott said, raising his voice as the wind picked up loudly.

She spread her hands out, palms up and shook her head as if waiting for him to continue.

He stepped in closer to her.

"What?" She asked.

"That was supposed to be a romantic moment," Scott said laughing. "You were supposed to look in my eyes and see the truth about how I feel about you."

"Oh, sorry, guess I'm not used to those," she said.

"Well, you better get used to them," he answered. "Like this…"

He leaned in and her open mouth met his. This kiss was different than the first two they had shared on the side of the highway. It was slow and relaxed. They took their time, with Destini placing her hands on his back and gently pulling him tighter to her body. His hands were loose around her waist, but all he could feel was the warmth of her mouth and her smooth tongue on his.

All the feeling in his body was localized to that one area where they had joined and he felt himself drifting away from every other sensation except for being locked together, almost as if he was disembodied save for that one act.

They remained like that for several minutes, neither wanting to be the first to break away or lose the moment. Finally, a strong gust of wind slapped them back into reality and they slowly pulled their faces away from each other.

"That was nice," Destini said, running her tongue across her bottom lip. "But I hope you know that it didn't mean anything to me."

"Liar," he whispered and they both smiled.

CHAPTER ELEVEN

Scott had his arm around Destini's shoulder and she was huddled against him as they returned to the car. To the few park visitors who noticed, he thought they probably looked just like an ordinary couple on vacation with no worries in the world – and certainly without any dead husbands hidden in the trunk.

"Um, by the way," Scott said, thinking about it, "what's the deal with Jerry now?"

"If we're lucky, we'll never see that bastard again," she replied. "But I'm not going to underestimate him again. I don't think we've seen the last of him."

"I'd have to agree," Scott merely said.

They saw that Eli hadn't made it back to the car, so they entered the curio shop and found her sitting at a small table at the snack bar area. She was dipping a white plastic spoon into a tall root beer float.

"Now that looks good," Scott said, as he and Destini each took a seat. "Man, I used to love those when I was a kid."

"I know," said Eli. "I used to make them for you when you were kid."

"That's right, I can't believe it's been so long ago," he said. "I remember riding my bike home from school in the afternoons and sometimes stopping at your house on the way just to have a float. Seems like you always had one waiting."

"I did," said Eli, with a smile. "And on the afternoons that you didn't show up, I ate them myself."

"Really?" Scott asked. "You mean you always had one made every afternoon whether I came by or not? Wow... that's pretty neat. I always thought you saw me riding down the street and that you were just really fast. So, basically, you cheated... I'm impressed."

"No, just a grandmother's little secret," she said. "You're my only grandson. I've always taken special care of you Scott. I love you for who you are, but you also are the only link I have left to Robert. We only had one child, your mother, so I was very excited when she had you – a boy. I see so much of your grandfather in you – not just physical characteristics, like your eyes and nose, but the strength of character, the honesty and integrity, and the trusting nature and willingness to help others."

Scott was about to thank her for the compliments, when she added, "Of course all it did was get him killed."

Destini shifted uncomfortably at that remark and looked away from the table, toward the window. Scott frowned, unsure if Eli had actually meant to make such a correlation to his own situation with Destini, but decided that he wouldn't put it past her.

"And now that you are doing this for me – taking me to see Wendell – it means just as much to me as all those delicious root beer floats meant to you," Eli added.

"Well, speaking of taking you to see Wendell... I think as soon as you finish that ice cream, we better get going," Scott said.

"I'm afraid I can't just yet," Eli said. "I hadn't taken my pills all day until now and I'm hurting very much. When that happens, I just have to sit still for a while and let the medicine kick in or I get really nauseous and pass out. I really can't be moving around right now. I'm sorry. I don't want to slow you down or anything. If you want to get a float or a coffee and give me a little time, I'd appreciate it."

"Yeah, sure, I guess," Scott said, noting that Destini had squirmed anxiously in her seat again at the mention of delay. "Um, how much time until you think you'll be feeling better."

"Not too long," Eli replied. "Maybe twenty or thirty minutes."

Scott glanced over at Destini, but she seemed to purposely avoid eye contact and continued to stare out the front window at the car. She did, however, speak – "I'll have a large coffee please, Scott."

After getting along so pleasantly at the start, Scott sensed a growing tension between the two women that made him a bit uneasy as well. But Destini's request gave him a good excuse to get out of their way. Maybe they can talk it out while he's gone, he thought.

He told them he'd be back shortly and headed for the counter on the far side of the room, but as he was going down an aisle of kitschy souvenirs a hand fell on his shoulder from behind and he froze. The possibilities raced through his mind as he slowly turned around, only to find someone he'd never seen before. Instead of wondering why some stranger was stopping him, he breathed a small sigh of relief and smiled at the short, bespectacled man before him.

"Sir, can you please come with me a moment," the man said, his voice cracking slightly as if he were nervous. Scott noticed a nametag on his crisp white shirt that said "Marty Mickelson, Curio Shop Manager."

The man started off toward an "Employee's Only" marked hallway, apparently assuming that Scott would follow.

I don't think so, not after the day I'm having buddy, Scott thought – remaining motionless in the aisle until the manager began talking again and looking to his left only to realize there was nobody with him. He turned around to see Scott still in the aisle behind him and his face flushed red with embarrassment. Almost sheepishly, he quickly looked around to see if anybody had noticed and then hurried back to where Scott waited.

"Sir," he started again, pointing to his little bronze nametag, "I'm the manager here and I must ask you to please come with me for a moment."

"You're not the real Marty Mickelson," Scott said, not exactly sure why he was messing with this harmless, stocky George Costanza look-alike, but finding it a welcome diversion from everything else. "I went to school with Marty. I've been over to dinner at his house with his wife and three children. I play 18 holes with him every other week. You are not Marty Mickelson, so who the hell are you?"

"I… uh… I am…" The man stammered, again bringing his hand up to point at his nametag as if that made it so. "I'm Marty. I am Mr. Mickelson. I… uh…"

His eyes began to frantically dart around as if he were looking for a curio shop employee to call over and back his claim.

"Hey, it's okay," Scott said. "Just kidding around a little. Sorry. Just thought it was funny because I actually do know a guy named Marty Mickelson and it's not a common name so what are the odds?

"I'm Hank, Hank Dobbins," Scott said extending his hand. Might as well keep on lying, he thought, using the name of one of his old college roommates.

Mickelson was visibly relieved, smiling and nodding his head vigorously as he grasped Scott's hand and shook it. With his other hand he wiped away the little beads of sweat that had started to form on his balding head. This guy was a typical smalltime manager, thought Scott, the kind who couldn't handle confrontations, probably hid in his little office most of the work day and let his employees walk all over him.

"What is it you need?" Scott asked.

"Well, um, really we should go do this in private Mr. Dobbins," Mickelson said. "Please, if you would be so kind as to come to my office."

This guy's pretty adamant about getting me away from the general public, Scott considered with some hesitation, or maybe I'm just too damn paranoid now. Still, he stood his ground.

"I'm sorry," Scott answered, "but I can't think of any reason why you would need to speak with me privately and..."

Shit, of course, you can, he thought, halting in mid-sentence and then trying to recover.

"...and, well, can you give me some idea of what this is all about?"

But he knew, dammit, of course he knew. It was Destini. Her face had been all over the news and this guy had recognized her from the television reports.

Mickelson leaned close to Scott and confirmed his suspicions in a hushed tone, "It's about the woman with you. I'm afraid she's done something and… um… well, it might involve the police and stuff…"

Fuck, did this guy already call the cops, Scott wondered.

"Please," the man said, now physically taking Scott by the elbow and guiding him toward the hall at the end of the souvenir section. There was a sense of urgency to his behavior that bemused Scott and he quietly walked along, his mind already going over options to get out of the park. He chuckled as an image popped into his head of Bogart holding a crowd of park guests at gunpoint in a restaurant while the police surrounded the place.

A girl at the snack bar counter gave them a puzzled look as they went past.

Mickelson's office was the last door at the end of the hallway, right across from the employee's washroom. He led Scott inside and then motioned for him to have a seat in one of the two straight-backed wooden chairs facing his desk.

"I'm fine, thanks," Scott replied, staying on his feet near the door. This seemed to disturb the already rattled manager even more and he appeared unsure whether to go and seat himself in his own dominating, large, black leather chair on the other side of the room behind his desk. It was obviously his perceived source of power and would make him feel more in charge of the situation, Scott gathered.

"Oh, okay," Mickelson said meekly and reached behind Scott to close the door.

They stood staring at each other a moment until Mickelson coughed to clear his throat and then proceeded.

"This is never easy and I'm not quite sure how to say this," he said, "but the old woman at the table you sat down with, well, she, um, placed an item from the shelf into her purse without paying for it."

Scott felt like a huge rock had just been removed from on top of his chest and he started laughing involuntarily.

Clearly mistaking his reaction for one of disbelief, Mickelson quickly droned on about the seriousness of the offense and how he didn't want to have to call the police because of the woman's age, but that he would, because – well, um, it was his job.

Scott waved his hand in front of him, imploring the man to stop because until he shut up about it, Scott was afraid that he wouldn't be able to control himself.

"No, really, she did sir," the manager went on, oblivious to Scott's unspoken plea. "I know this is something you'd rather not think of, but sir, I'm quite sure of this. We even have it on video if you don't believe me."

With that, Mickelson walked over to the small credenza on wheels in the corner by his desk and rolled it outward so Scott could see the four small black-and-white monitors wired into a main receiver on a shelf below that provided angles of the interior of the museum and curio shop. One of the surveillance cameras was still focused on the table where Eli and Destini sat.

Scott wandered over to the desk, his laughter trailing off. He saw that Eli had the float glass now lifted to her lips and was draining the last of the dessert. Destini, meanwhile, had found a pen and was writing something on her napkin. Neither of them was paying any attention to each other. So much for talking things out, Scott sighed.

Mickelson punched a few buttons and the image on the top monitor spun into rewind.

Scott watched with a frown as the camera was focused entirely on Eli and he watched her in reverse, high-speed get her float at the counter, pay for the float, order the float, walk to the snack bar counter, drop a small trinket into her purse, pick something up off the shelf, stop in the souvenir aisle … okay, he was getting dizzy and the gift shop manager had proved his point. He was just about to say he'd take care of it when the tape kept going and he felt that tightening in his chest once again.

As Mickelson fumbled with the buttons to stop the tape, Scott watched dumbfounded as Eli made a call from the pay phone next to the hallway by the snack bar counter.

What the hell? What is she doing? Who the hell could she be calling?

The screen went black.

"Whoa, whoa," Scott said. "Listen can you play that again at normal speed?"

"Yes sir, that's what I was about to do, but it rewound a little too far."

"No, it's fine – please let it play from there. In fact, would you mind backing it up to where she actually goes to the phone."

"I suppose so," the manager said, sounding as confused as Scott felt. "But at that time it's just an overall store shot because I hadn't trained the camera directly on her until she acted strangely in the souvenir section."

"Yeah, yeah, that's fine, whatever," Scott answered, concerned about what this could mean.

Mickelson rolled the tape back a little more on normal rewind mode so the screen remained blank. He then hit the play button again and a wide shot of the snack bar counter appeared on the monitor. The only person in the frame was the snack bar attendant behind the counter.

Mickelson coughed again and quickly reached his hand out to the control, but Scott grabbed it and stopped him.

"Um, I went back to far, let me just forward a little," he said, nervously pushing his glasses up on the bridge of his nose with his free hand.

"No, no, let it play," Scott said.

As they watched, the camera suddenly zoomed in on the face of the young teen behind the counter. She was kind of a pretty girl, thought Scott in an offhand way. Then the camera slowly panned down to the girl's chest – the little white top she wore revealing her smooth, tan cleavage. That, and the fact that her two uppermost buttons were undone and her well-endowed assets were very much on display.

"Nice view Marty," Scott said, holding tight to the man's right hand, which strained to get free no doubt to attempt to turn off the monitor. "Does Arizona have different laws for pedophilia that I'm perhaps not aware of?"

Mickelson attempted to stop the play with his left hand, but Scott pulled him away from the console by his right hand just enough to keep the controls out of reach.
They watched as the girl, obviously bored without any customers, leaned forward on the counter with both elbows and placed her hands under her chin.

"Ooooh, that's a sweet pose," Scott said, rubbing it in as the young girl's flesh strained against the skimpy material of the blouse. He figured the incidental shoplifting charge was not going to be an issue anymore.

The camera view tightened up even more on the counter girl's exposed cleavage and then the frame started vibrating up and down -- slowly at first, but then more erratically. It took Scott a second to make the connection and then he quickly dropped Mickelson's hand with disgust.

"Eeeeeeewww," he said, shaking his hand around in the air as if that would get rid of any germs or other unwanted substances.

Mickelson dropped back into his chair with a choked sob and let the leathery expanse swallow his shaking frame.

Scott, meanwhile, had turned his attention back to the screen while now vigorously wiping his hand on his jeans. He looked away from the unsteady view of the girl's chest to the current image of Eli and Destini. It was Eli now who was looking out of the window, the empty float glass in front of her, while Destini had her head down and continued to doodle on a napkin.

"See, what's up with that?" Scott asked, glancing back at the distraught manager but speaking more to himself. "I just don't understand women. They always say they want you to talk about your feelings and be open, yet it's like their own advice doesn't apply to them. I mean, look at them – they're giving each other the cold shoulder."

On the adjacent monitor, the image on the young girl's upper body steadied and then slowly zoomed back out to show the full counter.

"Damn, you're fast," Scott said. "And look, she's smiling, it was good for her too."

"Please," he heard Mickelson say from behind, "please sir, just leave. Take your friends and go."

"Not yet Marty," Scott said, pointing to the image of Eli entering the camera's line of sight. "This is what I've been waiting for. How do I zoom in on her?"

Mickelson didn't bother getting up as he replied in a dejected tone, "You can't zoom in on the recorded version, only while it's taping live."

Scott watched the small monochrome figure of Eli go to the pay phone, look around and then take something out of her pocket. She placed it on the metal ledge of the phone stand that held a worn copy of the Yellow Pages and began to dial.

"Son of a bitch, what is that? Who's she calling?" Scott said, completely amazed by what he was seeing before him.

Apparently someone answered the other end of the line because Eli started talking into the phone. Several times during the conversation she looked back toward the entrance. After about a minute, she hung up and wandered off the screen toward the souvenirs.

"Hey, hey!" Scott exclaimed as he noted that she had left the scrap of paper by the phone. He ran toward the office door, yanked it open and then sprinted down the hallway.

He reached the end of the hallway and stopped running so as not to attract attention. He turned and walked toward the pay phone. He could easily see the white square atop the yellow cover of the phone book and his heart began to race.

Fuck, fuck, fuck… he thought getting closer. I know what that is, good God, I know what that is. He stopped in front of the phone and looked down. Yep, sure enough, it was Ben's card. He had no idea why or how Eli would have gotten it, but what really bothered him was that she actually used it. She called the freakin' FBI, he thought. Jesus, she must have told them where they were … why else would she do it?

Her words at the table came back to him… "You're my only grandson. I've always taken special care of you Scott."

Oh man, she thought she was protecting him. And what else did say – she needed about 30 minutes to rest? She was stalling and that meant they were almost here.

"Fuck!" He yelled out loud, grabbing the card and stuffing it into the front pocket of his jeans. As he walked past the snack bar, the counter girl started to speak.

"Sir, please watch your language. This is a family…"

"Hey," Scott said, interrupting her, "don't worry so much about me. See that little surveillance camera up there? Your boss, Mr. Mickelson, sits at his desk and zooms in on you. There's a bottle of moisturizing lotion and a box of Kleen-Ex on his desk for a reason."

The girl looked up at the camera in disbelief, but that expression was quickly replaced by one of horror.

Scott didn't bother to see the gamut of her reactions. He made his way over to the table where Eli and Destini were locked in a silent battle of wills. As he approached, something else struck him as odd. Although the video of Eli's shoplifting incident had played in reverse and at double speed, he could have sworn that she had looked directly up into the store's camera both before and after pocketing the trinket. Good God, maybe she was hoping to get caught and that store security would call the police as a way to stall even longer and get the authorities on the scene. If Destini were recognized and apprehended as a result of Eli's petty theft, then she would be in the clear as to having turned her in outright. That seemed a reasonable explanation to Scott, because he just couldn't picture his grandmother ever taking something that didn't belong to her, especially committing a crime while doing so. Holy crap, was she really that diabolical?

"What took you?" Asked Eli, as he came up to the table.

"And where's my coffee?" Added Destini.

On impulse, Scott decided not to blurt everything out as he had intended. He casually took a seat, realizing, however, that whatever he said or did, it would have to be quick so they could leave.

"Um, sorry, had an argument with the counter girl and decided not to give my money to this establishment. Bitch…"

"You look a little flushed," said Eli. "What did she do? What happened?"

"Don't want to talk about it – just want to get out of here. You ready to go yet?"

"No," replied Eli, "in fact, speaking of giving money to this establishment, can you go pay for this for me?"

She pulled a small Petrified Forest refrigerator magnet out of her purse and pushed it across the table toward Scott.

Unbelievable, he thought, of course she wouldn't steal anything. She hadn't even left the premises of the store with any unbought merchandise, so technically how could that dumbass manager even accuse of her of a crime? Fortunately, Mickelson's inappropriate, knee-jerk reaction had provided Scott a temporary advantage, but he realized that time was quickly running out on him.

Eli confirmed that fact.

"Oh Scott, if you could just pay for this and give me 15 more minutes, I think I'll be much better," Eli said.

"Yeah, well... tell you what... cuz I really don't feel like having to put up with this shitty customer service in here... would you mind buying that yourself on your way out, while Destini and I wait for you in the car?"

Without giving her a chance to answer, Scott stood slid a ten-dollar bill toward Eli and got back up. Destini followed his lead, apparently more than ready to get away from the uncomfortable aura that had descended upon her and Eli.

"I guess, if you feel that strongly about it," Eli answered. "I'll be out in a little while then."

"Sounds great," Scott replied. As they turned to go, Scott reached back down for the napkin that Destini had been scribbling on. It was a poem.

"What's this?" He asked as they walked toward the exit.

"Oh, just something I like," she said. "We weren't talking, so I figured I might as well do something."

He read the words…

The Ninth Day

Remember that night

When we were together on the beach

The sun drowned in the sea

The waves reached higher

And higher

You couldn't let go

And neither could I

We were melted and grown

Into each other

Into the sand

That night we drowned

Our souls

Our spirits

Our hearts

Our bodies floated further

On the fierce waves

And washed ashore

On the ninth day

"I get it, pretty ironic," remarked Scott. "They loved each other so much that they couldn't just simply let go and save themselves, so they wound up dying together. Are you subtly trying to tell me something?"

"Must have been my subconscious," Destini replied.

"Well, it's pretty gloomy," Scott said.

"What did you expect? Do I look like a sunshine and rainbows kind of girl to you?" Destini asked.

"Well, even though it's a bit depressing, it's good. I like it. Did you write this?"

"Oh no, I'm not that talented. It's by some obscure Dutch poet. I probably didn't even translate it all correctly."

"Mind if I keep it?" He asked, folding the napkin neatly and placing it in his pocket atop Ben's card.

They had reached the Saturn and he unlocked and opened the passenger side door for her. As she got in, he scanned the parking lot and the outer road, but saw nothing unusual. He hurried to the driver's side as Destini reached across and unlocked it for him from the inside. He smiled at her through the window as he opened his door and got in. Then he started the car and put it in reverse.

"What are you doing Scott!? What about Eli!?"

"She called the FBI from the pay phone in there," he said matter-of-factly. "She can catch a damn bus to Kansas."

He backed out and shifted the car into drive when Destini yelled "Stop! Wait!"

He slammed on the brakes and looked around, half-expecting to see a dozen government agents aiming their guns at them, but the road was still clear. Destini leaned into the back seat and emerged with the framed photo of Ricardo Montalban.

She rolled down her window and flung it back toward the museum doorway. Scott turned his head back and watched as the frame cartwheeled off its edges, tumbling across the pavement, then landed on its back and slid the rest of the way to the entrance.

"Now you can go," Destini said.

CHAPTER TWELVE

"That was a bit harsh, don't you think?" Scott asked as he sped back the way they had originally come into the park.

"I'll make her a new frame in the prison workshop where I'll be spending the rest of my life if it makes you feel better," Destini replied.

Scott looked over at her, and in that instant, it was as if the dazzling glow of new love that had surrounded her in his eyes suddenly dissipated like a shimmering heat mirage in the distance on the blacktop before them. He saw her temper, moodiness and fear in her spontaneous action and the bitter sarcasm of her words, and he realized she wasn't the beautiful, flawless vision of a damsel in distress that he had created in his mind.

What she had said earlier now really sunk in: "This is what I am. This is what I'll always be."

Then he smiled, because he also realized that none of it mattered ... he did love her. Not just an ideal or a fantasy, but the alternatingly vulnerable and bitchy person who was now curiously staring back at him.

"I love you Destini," he said softly.

She started to smile, then bit her lower lip and looked away.

"Scott!" She yelled, pointing straight ahead.

He focused his attention back to the road just in time to see an old Wonder Bread truck stopped sideways across both lanes, blocking his way. He stepped hard on the brakes, but they were already too close, so he turned the wheel sharply to the left. In the blur of motion, he barely registered one of the black-suited Hispanic enforcers standing in the open side door of the truck, just behind the cab, a large handgun pointed at the oncoming Saturn.

"Get down!" He yelled at Destini just as the passenger side of the Saturn slammed into the bread truck at a good twenty miles per hour, tipping the van-sized vehicle back on its wheels and knocking the man with the gun into a stacked bin of bread. As the truck righted itself, the man inside lost his balance completely and in trying to grab onto a rack, brought a whole bin of bread down on top of him.

Scott, meanwhile, was desperately trying to start his car again -- the engine having stalled upon impact. He glanced at Destini, who appeared to be shook up and in somewhat of a daze. As she lowered her head into both of her hands he saw a wide smear of blood on her window.

"Jesus, are you okay?" He asked, still moving the key back and forth repeatedly.

"I think so," she said hesitantly, looking down at the blood on her right hand from the side of her face.

The Saturn's engine finally turned over and he peeled away to the left, the sound of metal on metal scraping loudly as the cars separated.

"Why are you going back into the park? You should have gone around the truck and toward the highway," Destini said.

Scott laughed at that. "Yeah, you're okay..." He said with a grin.

In his rearview mirror he saw the bread truck straightening out on the road and coming after them. The needle on his speedometer was passing 85 mph and the car was shaking badly.

"Well, this must be the big finish," he muttered. "The FBI's probably coming down one side of the park and the drug cartel is chasing us up the other. And if that wasn't bad enough, the bossy bitch next to me just blew me off when I said I loved her and didn't even say it back... Hey, not that I care, because I do love you and I'm just happy to say it to you. I just want you to know that. You don't have to feel the same way and…"

"My God, shut the fuck up already!" Destini yelled.

"Now that's a romantic moment to tell our grandkids someday," Scott said, turning toward her.

"Please quit looking at me and keep your eyes on the road!" She shouted. "Damn, damn, we don't even have a gun or anything."

"There's one in the trunk under… some stuff… I think…but maybe not…" He stammered.

"Is there any way to get to the trunk from the back seat?" she asked, starting to lean back between the front seats.

"No," Scott lied, knowing that the rear seats pulled down and allowed access. "Please, would you do me a favor, Destini, and put your seatbelt back on?"

She frowned and kept her eye on the bread truck, which seemed to be catching up to them. They blew past the museum just as an RV was about to turn out from the parking lot. It couldn't stop in time and bounced onto the road just behind Scott, who had to swerve himself to avoid broadsiding it.

"Good going! That'll slow 'em down," Destini said.

"Oh yeah, like I planned that," Scott replied, his knuckles tight on the steering wheel. "For God's sakes, please put your seatbelt on!"

He noticed the car wasn't shaking so much anymore, and then got a bad feeling he knew why. His suspicions were confirmed as he noticed the needle on his dashboard slowly descending… 75… 70… 65…

Destini saw it too.

"Shit," she said. "That crash must have busted something. What now?"

Scott didn't answer. He had no answer. He just kept pressing his foot down harder on the accelerator as if that would help. The Saturn finally bottomed out at the 50mph mark as white smoke started to escape from under the hood.

"Turn right up there!" Destini yelled as the road split off up ahead.

He began to brake for the turn and saw that the bread truck had managed to get around the RV with no problem and was close enough now that he could make out the driver's features – long hair and baseball cap. I'll bet she wants to get back into my pants again, and not in a good way, he thought. He had slowed the Saturn just enough to attempt the turn but then saw a sign through the billowing smoke flowing over his hood that read "Long Logs/Agate House."

"Hey, I think it's a …"

He never got to finish his thought that it was more than likely a dead end before Destini grabbed the steering wheel with both hands and yanked it hard to the right.

They overshot the turn and skidded out into the desert just beyond, leaving a wide trail of dust. Scott managed to straighten the car out and bring it back up on the asphalt in the direction they had just come. He couldn't see anything through the windshield because of the dust and smoke enveloping the car, but he punched the gas and when they finally broke through the haze they saw the bread truck bearing straight down on them.

The collision was so imminent that Scott didn't even have time to swear about the situation. He instinctively turned the steering wheel hard to the driver's side again just as the truck swerved in the opposite direction and the two vehicles again scraped each other in passing as they both went off the road.

Destini, meanwhile, was trying to heed his earlier advice and snap on her seat belt as she bounced around the front seat.

He was getting ready to try to accelerate again when he shot a quick glance into his rearview mirror and noticed the stocky, black-suited little hit man picking himself slowly up off the desert floor and dusting himself off. Apparently his equilibrium had failed him again and when the cars had side-swiped each other, he had fallen completely out of the side door. Scott watched a second as the man limped back toward the truck, which was swinging in a wide arc to come back for him.

Without thinking, Scott put the Saturn in reverse and floored it, heading directly for the guy.

"Holy shit…" Destini said, her eyes growing wide as she saw what Scott meant to do. "I didn't think you had it in you."

Scott almost hit the brakes when she said that. What the fuck was he doing? But then he thought that if he didn't seize the opportunity and take this guy out now, that guy wouldn't hesitate to take them out later. He was using the only weapon he had. The man heard the Saturn's straining engine as it got closer and turned to see Scott aiming the car at him. He tried to pick up his pace, but he had obviously hurt one of his legs badly and couldn't manage more than a staggering half-run. Meanwhile, the bread truck was now racing back toward them from the other direction.

Scott knew he would get there first, and that fact was also evident to the stocky, sweating South American by his actions. Scott watched as the man turned again to face his impending fate, dropped to his knees, looked up to the sky and made the sign of the cross over his chest while mouthing some kind of prayer.

"Sonofabitch!" Scott yelled, turning the wheel hard and braking at the last second. The car missed the kneeling man by a matter of feet and kicked up another huge reddish, dust cloud that consumed the intended target, who had lifted his hands up as if waiting for deliverance from God.

The Saturn's engine sputtered on the sharp turn as Scott fought to regain control and straighten the vehicle. He overcorrected and it fishtailed before he finally righted it. The tired, overheated car jerked forward a short distance and then completely died with its front bumper just over the edge of a small precipice overlooking a vast expanse of petrified logs resembling rusted tree stumps. It appeared to be about a fifteen-foot drop to Scott, who was futilely trying to start the ignition again.

After several attempts, he let out a huge sigh and he and Destini both turned to look behind them, just in time to see the shimmering black silhouette of the previously-spared hitman emerging slowly out of the dust -- gun raised and pointed in their direction. It actually looked like he was coming at them in slow motion because of the swirling dust storm around him.

"Oh fuck me," Scott said incredulously as the gunman steadily limped on.

Just then, the remaining wall of dusty fog behind the man spread back like a stage curtain hurriedly being opened and the sun reflected blindingly off the grill of the bread truck as it shot out and struck its former passenger without slowing.

Scott and Destini watched in morbid fascination as the man was knocked straight to the ground and run over by the van. They continued to watch in curious disbelief as the speeding truck continued on course right for them.

"Jump! Jump!" Scott yelled, unbuckling his seatbelt with one hand and leaning hard against his door while pushing the handle down to open it with his other hand.

He fell out, more than anything else, and rolled over twice to get clear of the vehicle. When he looked back he saw Destini still in the car, struggling with the seatbelt he had told her to put on. Apparently the locking mechanism had jammed somehow. He felt his chest tighten as the bread truck swerved and hit the rear right bumper of the Saturn, sending the little car's back end swinging toward Scott. He threw himself over the side of the drop-off as the Saturn came down behind him. His eyes were closed as he tumbled down the uneven, rocky decline so he wasn't quite sure when the blackness changed from that of a lack of vision to one brought on by a lack of consciousness...

Scott heard laughter.

It was faint at first, but grew steadily louder. It was a pleasant laughter and it surrounded him – as if he had told a joke in a crowded room. Then he heard applause – lots of applause.

He was sitting in an overstuffed chair facing a studio audience, and as he scanned the crowd he realized it was comprised entirely of women. He didn't feel uncomfortable or unnerved, in fact, he welcomed the obvious adoration that he could see on their faces as they smiled at him and clapped loudly.

Then he felt an arm on his elbow from next to him and turned to see Ellen DeGeneres.

"Scott," she said, "I think we are all inspired by how you've overcome this handicap in your life. You could have easily given up and let the situation take control of your emotions and your life, but your bravery in the face of such a horrible tragedy serves as an example of inner strength and gives us all hope that we can rise above the unfortunate events that befall us."

Again, the room erupted in applause and many of the women were nodding their heads in agreement with Ellen.

"Scott, Scott," the popular talk show hostess continued as the applause trailed off, "would you share with us exactly how it was that you first realized you had broken your appendage?"

"What?!" Scott replied, quickly looking down at his lap in horror to find a small penis-shaped cast protruding from his open zipper. Then Ellen's hand came into view. She had a pen and began to sign the penis-shaped cast. He watched as her neat handwriting spelled out: "Rise to the challenge." Then she added a little smiley face at the end.

"Sorry," she said. "Couldn't resist the pun."

"What the…"

"…fuck," he muttered, half-conscious, spitting out a mouthful of dirt and blood as he slowly regained his awareness of where he was and what had happened. His whole body ached, but the pain between his legs was overwhelming. He wondered if it was possible to actually break one's dick. Then he shifted slightly and felt the pressure on his groin substantially subside.

Holy shit, I must have landed right on top of a petrified log, he thought. Now there's a human interest story for Ellen. Several tasteless jokes popped into his mind, foremost was giving a new meaning to 'sportin' a woody.'

Can't be hurt too bad, he thought, if I'm still coming up with bad one-liners.

He painfully rolled himself over a little more and slowly opened his eyes. The bright sun off the desert sand was blinding and he had to blink several times before any semblance of vision returned. The first thing that gradually came into focus was his little lightning bolt kachina doll. Apparently that's what he had come to rest on. He tried to laugh, but wound up spitting out more blood. Now what the hell were the odds of landing on that? It had been in the car and…

Shit! The car… where's the car?!

He pushed himself up on his hands and knees and scanned the area. Shards of shattered glass littered the sand and reflected the sunlight like small glittering diamonds. They refracted a kaleidoscope of colors across the shimmering vista and it took him a second to realize that the small rainbows he was seeing weren't actually in his head as a result of the fall, but were real – dancing in the air just on the periphery of his vision.

He found the Saturn sitting upright at the bottom of the slope about 10 feet further down and to his right. He saw Destini still in the passenger seat, hanging forward in her seatbelt. She wasn't moving.

"Oh fuck," Scott said as he tried to stand up. His knees buckled from the effort and the world around him spun as if he were viewing it from a carnival ride. He fell back on his butt and grabbed his head with both hands, hoping somehow that would steady things.

"Aw, that's sooooo sad. Can't even go to the aid of your lover. Just a helpless, weak and broken little man."

Scott didn't have to look behind him. He recognized the voice of the tomboy bitch from the rest stop bathroom. No doubt there was a gun pointed at his back.

"Hey you wild, sexy thing," he said, turning slowly and getting on his knees. That was the best he could manage as the vertigo kept him grounded. "I've never had a stalker as pretty as you before."

"Well try not to wet your pants with excitement again," she answered.

Despite his contempt for her, he found himself genuinely laughing at that remark. He squinted up at the top of the ridge where she stood. Sure enough, there was a pistol aimed in his direction.

"I've got a bullet in here with your bitch's name on it," she said. "Looks like an easy job. I might not even have to use it. The other five bullets are for you. Got any last words wannabe hero?"

His mind raced in search of options… start talking Scott… start talking and stalling your ass off because she's about to kill you and Destini.

He filled the silence with more laughter, but this time it sounded forced and unnatural.

"Time's up," the woman above him said, bringing her left arm up from her side to clasp the gun with both hands as she methodically took sight.

"You really don't know, do you?" Scott asked, not even sure where he was heading with that statement, but he figured a question was always a good way to keep a conversation going. Everybody wants answers … he hoped.

"That's just pathetic. That the best you got?" She replied.

For now, he thought, but at least she asked him a question in return and they were still talking.

"If you want to squirm a little, go ahead – I've got nothing but time," she added. With that, she glanced back over her shoulder toward the main road and apparently decided to get out of the sight of any possible park visitors passing by and took a few steps down the slope toward Scott until she was also below the ridgeline.

"Oh don't get your hopes up," she said. "I don't plan on getting close enough for you to shoot me with your little squirt gun again…"

Scott ignored the reference as it was obvious he had pissed her off, so to speak, with his earlier get-away tactic. No point in making it worse by staying on the subject and reminding her. She's got the upper hand, so make her feel big and bad now to redeem herself, he thought.

"Okay, this is me squirming," he said, realizing suddenly that she didn't want to just put a quick bullet in his head. She wanted to exact a little revenge for the way he got the best of her. "Look, I'm just a damn bystander who picked up the wrong fuckin' hitchhiker. I don't know her and I don't care about her.

She's the one you're after, so just do your job and I'll quietly get out of the way."

As he spoke, his eyes darted all around for something he could use to his advantage. At first he thought about trying to throw sand in her face and blind her long enough to either rush her or make it to the Saturn for the gun in the trunk. Nope, she was just a little too far away and he'd be dead before he got halfway in either direction. Then he saw some of the broken glass and he momentarily thought of blinding her with the reflected sunlight off of that. Yeah right, he could picture himself trying to angle the glass so the reflection hit her eyes – as if she would stand there patiently and wait for him to line it up. Not only would he look stupid, but again he'd be dead before he even picked a piece of glass all the way up. He dismissed that idea as well.

Meanwhile, the woman started laughing again. "You think I believe that? You really disappoint me. I think I'll put a bullet in her head first, just so we can see how much you don't care about her. What do you think of that?"

"I think I'm strangely attracted to you, what's your name?" Scott said, trying desperately to change the subject.

Her reply rang out in the form of a shot and a small dirt cloud that rose from the ground about a foot in front and to the right of Scott. Now there's an idea, he thought, I'll just keep annoying her until she's out of bullets…

"Um… you really shouldn't have done that…" he said, slowly reaching for the Kachina doll on the ground near where the bullet hit. "Not smart at all… Now… you've angered… the storm god!"

With dramatic flair he lifted the dancing Indian figure high above his head, raised his face to the sky and started making up a chant. If I can just distract her long enough to throw this heavy block of wood at her head, he thought...

"Kachina of the storm, Kachina of the storm, I call on your powers. Hear me now as your servant and believer," he yelled loudly, then muttered under his breath – "God, I am so fucked…"

He stole a quick glance at his captor. She was still looking directly at him with the gun raised. Her expression was one of growing impatience. He chanted louder and faster…

"Oh vengeful stormbringer, I command of your powers to strike down the enemy. Gather up the forces of nature and bear them upon the evildoer! Hear me and obey master of the skies! Father of the desert clouds!"

There seemed to be a slight change in the atmosphere, almost imperceptible at first, but one that became quickly noticeable as Scott went on. The wind, which had not been blowing as hard as before, started to pick up again and there was even a low, persistent rumbling that echoed across the desert. Sand started to blow over the top of the ridge and swirl down around Scott and the woman.

Holy shit, this motherfucking Indian magic is working, he thought, raising his voice louder against the rushing air and waving the doll wildly above him.

"Oh ruler of the wind, show your might! Darken the skies and bring your strength against those who would…"

At that moment, a large shadow fell across the slope where they stood and blotted out the sun and the wind whipped crazily about them.

A second later the black shape of a low-flying helicopter cleared the ridgeline above them and hovered less than 20 feet over their heads. The distinctive whoop-whoop of the rotor blades was now evident as the growing rumble he had heard and the reason for the blowing wind and sand. Oh well, so much for magic, he thought as he noted the big yellow letters on the side of the chopper – FBI. He saw that the woman had turned her attention away from him and was focused on the helicopter as well and that was all he needed.

As she turned back around from the distraction to face Scott, she was met with the Kachina doll smacking her squarely in the forehead.

Unfortunately it didn't have the desired effect Scott had hoped. Instead of knocking her down or making her drop the gun, it merely bounced off her head. The look she gave him in return was one of utter contempt as she squeezed the trigger again.

"Oh shit!" Scott said as he threw himself down the rest of the hill and rolled to the bottom. He heard the low repeated pop of what he thought were several shots amid the almost-deafening noise of the helicopter.

He lay at the bottom, a few feet away from the back of the Saturn, and although his body was sore and hurt, he didn't think he had taken any hits. Just as he was raising himself up to view the situation, he was roughly knocked back down.

It took him a moment to realize that it was the body of the woman that had rolled down the hill behind him and slammed into him. He pushed her off and saw that she had several gunshot wounds in her chest and was covered in blood and dirt. Her eyes were open and vacant.

Scott closed his, and shook his head.

CHAPTER THIRTEEN

He knew he was going to have to get up, but he didn't want to move.

This time the world around him was black by choice. He wondered how long he could stay frozen in this moment in time, feeling his accelerated heartbeat gradually slowing back down in his chest.

How long could he just sit there with his eyes shut and pretend he was sipping the last vestiges of root-beer flavored, melted vanilla ice cream through a long, blue twisty straw with that familiar slurping sound as he sucked up the last delicate bubbles of childhood innocence?

How long, when all he could taste in his mouth were coarse, dry granules of sand?

How long could he fool himself into believing that, for now, time was suspended just for him? He cupped his hands over his ears to try and block out the sound of the helicopter landing just beyond the ridge. As long as he remained motionless and oblivious to what his senses were telling him, he could stay in the dark for at least a few more minutes. But those minutes would seem like precious hours. He knew he needed that time before his world crumbled.

He needed that silent darkness where she still existed as he remembered her. He just needed a little time before going to the side of the car and seeing her lifeless body and having everything instantly change. Once it's real then he'd have to deal with it, but he just didn't think he could do that. Not now. He couldn't believe it could all be over so quick. So he sat there, knowing deep down that he should be rushing to the side of the car just in case there was any hope that she was still alive, but unable to move because of the greater fear of the alternative.

He felt almost childish – in the way one would ignore something in hopes that it would just go away. Dammit, a voice cut through his mind, get your ass up and see if she needs help, you stupid motherfucker. His own thoughts were rebelling against his inaction, yet he couldn't make his body comply. He was paralyzed by what he expected to find.

So instead, he focused on the memory of their embrace against the wind outside the curio shop. It had only been less than an hour before, but he knew that soon the memory would be days old, then weeks, months and years. He knew it would relentlessly drift away from him on the unforgiving tides of time, carried further and further until the image was lost beyond his mental horizon. He had to make it last. Burn it into his consciousness now. Her eyes. Her smile. The words whispered from her lips – "I love you too."

Damn, already his mind was betraying him. As much he had wanted to hear her say that, she never did. She never said "I love you too" even though he could hear it in his thoughts, distant and muffled, over and over again...

Wait a minute, he thought, taking his hands off his ears and hearing it more clearly.

He opened his eyes and saw her kneeling in front of him.

"I know, I know," she said, seeing his shocked expression, "my hair looks like shit."

"Oh my God, you've never looked better," Scott said, pulling her onto his lap and kissing her eyes, her nose, her lips...

He pulled back and looked at her in disbelief. The blood was dried and matted to the side of her face from where she had hit the window earlier and there was a large bluish knot just above her right eye. But her eyes seemed lighter, almost milk-chocolate brown, and they seemed to sparkle as they peered at him.

"I… I was so afraid you were..." He let it trail off.

"Well, I was getting a little worried about you just now," she said. "I thought you were in shock or catatonic, or something. Are you sure you're okay?"

Before Scott could answer, the familiar sound of Ben's voice cut in.

"The love and concern here really touches my heart," he said sarcastically. "I have to wonder what kind of dumb luck it is that allows a conspiring murderess and a philandering family man to come out of this with cuts and scrapes while trained professionals lose their lives in the line of duty? It sickens me, really."

Scott and Destini watched him slowly come down the side of the drop off, observing his footing as he went, instead of looking at them as he spoke. Behind and to either side of him were two other agents, similarly attired in dark windbreakers, black slacks and reflective sunglasses. They both had one hand casually resting on the butt of MP-5 machine guns hanging off their waists from long straps around their necks as they also made their way cautiously down the slope.

Scott glanced to his right – the dead woman's pistol was laying just a foot away. Looking back at the approaching men, Scott reached a hand quickly toward the gun and slid it behind his body. He exhaled a deep breath as his action appeared to have gone unnoticed.

"In fact," Ben continued as the trio reached the bottom and stood before them, "it now seems to me that it would be more fitting if the bitch had broken her neck in the car accident and her bumbling accomplice had been plugged between the eyes by the little blonde. Come to think of it, I believe that's exactly what happened here… as far as anybody else will know."

"You goddamn bastard!" Destini yelled. "I didn't set those men up, but if it's me you want, then just let him go."

"That's so noble. Well, that was the original deal we'd made with dear old grandma in return for your whereabouts," Ben said coolly. "And I was hoping that your motionless body in the car could have made that a possibility. But, here you are, too alive for your own good. And to remedy that little problem, we have to get rid of all the loose ends."

"God, you are pathetic," Scott said laughing. "It's 'tie up' the loose ends, not 'get rid of' them.' What kind of a second-rate, improper cliché'-spouting, crooked FBI agent are you?"

"Scott, what the hell are you doing?" Destini whispered through clenched teeth.
Something he'd come to learn to do well lately, he thought – improvising to buy more time.

"Hmmm, that's a new one," Ben mused, unruffled. "Most guys would be begging for their lives at this point instead of casting insults. Maybe you've got some balls after all. Or maybe you just realize that you're a dead man either way. But, okay, I'll give you that – 'tie up' loose ends. That's what happens sometimes when English isn't your first language."

He looked at Destini and said something to her in Spanish that Scott didn't understand, but Destini made it clear with her reaction.

"Oh my God, you work for my father."

"Yes, and Daddy wants you back dead or… well, just dead, actually. You're too much of a liability. Although I am curious," he said, looking back at Scott. "How did you know I was on the take?"

"Besides the fact that you're talking about killing us in cold blood? Maybe it was that little cell phone call to Jerry this morning."

Recognition slowly dawned on Ben's face and he nodded – "Not bad, I'm impressed."

"What? Scott, what are you talking about?" Destini asked.

Scott didn't answer. Instead, he shoved the barrel of the gun halfway down the back waistband of Destini's pants as he slowly got up, pretending to use her to steady himself. As he stood, he spread his arms out with palms open to show he wasn't going to try anything. He took a few steps toward the car's trunk, which had been jarred open a crack during its downhill tumble. He lifted it the rest of the way, sat down on the open end, reached in deliberately and propped Jerry's body up next to him by his shirt collar.

He heard Destini gasp, but he wasn't sure whether her reaction was because of the shock of seeing him dead or the fact that her husband's body had wound up in their car somehow.

"Here's the deal," Scott said. "You take Jerry here and implicate him as the person who set up your DEA guys – which shouldn't be too hard to do – then you put the blonde in the Saturn and torch it. I'm sure you guys can cover it up so nobody knows that it wasn't Destini in there who was burned to bones."

"You know," Ben replied slowly, as if considering the option. "I like that kind of initiative and thinking, in fact your idea could probably work. But call me an asshole for not playing along, I still think I'd rather see you both dead. It's just less paperwork for me to have to worry about later. Besides, there's one important ingredient you're missing – usually when folks try to make a deal, they have something to offer in return."

"Well, that's where the briefcase full of four hundred thousand dollars in drug money comes in," Scott said, slowly reaching his right arm across his body back into the trunk while straining to hold Jerry's corpse steady with his left. He kept his eyes on Ben's suddenly confused face, and saw the creases of a smile forming at the edge of his lips. Greedy fucking bastard, he thought as his hand closed around the gun in the trunk.

"Or…" he continued, as he brought the weapon out and pointed it at Ben, "we can work some other kind of deal, don't you think?"

Taking Scott's cue, Destini pulled the other gun out from behind her and aimed it at the closest of the two men behind Ben. Both had started to raise their machine guns slightly, but stopped.

"Well, well, well," Ben remarked with an amused tone. "You two really are something. I sure as hell didn't see this coming. I guess I deserve that for underestimating you. Here I thought it was just plain dumb luck that got you this far, but apparently you've got a little fighting spirit as well."

Ben cupped the elbow of his left arm in the hand of his right as he brought the other hand up to his chin in a thoughtful pose. He paced a few steps over to the dead woman.

"So…" he went on as he absently nudged the blonde's limp form with the toe of one of his dusty suede shoes. "I think one dead, badly burned female body in a fiery car crash would pretty much resemble another. It's a plausible alternative."

"You adapt pretty quick to changing situations, but I don't trust you," Scott said.

"You shouldn't," Ben replied, looking up at him and smiling. "I'll turn on you just as fast again if you lose the upper hand. But right now, you're calling the shots and I respect that and am willing to make the necessary concessions. It's all give and take – finding a happy compromise."

"You're too damn calm about all this," Scott said. "What am I missing?"

"Boy oh boy, you are good," Ben said, chuckling. "You're right. I still have a couple of things going for me. First, I have one of my guys sitting with your sweet, old granny to make sure she's… taken care of. And for another, I'm a good judge of character and neither of you are killers. I'm not so stupid as to say that I don't think you'd pull that trigger if you were forced to in self-defense, but I can't see you shooting us if we were to just turn around and walk back up the hill."

"He may not," Destini said, "but you better look into my eyes again because I won't hesitate to put a bullet straight into your fucking head."

Ben gave a short nod and paced back in her direction, still assuming the posture of a man in charge of a situation.

"Hmmmm… yes, yes you would shoot," he said matter-of-factly. "I guess that should be obvious by the present state of your marital situation."

There was an uncomfortable pause, at least for Scott, as everyone seemed to wait for a response from Destini, but her expression didn't change and she said nothing in return.

Scott, meanwhile, had maintained his grip on Jerry throughout the proceedings, resembling a twisted version of a ventriloquist about to do an act. He had wanted a possible shield in case events disintegrated into a shooting match, but he felt comfortable enough now to let Jerry drop back into the trunk. Scott got up and moved parallel to Ben, who was heading back in the direction of the dead blonde.

"Well then, it's your game," Ben said, "so let's strap this one in and…"

"Stop there and don't move," Scott interrupted, as Ben was about to bend down for the body.

Ben straightened back up and shrugged. "Just trying to help."

"You still have a gun on you," Scott said, using his thumb to cock the weapon. "Take it out very slowly, drop it at your feet and then move away."

"Whoa there buddy," Ben said, his eyes widening a bit. "Be very, very careful pointing that at me with the hammer cocked. I don't know how familiar you are with firearms, but that's an extremely sensitive position to place your gun in. It could very easily slip and go off, and I really don't want that to happen."

"Then you better quit wasting time talking," Scott replied, hoping not to let Ben see that he had already realized the consequences of his act. He didn't know a damn thing about guns and wasn't sure how he was going to let the hammer back down now without discharging the weapon. He was already exerting a lot of pressure with his thumb just to keep it steady.

Ben removed a 9mm in deliberate fashion from an inside shoulder holster beneath his coat, pulling the butt of it out by his fingertips and then letting it fall to the ground before him.

"Good, now move back over to your buddies," Scott instructed.

"Your turn," Destini said, addressing the other two agents. "Slowly reach both hands up to your necks, bend your heads down, loop your gun straps over your heads and let them fall in front of you."

Neither made a move to heed her instructions until Ben spoke: "Go ahead – do as she says."

After they had dropped their machine guns, Destini ordered them to move back up the hill a few feet and sit down on their hands. Scott still had his gun pointed at Ben and was trying to figure out how to uncock the thing – if that was even possible, he thought. His thumb was starting to throb from maintaining the steady pressure and the rest of his hand was shaking a little as well. He was hoping nobody else had noticed.

What the fuck do I do with this, Scott wondered. It's not like he could ask Ben for advice – that would certainly diminish his intimidation factor.

Ben, meanwhile, had remained standing about five feet away from Destini and was now raising a curious eyebrow at Scott, who it seemed to him was intently looking down at the cocked gun as if it were a giant turd in his hand and he was too shocked to know what to do with it.

"Jesus Christ, you fuckin' amateur," Ben said, exasperated. "You're gonna wind up getting somebody…"

That's when the gun went off as if to punctuate his concern.

Scott had barely registered Ben's voice – his thumb had built up a thin layer of sweat between the skin and the metal from the strain and he had watched transfixed as it slowly slid off the hammer.

After the loud report cut through the air, he looked up.

Ben was sprawled on his back, both hands across his chest.

"Oops," Scott said sheepishly.

"Well, this complicates things a little bit," Scott said, slowly enunciating each word as he tried to take in the rapid change of circumstances.

He looked at Ben's prone figure and could still hear the shot ringing accusingly in his ears. This is a fucking nightmare, he thought. Now you've gone and killed an FBI agent.

"Oh, he's okay," Destini remarked casually. "He's wearing a bulletproof vest."

With that, Ben slowly sat up and glared at Scott.

"It still hurts like a bitch and now I am really pissed," he said, with a cough. "I'm pretty low-key, but you're trying my patience."

"Holy shit," Scott said, unable to suppress his smile. "I am so sorry, man, I can't believe that I did that, I just … hey, wait a minute, why the hell am I apologizing to you? You were about to kill me. Fuck you. I'll shoot you again if I have to."

Ben shook his head and sighed, then he looked to Destini and raised his eyebrows as if to implore her to make some kind of decision to resolve the current predicament.

"Okay," she said, taking his cue, "here's what we're going to do. Scott, come over here and give me your gun…"

"What?!" He started to protest. "I can handle…"

"Please let me finish," she interrupted, wiping some of the dried blood off the side of her face. "I want you to give me the gun and then you're going to leave. Go back up, take the van, get Eli and get the hell out of here. I'll keep an eye on these guys so that you can get far enough away."

"Um, no, that's not a good plan at all," Scott countered. "I'm not just going to leave you."

"Please don't argue with me," she said. "The five of us can't just expect to walk out of here. This is my problem, and I'll take care of it. But you and your grandmother need to get away from this mess while you can."

"I'm sorry, but I'm not going," he said. "We'll just have to think of something else. In fact, why don't you get away while I watch these guys? Give me your gun and you can leave."

"Oh God, please don't do that," said Ben. "I'll help you think of some other plan myself…"

"Shut up," Scott and Destini both said at the same time.

Ben threw his hands up in mock exaggeration.

"Look Scott," Destini said, "this isn't worth your life. You've known me less than 24 hours. Just go back to the world you knew before. Erase the last day and go back to your life."

"Yeah, because the problems of two little people don't amount to a hill of beans in this crazy world, blah blah blah," said

Ben. "This is truly a touching Casablanca moment. But you and I ain't walking off in the horizon together all buddy-buddy Scott, so listen to the woman and move along. If you go now and forget everything, we won't come looking for you later."

The sudden sound of another gunshot startled Scott.

He ducked down by reflex, eyes wide and looked at the gun in his hand. He didn't think he had fired it again accidentally, but hell, how could he be sure? He then glanced up at the hill, where once again Ben was flat on his back.

"I told you to shut up," he heard Destini say.

"What the fuck is wrong with you people?!" Ben groaned, slowly repeating the process of sitting up. "You're a bunch of goddamn lunatics. This isn't funny."

Scott laughed, but it sounded more like a nervous chuckle. He looked at Destini and that unnerved him even more. She appeared calm and unruffled, and she obviously knew how to use a gun. He couldn't help but wonder if he agreed to give her his gun and leave whether or not she would shoot all three of these guys in cold blood. A slight chill ran down his spine at the thought.

He fixed his gaze back on Ben, who genuinely appeared to be pouting as he examined the matching bullet holes in the front of his jacket.

"I got it!" Scott suddenly shouted. "You guys all take off those cool FBI jackets and throw them over here. While you're at it, give us the bulletproof vests as well."

"Hey, good idea," Destini said, nodding as if she were impressed by Scott's unexpected input. "Then what?"

"Um, uh... huh? I mean, that was it," Scott answered, a little embarrassed that he hadn't thought things through beyond that point. "Hey, it's a start. Maybe we can put on their jackets and lead them out of here and hopefully nobody will stop us."

"Too many variables," Destini replied. "The best plans are the simplest plans. Keep it basic and there's less that can go wrong."

"You're scaring me a little, I hope you know," Scott said.

Ben snorted at that comment, but didn't say anything. Meanwhile, the two agents behind him had taken off their jackets and tossed them towards Destini.

"You too, let's go," she instructed Ben, who grudgingly complied. After they had all removed their jackets and vests, Scott yelled enthusiastically, "Wait! I have another idea!"

This time it was Destini's turn to chuckle. "You are so fucking cute," she said, looking at Scott as if he were a little kid.

"Gee, thanks, that makes me look real menacing to these guys," he said. "Good thing I have the gun or they'd be kicking my cute little ass."

He saw Ben open his mouth as if the temptation to comment was too much to resist, but then he grimaced and held it in.

"Anyways," Scott continued. "We handcuff two of these guys together and leave them down here, and we get the helicopter pilot to fly us out of here… maybe even across the border to Mexico."

"Scott…" Destini began, then stopped a moment as if thinking it over before going on. "Actually, that's a pretty damn good idea. We can fly low enough that hopefully we can go across undetected, but if we are, the pilot can radio in that he's in pursuit of us in a vehicle on the ground. We can be across before they realize what's going on. That's not a bad idea at all."

"Gee, don't sound so surprised," Scott said.

"Well I'm surprised," Ben finally spoke. "It could work, but may I still suggest that we put the other two bodies in the car here and torch it. That way nobody's looking for the two of you later if they think you died here."

"Why are you being so helpful?" Scott asked.

"I have to work the circumstances to my benefit somehow," he replied. "As long as it looks like you two didn't get away, then I won't have to answer a lot of questions and be held accountable later."

"You two," Destini said, waving the gun at the men behind Ben. "Do it."

Neither moved until Ben again approved the instructions, "Come on, you heard her, let's make this happen and get the hell out of here."

While the two men went about their task, Scott and Destini each took turns putting on the discarded bulletproof vests and FBI jackets.

It didn't take more than a couple of minutes before Jerry and the blonde were positioned in the front of the Saturn and strapped into the seatbelts. Scott then followed Ben up to the helicopter, where he had volunteered to get a gas canister to splash the interior of the Saturn with and then set it ablaze. But as they neared the chopper atop the ridge, Scott became more cautious.

"Hang on a minute," he said as Ben was about to climb into the helicopter. "I'm sure you probably have some guns in there and wouldn't put it past you to try something, so why don't you just come over here and stand directly in front of the helicopter where I can see you, while I get the canister out."

Ben turned slowly and smiled.

"I really need to start giving you more credit," he said. "There is no gas canister. I just wanted a chance to talk with you alone. It's not too late to save your ass. I want to give you the opportunity to…"

"Oh just shut the fuck up already," Scott said.

"No," Ben replied. "You still have no idea the magnitude of what you're involved in here. That woman down there who you're so in lust with doesn't give a shit about you. She's used you since the moment you picked her up. And once you've served your purpose, she'll discard you just as easily, and maybe even as permanently, as she did her husband. Think about that. What kind of person puts a bullet into the head of their…"

"Ben," Scott interrupted. "I know what you're trying to do, but you're only wasting your breath. I don't know if she killed him or not. For all I know, it could have been you trying to set her up. Or it could have the blonde and her two henchmen closing in. Or maybe it was Destini who shot him. I don't know, but even more importantly … I don't care. It really doesn't matter to me at this point. It's a fucked up world and you just make the best of it."

"I like that," Ben said, laughing. "Now there's a quote that should have been in 'Casablanca.' Yeah, I can see Bogart saying that. Could have been a classic line. Well, here's another classic line for you – 'No one here gets out alive.' Think about that and ask yourself if it's worth it. Personally, I'd rather live in a fucked up world than be dead."

"But Ben, don't you see the irony," Scott asked with just a hint of sarcasm in his tone. "It's a fucked up world because of people like you. So if you were dead, maybe the world would be a better place."

Ben's eyes narrowed and then he spit on the ground.

"I don't know why I'm wasting my time trying to save your ass," he said. "I don't much even like you. I just feel sorry for you that you and your grandma got involved with that double-crossing, homicidal bitch down there. But fuck it, maybe you two deserve each other. You're sadly mistaken, however, if you think you're getting away."

"Daaaamn…" Scott sighed dejectedly. "You really don't like me? Because I thought we were bonding with some meaningful dialogue here. I mean… I like you Ben. Now I'm kind of hurt to think you were just toying with my feelings."

"I'm going to kill you, you little fucker," Ben replied slowly, past the pretense of being cordial.

"I don't think…" Scott started, but suddenly stopped at the sound of sirens in the distance. He looked around the back of the helicopter and saw three police cars speeding towards them, blue lights flashing.

Ah fuck, he thought, this is so not good.

"Playtime's over," he heard Ben say. "Even with that jacket you're wearing, it'll take me two seconds to convince them of the truth."

"You know what's sad," Scott said, looking back at Ben's smug face. "You still can't get your clichés right. It's 'game over.'"

And with that Scott squeezed the trigger of the gun.

The bullet hit straight in the abdomen and a large pool of blood spread across Ben's white shirt as he looked down in disbelief. But he was still on his feet and that wasn't a good thing, Scott figured. He heard the sirens getting closer and fired again. This time the bloodstain began forming outward from Ben's upper left chest area.

Scott watched with a complete feeling of detachment, as if he wasn't really there and was seeing things happening through the eyes of someone else. He was dimly aware of the fact that he had heard two gun shots around the same time from the ravine where he had left Destini, but wasn't sure if they was just the echo of his own weapon or separate firings.

Ben opened his mouth to say something, but a thick, dark red bile oozed out instead. He dropped to his knees in the dirt, still looking incredulously at Scott.
Scott put his arm with the gun down and walked closer to Ben, stopping about five feet away and then kneeling down to look straight into the dying man's fading eyes.

"Both quotes were pretty good," Scott said, "but I think if we combine them, we get to the real gist of things – It's a fucked up world *and* nobody gets out alive."

Ben's lip curled up in a slight sneer and then he toppled forward as the police cars skidded to a halt around them.

CHAPTER FOURTEEN

Scott remained kneeling and looking down at Ben as he heard the car doors open up and people running toward him.

Don't panic, don't panic, don't panic, he repeated to himself over the swell of thoughts rising up in his mind – Oh my fucking God, I just killed a man. Stay calm. Yeah right. What the hell have I done? This can't be happening. I've lost my mind. I'm insane. Now I'm hearing voices in my head. Oh shut up you dumbass, that's normal. Just... don't... panic!

"That's him! That's the bad man!" He heard a familiar voice yell.

He looked up to see Eli pointing at Ben's body as she approached with a very overweight, white-haired man wearing a sheriff's badge on his uniform.

"That's the man who kidnapped my granddaughter! Oh my goodness – where's my Sally?"

Holy shit, Scott thought, this is just one big fucking lie and now my grandma is getting in on the action. He took a deep breath and realized that the next few seconds would determine whether or not he and Destini spent the rest of their lives in jail. He laid the gun down in the sand and stood up slowly.

"I'm a federal agent," he said, looking directly at the grizzled sheriff. "This woman's granddaughter is a material witness in a crime in California. She's been abducted and the felons have crossed state lines. I have jurisdiction over this pursuit and I'm going to have to ask you and your men to cooperate fully."

Scott paused for an instant, hoping that would be enough and he didn't sound like the dramatic TV dialogue-spewing retard that he felt like. The cautious look on the face of the sheriff told him he'd better keep talking, and fast, or he'd get peppered with questions that he wouldn't have the answers to – the first of which would probably be to see his badge.

"The witness was taken from this scene approximately 5 minutes ago in a black SUV, I think it was a Yukon," Scott went on, talking at a rapid clip to entail a sense of urgency. "They were headed north and might still be in the park limits. I need you to get a car at that gate as soon as you can and send your men after them in that direction. Now… please!"

The sheriff's eyes narrowed as he kept his gaze directly on Scott. He seemed to be processing the information. After what seemed like an eternity to Scott, the sheriff looked at his men, pointed north and simply said "Go."

Scott felt a huge sense of relief wash over him as the other cops ran to their cars and peeled out.

At the same time, Destini emerged from the ridge below and walked over to where Scott and Eli stood with the sheriff.

"My partner," was all that Scott mumbled by way of explanation, and since she was also wearing one of the FBI jackets, it seemed enough to satisfy the sheriff, who then made his way over to the helicopter. Eli, perhaps uncomfortable with the thought of having betrayed Destini who was approaching with a gun in hand, followed closely behind the sheriff.

Destini seemed to be surveying the scene as she came.

"Oh my God, did you really kill him?" she whispered to Scott, stopping less than a foot from him. Meanwhile, the sheriff climbed inside the helicopter to take a look around.

"Uh, noooo," Scott answered sarcastically, "I didn't kill him anymore than you didn't kill your husband."

"Are you crazy?" She replied in a sharp, yet hushed tone. "How can you even fucking think that?"

"Hell," she continued, pointing at Ben's motionless body, "he could have killed Jerry. Either because Jerry knew too much about his affiliations outside the bureau, or to set me up. Possibly both."

Scott bit his lower lip and mentally cursed himself. It appeared as if she was telling the truth. She certainly had no reason to lie about it at this point.

"What about the two guys down below?" He asked.

"They're both tied up cozy in the trunk."

"I thought I heard two shots down there…" Scott began.

"So what do you think, I executed them gangland style with a bullet to the back of their heads?" Destini snapped. "Is that what you think of me? I put a couple of air holes in the trunk so they could breath."

"Great, just fuckin' great," Scott mumbled. "Well then, tell you what, go ahead and plug the old sheriff there and we'll just call it even."

Destini's mouth fell open and her eyes widened at his statement.

"I'm kidding!" Scott yelled in frustration.

"Kidding about what?" The old sheriff in question asked as he climbed back out of the helicopter, his knees cracking sharply as his feet smacked the ground. Eli positioned herself cautiously behind him as he walked back toward Scott and Destini.

"About trying to take back off in this thing," Scott said quickly. "We made a hard landing and the rudder controls were damaged. We'll all have to go in your vehicle."

He waited nervously for the sheriff's response. He hoped that the cop knew as little about helicopters as he did, because he wasn't even sure if helicopters had rudders. Maybe that was just on boats.

He felt he was starting to spout too many lies and it was just a matter of time before the experienced lawman called him on one.

"Sure," the cop replied somewhat hesitantly, "I guess we can do that as soon as we get another unit out here on the crime scene. I can't just leave it like this in case it gets disturbed. Let me go call in for another car to..."

"Stop," Destini said, raising her gun toward the sheriff, who, Scott noted, didn't seem to look all that surprised by her sudden action.

In fact, it was Scott, not the sheriff, who blurted out "What's going on?"

"You forget I'm a lawyer," she answered. "He wouldn't call this a crime scene if he thought you were really an FBI agent shooting a felon in self defense. Obviously he could tell you were lying. You're not very good at it, you know."

"Well, actually ma'am," the sheriff interjected, "he's pretty darn good. He had me completely convinced, I'm sorry to say. The only reason I figured things weren't quite right is because I've seen your pretty little face all over too many bulletins in the last 24 hours."

"Ha," Scott said, smirking at Destini like a little kid.

"Sheriff," Destini said, ignoring Scott completely, "please put your hands up behind your neck while my partner Lou

Costello walks behind you and slowly removes your gun from your holster. If you cooperate, I promise you won't get hurt."

"Yeah, is that what you told the real FBI guy over there? I can see you're just a couple of adventurous kids out having some harmless hijinx," the sheriff answered, raising his hands and clasping them together behind his head.

"Hey, no need to get all accusatory, you have no idea what's going on with…" Scott started.

"Just… get… the gun," Destini said through clenched teeth.

Scott did so and then walked back over next to Destini, who was about five feet in front of the disarmed sheriff. At the same time, Eli stepped in front of the cop.

"Oh no," she said. "You two have gone far enough. You are not shooting this gentleman."

The sheriff quickly proved her choice of words describing him as wrong by throwing an elbow around Eli's neck and pulling her towards him as a shield or bargaining chip.

"That looks like a fair deal to me," said Scott as he turned and walked toward the patrol car. "You keep my grandmother and we'll take your vehicle. Sorry, all transactions are final."

"We don't have time for this," Destini said. "We're all going, now let's get in the car."

She waved her gun toward the vehicle. The sheriff seemed to weigh his options, released his grip and led Eli toward the car.

"Good choice," said Destini. "I haven't killed anyone yet." Then just under her breath, Scott could have sworn he heard her add "...today."

"Now what's the plan?" Scott asked after they were all seated. The sheriff was behind the wheel, with Destini beside him in the passenger seat, gun still aimed at him. Scott sat behind the sheriff and Eli next to him in the back seat.

"There is no brilliant plan," Destini answered, the frustration evident in her tone. "Let's just start driving toward the interstate and we'll try to think of something along the way. I'm open to ideas."

"How about letting the old folks go and turning yourselves in," the sheriff offered as he started the car and pulled back toward the road.

"Speak for yourself asshole," Eli said, massaging her neck.

Scott chuckled.

"How far to the New Mexico border from here?" Destini asked.

"About half an hour, once you get back on the interstate," the sheriff replied.

"And how long before we hit the interstate?" She asked.

"I'd say another 15 minutes through the park here," he replied.

"And how long do you figure before your other two cars turn back around and meet us on the way?" She added matter-of-factly.

"I'm hoping within the next 10 minutes," came the sheriff's reply.

They drove on in complete silence for a few minutes after that. Scott mulled over the rapid turn of events of the last 24 hours. My God, I actually killed someone. Killed him dead. He realized it was a redundant thought – a cliché even, but he could think of no better statement to describe it. Killed him dead, killed him dead, killed him dead...

He'd get the death penalty for this for sure. So much for his idyllic, romantic visions of running off with his newfound love.

And he really did love her – that was the crazy part. Hell, he shot Ben to save her from going to jail. No, he can't blame her for this, he realized.

"Hey bitch," he said.

Destini glared at him and raised an eyebrow as if to say "What?"

"I just wanted to say it again... I love you."

Her lips curved upward slightly, almost imperceptibly, as if she were forcing herself not to smile. She merely nodded at him in acknowledgment and turned her gaze back at the sheriff.

"That went well, you've really got her now, smooth talker," Eli remarked casually.

"As for you…" Scott started, "I can't believe you fucking called the FBI, and then you called the cops too, didn't you? We wouldn't be in this goddamn situation right now if you hadn't taken it on yourself to try and do what you thought was right."

"We all make mistakes trying to protect the people we love," Eli simply said. Then she reached inside her sweater and pulled out a torn, soiled and ragged paper. Scott saw that it was the photo of Ricardo Montalban, now frameless and fragile. He watched a single tear slowly run down the side of Eli's nose, pause on the edge of her wrinkled lips, then continue its crawl to her chin where it hung like a drip clinging determinedly to a leaking faucet before letting go. It splattered across Ricardo's glossy visage as if to punctuate her comment.

Scott came close to saying "Ooooh very dramatic. Extra points for timing." But he decided not to verbalize that thought. She could very well be hurting somehow, and just when did he become so fucking cynical?

"Yes!"

Destini's exclamation jarred him from his sudden introspection. He looked at her and then in the direction she seemed to be focused on. Ahead in the distance on the left he saw it and knew exactly what she was thinking.

"Um, I would strongly advise against this wild west Hollywood ending," he said, watching the eastbound train cars, most of them reading "Santa Fe" on the side, moving along the tracks at a high rate of speed.

"That train's gotta be pushing 60 miles per hour," Scott continued. "There's no way we're jumping that. Our dismembered torsos would be as petrified as these old logs around here before anybody found them. Kids will be buying souvenir pieces of my large intestine for three bucks."

"I think you can make it, just give it a try," the sheriff deadpanned.

"He's right," Destini said. "We're catching that train."

The sheriff shook his head incredulously as he watched the last train cars fade out of sight down the track. The sun was starting to set behind him and the darkening shadows lent a surreal feel to the scene as the caboose vanished into the dim horizon.

"This is Sheriff Murphy," he said calmly and with no sense of urgency into his patrol radio. "We have three fugitives heading east on a Santa Fe train they boarded in the Petrified National Forest. Do you copy?"

"Hey Sheriff, this is Baker," a voice crackled back. "We lost pursuit, but have set up a road block at both ends of the park just in case, and we've got state troopers on lookout in both directions on the interstate."

"I repeat," the sheriff said slowly, "the fugitives are no longer within the park confines. They are on a train going east. Get your asses off the entry points and head toward the next town to stop that train. Have dispatch contact the rail lines and notify the engineer to stop at the next station."

"10-4!" Came the reply.

Sheriff Murphy let out a prolonged sigh, placed the hand transmitter back into its slot on the dash and turned to Destini. "There. But all you've done is bought yourself a little more time."

"And so have you," Destini replied with a saccharine smile.

"Wow, I guess we did catch that train," Scott said from the back. "I gotta tell you, that was a great idea. And as much as I hate to ruin a good moment, I have to ask … what now?"

"I'm still working on that part," Destini replied. "We have maybe 30 minutes before they stop and search that entire train and realize we aren't on it. I'm just not sure what to do or where to go in that time."

"I think I have an idea," Scott said.

Destini and Eli turned to look at him. Even the sheriff craned his neck around.

"Oh come on," Scott said, "like that's so hard to believe?"

"Okay, we're listening," said Destini.

"Um, well, I'm still working out the details in my head," Scott replied, "but first, the sheriff and I are changing clothes, and let's make it quick."

A few minutes later Scott was checking out his new look in the rearview mirror as he led the patrol car toward the park gate. The shirt hung off him a little baggy and he'd had to tighten the belt as far as it would go to keep the uniform pants up, but it was passable.

He noticed Destini staring at him from the back seat, where she had moved to keep an eye, and the gun, on the sheriff – even though he now had one hand handcuffed to the door and sat shivering in his T-Shirt and underwear.

"I can keep this on later, if you like the look," Scott joked.

"If there is a later," she answered.

"Hey, now is not the time to give up," Scott shot back. "Look at all the shit we've been through. It's amazing we're still alive. We're gonna get out of this. I have a good feeling."

The Interstate 40 on ramp was right outside the park's north gate. Scott veered left onto the four-lane and less than 20 minutes later, just as the last scrawny trails of sunlight were consumed by the darkness, he saw what he was looking for.

"There we go," he said, pointing to a green highway sign that read: Weigh Station, All Trucks Exit, 2 Miles.

"Most state borders have these," he explained. "It'll be easy enough to do a spot inspection. I'll actually tell the truckers I'm looking for some fugitives. After they open their trailers, I'll distract them up front. You'll throw the sheriff into the back end of one and send him on his way, then we'll sneak the two of you into another. Free ride out of here."

"That's a stupendous idea," Destini said with enough comic inflection to let them know she thought it was nuts. "Except for one thing…"

Scott looked back out to the right where she was pointing ahead and saw the sign: "Weigh Station, Exit Now" was covered by a large diagonal plate that read CLOSED in tall, reflective letters.

"Son of a bitch," Scott said, but then he began to brake and put on his turn signal.

"Actually, this works out better," he said, smiling. "We'll just remove that magnetic strip that says closed and place the cop car toward the road with lights flashing. We'll get them to pull in anyways."

"No offense, Scott, but keep driving," Destini said.

"What? You don't have a better plan. Trust me on this."

"I do have a better plan, so keep driving," she said calmly.

Scott thought about it for a second, then flipped the turn signal back off and stepped on the gas. He watched the empty weigh station parking lot pass by and hoped she was right.

"Okay, we're gonna do it like you said," Destini told him. "But not out in the open like that. Find a truck up ahead, turn on your flashing lights and pull it over. Go with a drug smuggling cover. The driver will be so happy he didn't get stopped for a ticket, and so sure that he has no contraband in the back, he'll be more than happy to open his load for a look. I'll be your partner from the DEA. After he gets it open, ask to see his license and vehicle registration. While you two go back to the cab, I'll pretend to inspect the truck..."

"And throw the sheriff in the back of it," Scott finished.

"Can you two talk a little slower," Eli asked. "I'm trying to write all this down for my National Enquirer eyewitness article on how you two idiots were caught. Don't worry Scott, I'll still give you credit for this lame-brained idea, but I'm not sharing the money from the exclusive."

"If we get caught, then it was her idea – oh and put in a part about how I'm virile, charming and a lady's man. Sex sells," said Scott, regaining some of his smartass attitude.

"I already thought about the sex angle," Eli said. "Ben was your gay lover, whom you shot after he spurned you for another man. Hmmmm... I wonder if there's any way to work aliens into this story?"

"Hey, there's a truck up ahead," said Scott, changing the subject. "Let's pull it over."

"Is that really how you are?" Destini asked.

"What?" Replied Scott, totally confused.

"You just go for the very first one you see? You don't even bother taking a close look at it or weighing the consequences. What if there are other, better trucks out there?"

"You know," he sighed, "if this is a metaphor about how you think I approach a relationship, well... let's just say I believe in truck at first sight... besides, that one's got a nice set of wheels on it..."

"You people are fucking insane," the sheriff said, breaking his long silence.

"Opinion is duly noted, and a sound basis for your assumption does exist," said Scott, slowing down behind the truck, which featured the face of a big, fat cow on the back. "But instead of debating the subject, just tell me how I turn the pretty, flashing blue lights on."

Murphy told Scott what to do, but as his hand reached for the light switch an unexpected southern-accented, female voice cut through the quiet.

"Sheriff Murphy, this is dispatch, what's your 20?"

"Jesus Fucking Christ! That about gave me a heart attack," yelled Scott, grabbing the mike and stretching out the cord. It was just long enough to pass through the Kleenex box-size opening in the center of the wire grate barrier that separated front from back.

Destini took it from him and then passed it to the sheriff's free hand. Looking at the nervous old man, she said, "tell them you took 40 to the state line, but are turning around and will be back at the station in about 30 or 40 minutes – or however long it would normally take you to get there from the border."

Murphy did so, and received a short reply from the dispatcher.

"Copy that, just wanted to let you know that the train is being stopped right now. State police and federal agents are on scene to conduct a search."

"Thanks for the update," the sheriff replied. He was about to hand the mike back to Destini, when he pulled it back and depressed the talk button.

"I love you Marlene," he said, his voice a bit shaky.

Destini knocked the mike from his hand and it fell against the wire. It dangled there from its extended cord.

"Oh Good God," said Scott. "That fuckin' blows it for us. Gimmie the goddamn radio."

Destini now had the barrel of the gun pressed next to the sheriff's temple and with her free hand passed the mike back up front to Eli.

They all sat speechless, waiting to hear what the response on the other end would be.

"Well, I love you too, you old coon dog," Marlene finally replied after what seemed a lengthy pause. "You just hurry up and get on back here. I'll have the coffee waiting."

"What's that mean? Huh?" Asked Scott. "I'll have the coffee waiting. What is that, code for 'I'm sending out reinforcements because you're in trouble?'"

"No code," the sheriff answered. "That's my wife on the controls."

"Bullshit," said Scott. "I don't buy it. You just set us up."

"It doesn't matter now," said Destini. "Pull that truck over and let's do this fast."

"Hey, do these police vehicles have GPS in them?" Scott suddenly asked as the thought struck him. "I mean, are they tracking us right now?"

"Do you think I can afford that kind of technology in our annual budget?" The sheriff answered. "Hell, it's been four years since I've even gotten a raise. You're safe…for now."

"I thought I mentioned I was a lawyer," Destini said to him, "so please quit lying."

"Let's do it," Scott said as he turned the flashing lights on.

They followed about three car lengths behind the truck, waiting for it to signal that it was pulling over, but it just kept going.

"Okay, where's the freakin' siren?" Scott asked.

"Scotty, you're language has been deteriorating all day," said Eli. "I'm not very happy about that."

"I fuckin' said freakin,' okay?" He said, clearly agitated. "Thanks for saying my name. Want to give him my last name and address too?"

"Oh," said Eli, "I didn't realize…"

"The siren control is the switch to the left of the lights… Scott," said the sheriff.

Scott moaned as his name was repeated and turned the siren on.

It appeared for a brief second or two as if the truck picked up speed in response to the siren, then the red glare of the brake lights finally came on and the big rig began to veer to the shoulder.

"This should be fun," Scott mumbled to himself as he followed the truck over to the side and came to a stop about ten feet behind it. "First I'm an FBI agent and now I'm a cop."

"You can do it," Destini said encouragingly.

Scott opened his door and eased himself out. He walked toward the driver's side of the cab with his right hand instinctively on the hilt of the gun in his holster -- which helped to keep up the baggy pants as well. A few cars sped by, oblivious to what appeared a routine traffic stop. From the headlights shining behind him he could make out an assortment of colored ice cream cones on the side of the large trailer. "Udderly Smooth & Refreshing" was stenciled above the display.

As he pulled even with the cab, Scott saw a young man staring down at him wide-eyed. He looked like he was in his early 20's and he looked visibly upset.

"Uh, hi-i-i," the kid stammered apprehensively. "I'm sorry, was I going a little too fast? I didn't realize."

Scott immediately felt sorry for him. Wow, he thought, cops sure wield a lot of power over people.

"Hey, no worries," he answered quickly. "You're fine. You're not in any trouble. This is just a random inspection stop we do. I'll have to ask you to open your back end so my partner can take a quick look and we should have you back on your way in no more than 10 minutes."

"Uh, o-o-okay," the young driver replied. "Um, but is that necessary? I mean, I'm so waaay late on my run already."

"I promise," Scott said. "This won't take long."

The kid slowly climbed down from the cab and led Scott to the rear of the truck, where Destini stood waiting. She had her arms folded inconspicuously and Scott guessed she still had a firm grip on her gun hidden away.

"This is agent Garcia from the DEA," Scott said. "We'll just take a quick look for illegal substances and then you can get back on the road."

"Oh crap," said the trucker. "I'm sorry, this is my first time operating for this line and I forgot that I can't open this. It's pressure sealed and refrigerated. See the little temperature thingy on the lock. It's below 32 degrees in there and there's no-o-o way to o-open it without ruining the frozen goods."

"Son, I don't want to take up a lot of time but you're just…" Scott started to say before Destini interrupted him by bringing her gun out and pointing it at the driver.

"Just open it," she said and her tone left no room for discussion.

"Oh shit, oh shit, oh shit," the driver repeated awkwardly. "O-o-okay."

It only took him a moment to unlatch and unlock the big doors, despite his nervous fumblings. When he swung them back, two things happened simultaneously. A previously unnoticed passenger up in the cab jumped out of the truck and started running away into the darkness. He didn't get far when they all heard him trip and fall, accompanied by a loud crack, and subsequent screaming "Oh my God! My leg! I broke my fucking leg!"

The other occurrence was a collective, startled gasp from the twenty-or-so Mexican men, women and children sitting in the otherwise empty trailer.

"Holy shit son," said Scott. "Did you know these people broke into your truck and ate all your ice cream?"

"Oh God, I don't wanna go back to ja-a-ail," the driver cried as he automatically dropped to his knees and placed his hands behind his head.

"Wow, I really need to get out more," said Eli in awe as she came walking up. "There's some crazy stuff going on the world."

Just then, another wailing imploration came from the darkness. "Jesus, somebody help me, I broke my leg! Goddamn it hurts!"

Destini, meanwhile, had walked to the back end of the trailer and was addressing the crowd inside in Spanish. An elderly gentleman spoke with her briefly in return.
Destini turned back to Scott and told him she would get their package, then she went back to the patrol car.

"Look buddy, it's your lucky day," said Scott to the sobbing driver. "Hey, are you listening to me? Get up already. You're not in trouble."

It took a moment for Scott's word to sink in and when he did finally look up, he saw Destini leading the shackled, semi-clad old sheriff to the truck.

"Hu-u-u-h?" He managed to sputter.

"We're not really cops, you lucky bastard," said Scott. "In fact, we stole this car and this is the real cop. You're gonna help us out by just taking him for a little ride to wherever it is you're going and we'll both be on our way. Sound like a deal?"

"Oh yes sir, yes sir," the kid replied scrambling to his feet. "Absolutely. You got it."

"Do me a favor," Destini said to the trucker as she came back from having had the folks inside the truck lift the sheriff up and in the back, "please drop our package off somewhere in an open field before you make your delivery. Your employers probably wouldn't appreciate having a law enforcement witness to have to deal with and that wouldn't be good for you either. Just deposit him someplace alone before you reach your destination. Got it?"

"Oh yes ma'am, you bet," the driver agreed, vigorously nodding his head, still trying to grasp his good fortune.

"Good," she said. "Now lock it back up and hit the road."

"Hey, wait a minute," Scott whispered to Destini as the grateful trucker moved to comply. "Why don't we all just jump in the back and sneak out of here. It's perfect."

"Until they find the abandoned police car and set up more road blocks – which they're bound to do anyhow within the next few minutes after they realize that train is empty," Destini replied. "I doubt this truck will make it as far as Albuquerque, before it's searched."

"So back to the reoccurring question du jour… what's our plan?" Asked Scott.

"Oh, I've got a good one," Destini replied. "It's your turn to trust me."

"Will all you motherfuckers up there quit gabbing and somebody help me!? Please?!!!" Came the renewed plea from the darkness beyond.

CHAPTER FIFTEEN

"This has been the longest day of my life," said Scott absently, as the car's flashing blue lights disrupted the desert's stillness. He peered down the tracks to his left from the desolate railroad crossing they were parked at and was met with nothing but blackness.

"I like your idea, in theory," he said to Destini, now back up front and next to him. "In fact, it's pretty damn clever – getting on the very train that's already been searched. But what if the engineer doesn't stop?"

"You're a cop. He'll stop," she said. "Just remember the plan and trust me."

"You keep saying that, but it's not like I have much choice," he said.

"So, what's the plan?" Destini asked.

"What?" Scott answered, confusion showing on his face.

"For us, dummy. What's the plan for us?"

"Oh," he said, smiling. "Well, I'm thinking a luxurious double-wide in a trashy trailer park in Florida. Me doing odd jobs for cash, like carpentry or woodworking, when I'm not soaking up the sun and a six-pack. You punching out a few little ones, hand-washing dirty cloth diapers and doing some alligator wrestling on the side. If we really get strapped for cash, we can always sell off one of Eli's kidneys."

"Hmmm... so you are thinking long-term though," Destini grinned. It was the first time he'd seen her smile since they had left the small café at the park.

"You're all I have now... literally..." Scott said with a shrug.

"What's your plan?" Destini asked, turning back to Eli.

"I'm just hoping to make it through one more day to see Wendall," she replied. "I just hope this train goes toward Kansas."

"We're kind of at the mercy of wherever it's headed," Destini said. "But we'll get off somewhere convenient so we can do that for you."

"What?" Eli said, genuinely shocked. "You'd do that for me, even after all the trouble I've caused you today?"

"I am still pretty upset about that," Destini said. "But I do realize that you were only looking out for Scott and doing what you thought was best. I'm okay with that. We'll make a stop in Kansas so you can see your boyfriend."

"Thank you Destini," Eli said quietly. "And for what it's worth, I'm sorry. Very sorry."

"Hey, hey, I see a light in the distance," Scott said with some excitement. Then his face changed to one of concern as a new thought struck him.

"What if there are no box cars with any doors open?"

"Is he always so pessimistic?" Destini asked, looking back at Eli. "We'll have to find a way on, because we won't get much further the way we are now."

"God I hope he sees us and stops," Scott said.

Destini climbed into the backseat with Eli, where they both crouched down low.

"I can't tell if he's slowing down or not," Scott said. "It looks like he's just coming straight at us. He's gotta see these lights for miles, there's nothing else out here. C'mon you dumbass -- brake the train already."

"I'm sure he's too busy cussing you out right now," Destini said. "Give him a minute."

"Did I mention this has been the longest damn day of my life?" Scott asked rhetorically.

He watched the digital clock display on the dash. It went from 8:22 to 8:23.

"Christ, I still can't tell," Scott said. "He must be like five miles away still for all I can judge, but that light doesn't seem to be getting any bigger."

8:24.

8:25.

"Well Scott?" Asked Eli.

"I hear your voice grandma. I see the bright light getting closer. Keep talking, guide me home, I'm coming."

"Funny, but we're not dead yet," Eli replied.

"You know, while we're on the subject," said Scott, "do you think it's such a good idea that we're actually parked directly on the tracks? I mean, I'm sure he can see us just as well if we were 10 feet back."

"Oh my God!" Yelled Destini, sitting bolt upright in the back. "You're on the tracks!?"

"Um, hello, you were sitting right next to me as I stopped the car on the middle of the tracks."

"Apparently it didn't register," she replied. "I've got a lot on my mind."

"How could you not notice?" Scott asked. "I pulled to a stop right on them. Didn't you feel the bumps?"

"If I had, don't you think I would have said something? Only an idiot would try to stop a speeding train by parking his car directly in front of it."

"Well only a complete moron wouldn't even be able to tell that an idiot had parked his car directly in front of a speeding train," Scott answered in a childish tone.

Eli looked incredulously back and forth at the exchange, while throwing alternate glances at the rapidly approaching train light.

With a shake of his head and a sigh of resignation, Scott put the patrol car in reverse and rolled it back, just off the tracks.

"There, is that better?" he asked, looking at Destini.

She didn't answer, but instead focused her gaze out the front window and raised an eyebrow. Confused, Scott turned around in time to see the descending mechanical signal arm at the crossing bounce off the hood of the cruiser. Although the impact was slight, it set off the car's panic alarm -- the horn began to beep and the inside dome light began to flash.

"I can't remember the last time I had so much fun," said Eli laughing.

"Gee," Scott replied sarcastically, "it's a shame the airbag didn't deploy for your entertainment."

That only made Eli laugh harder as she nodded her head in apparent agreement.

Scott fumbled with the keys in the ignition, looking for a button on the key pad that would silence the alarm. Unable to find it, he simply turned on the police siren to try to drown out the horn. Destini was saying something in the back but he couldn't quite make out the words over the din.

Frustrated, Scott opened his door and got out of the car. The desert air was unusually crisp, he thought, as a cool breeze made him shiver. He watched as the train approached ever more slowly -- at least the engineer had applied the brakes and was bringing the metal behemoth to a stop. Perhaps pissed about the unscheduled delay, he was also laying hard on the train whistle as the long Burlington Northern/Santa Fe line ground to a screeching halt.

"Jesus!" shouted Scott, barely able to even hear his own voice. He covered his ears with his hands and watched as the locomotive finally came to a complete halt about 25 feet away from the crossing.

He took a step toward the tracks and realized that from this position, there was no way Eli and Destini could get out of the car and not be seen in the train's headlight. Cursing under his breath, because he knew how ridiculous he looked, he got back in the car and drove it off the pavement and onto the desert just past the locomotive, then angled it back toward the crossing so his headlights were aimed at the front of the train.

"Just head down the line to the first open box car you see," he told Eli and Destini. Then he stepped out of the vehicle again and walked slowly up to the front of the train. As he went, he could feel the oversized sheriff's pants start to come down off his hips so he jerked them up with his left hand and kept it there, trying to assume a pose of laid-back, southwestern indifference. He rubbed his chin thoughtfully with his other hand as he slowly neared and saw an elderly conductor waiting atop the back of the locomotive.

"What the hell is going on?" The old man asked indignantly. "You all just held me up for 45 minutes to search this train and now you're stopping me again? I'm going to file a grievance. Do you have any idea what a pain in the ass it is to stop and start this old bitch?"

Scott stood silent for a while, continuing to rub his chin as if to assess the situation. He wished he still had his kachina doll so he could watch it bounce off this stodgy old fucker's head. After sizing up the guy, he decided to try a polite, remorseful approach.

"Well, I do apologize sir," he said, "I'm sure it isn't easy and I certainly wouldn't stop you for a routine matter, but we have kind of a dangerous situation on our hands and reason to believe that some fugitives may try to board this train further down the line -- especially knowing that it's already been searched once."

"Well, I don't rightly see how the hell anyone's gonna jump a train that's traveling nigh on 70 miles per hour," the conductor answered. "And I sure as hell ain't stopping again until I reach Amarillo."

Scott noticed that he pronounced the name of the Texas town as if it ended with an 'a' and he also found himself wondering where the term "nigh" originated.

"Well, these particular outlaws are a downright clever lot," he replied, trying to affect the local dialect. "They might could possibly get you to stop this here train using subterfuge."

Scott beamed inwardly -- the redundancy of might/could/possibly was sheer genius.

"Is that like dynamite?" The old man asked.

"Huh, what?"

"That there subterfuge stuff you mentioned. Is that some sort of explosive?"

"Oh, uh, have you heard of C4?" Scott asked.

"Hallelujah son, I wasn't born on a farm, of course I know ... oh, wait a minute, I was indeed born on a farm," the conductor said, then chuckled at his own comical observation.

"Well, this stuff is C8," Scott ad-libbed. "It's twice as powerful."

"With all due respect to the law, you are quite the smartass," the old man replied. "Don't you think that I know that subterfuge is just a fancy way 'o saying by deception, deceit or an act of trickery? How dare you insult my intelligence. Do you know it requires a college degree to do this job? I ain't just some glorified truck driver on iron rails here boy."

Whew buddy, touched a little nerve there, Scott thought.

"Hey now Mister Webster, you were the one who asked me if subterfuge was like dynamite, so if you already knew it wasn't, then you, my good man, are the smartass," Scott answered, emphasizing the last word.

"Just go 'bout your business and be quick so I don't get shifted down the line for being off schedule," the conductor replied with a sigh and disappeared back inside his compartment.

Scott looked back at the patrol car thinking that this little exchange should have given Eli and Destini plenty of time to find a ...

"Ah fuck," he muttered. Despite the bright lights doing their best to blind him, he could make out the shadowy form of someone pounding on the backseat window. Of course, they can't open the back doors from the inside.

Instead of going back to the cruiser, however, Scott climbed up on the locomotive and entered the train car. He didn't have a good feeling about the old man. For all he knew, the guy was on a radio calling the cops right now to complain about being stopped again. He saw the guy making some notes in what looked like a logbook. Although he was sideways to Scott, he either didn't notice that Scott had come in or didn't think it important enough to acknowledge. Scott found out it was the latter as the conductor finally spoke up, "How long is this gonna take?"

"Do you have someone in the back?" Scott asked, ignoring the man's question and coming back with one of his own. He felt he needed to display a little authority.

The conductor turned his head to face Scott and stared intently at him, as if it were his turn to size up the disheveled-looking lawman before him. After a long pause he responded, "Yeah, Jasper sits in the rear."

Scott nodded, as if there were now an understanding between them to concede that while the old man was in charge of the train, Scott was in control of the situation.

"Okay," he said, again tugging his pants up to his waist. "I'll take a little ride down to the end and just make sure everything looks okay on the way and that Jasper doesn't have any unwanted company. Hopefully this won't take more than five minutes. I'll have Jasper let you know when you can start her up again. Thanks for your cooperation in this matter."

"Uh huh," the conductor replied resolutely, and with that turned his back to Scott.

Scott made his way to the police car. The siren was still on, as were the flashing lights. As soon as he opened the door and sat back down, Destini screamed at him.

"Turn that noise off! My head's about to explode!"

He found the switch to cut the siren and then started the car.

"So glad you could come back for us, since we're trapped!" Destini yelled at him.

"Hey, the siren's off; no need to continue shouting, we're not married yet," Scott replied as he turned the car around and drove along the tracks toward the back of the train. The ground was uneven and the cruiser bounced roughly along.

"Sweet Mary, I don't feel so good," Eli said.

"Sorry, we're almost there," Scott said, slowing down to a crawl.

"Almost where?" Destini asked, poking her head back up to peer out of the window.

"The end of the train. So far I haven't seen any options for stowing away, but if we have to, we'll just all get in the caboose with Jasper and ride to Amarilla."

Apparently his passengers didn't find the pronunciation as humorous as Scott had earlier, as he was greeted with utter silence -- followed shortly thereafter by the sudden gut-wrenching sounds of Eli throwing up. The sound, combined with the pungent smell of stomach bile and what Scott perceived as an odor much like cheese-gone-bad, made his own abdominal reflexes start to contract. He quickly rolled down the window and stuck his head out to keep from gagging -- and promptly swallowed some kind of large bug.

"Ggggrraaahhhrrr...wa-a-a-a! Son of a bitch!" He gargled, then proceeded to spit numerous times as the car veered from left to right and back as a result of Scott's unpleasant ingestion. The jerking of the vehicle did little to help Eli, who started vomiting anew.

"If this is some kind of new gross-out Fear Factor stunt, you win!" Destini shouted. She managed to get the sentence out just before Scott slammed on the brakes and sent her flying into the iron-mesh divider between the front and back seat. Her face was still pressed sideways against the barrier as the car came to a stop and Scott turned back to look at her.

"I do not like you," she said slowly, the words slightly distorted as part of her lip was bleeding and stuck to the criss-cross of the tiny bars.

"How the hell did we get this far?" Scott asked rhetorically. "We are the sorriest bunch of losers ever. Maybe we should just turn ourselves in and console ourselves with the fact that a lethal injection would be less painful than this bullshit."

"Get me out of here!" Eli began yelling repeatedly.

Scott saw that the end of the line was only about four train cars away, but with Eli's insistent hysterics, he decided it best to honor her wishes. He got out of the car, opened Eli's door and helped her out. She leaned herself a bit unsteadily against the side while Scott walked around the back of the car to let Destini out of the other side, as she had looked unwilling to cross over the pool of puke on Eli's floorboard.

The three of them gathered in front of the police car.

"Okay, here's the deal," Scott said, pausing to scrape his right index finger across the inside back of his throat. After hacking up some more spit, he continued. "There's a guy named Jasper in the caboose. We'll hang out with him until we cross the Texas border and then figure out the rest from there. I'm just not gonna worry about planning any further ahead than that at this point, especially with the way our day's been going."

Receiving no responses, Scott considered that as approval and started toward the caboose. Eli and Destini followed a few feet behind on either side.

The gunbelt dangling loosely on his hip, the rusted, old train and the wild west feel of the desert led Scott to start whistling the theme from some old Clint Eastwood spaghetti western. The tune re-energized him somewhat and he envisioned what the current scene must look like as he and his bedraggled comrades triumphantly made their way to the end of the train. In his mind, he could picture a dramatic, slow-motion walk as his modern-day band of outlaws kicked up the dust behind them on their march toward freedom. A slight smile creased his lips at the romantic notion and he glanced back to his right.

There, Destini was pathetically cradling her bloody mouth with a trembling hand and limping gingerly along. Scott furrowed his brow and looked to his left. He saw that Eli was stooped over and convulsing with a bad case of dry heaves. Oh well, he thought as he ceased his whistling and tugged his pants back up over his exposed butt crack, he could always embellish the events later as he was describing it all in detail to his cellmate Bruno.

He went back to hold Eli as she finished shuddering and wiped her mouth with the sleeve of the police uniform.

"Still having fun?" He asked somberly.

"Oh yes!" Came the unexpected reply. "This beats the hell out of bland orange Jell-O and bingo night."

Scott laughed. "I thought I was the only one with a psychological aversion to orange Jell-O. It's good to see we have a common phobia."

The sharp, hollow cry of the train's whistle made them all jump.

"Geez, let's get on board," Destini said and led the way to the back steps of the caboose.

"Hey, hey, wait a minute," Scott intoned a bit childishly again, "I'm first. Uh, I mean, it's better to let me go in first so we don't startle the engineer. He's only expecting a cop."

Scott stepped up onto the back platform and stuck his head around the open doorframe. Inside he counted one gray-haired engineer and four dark-suited guys with guns pointed in his direction.

"Okay," he called back to Destini, "you can go first."

CHAPTER SIXTEEN

"You know, I just can't decide," said one of the suits as he shook his head and eyed Scott, whose immediate thought was to ask if the man's dilemma involved shooting them or not. He bit his tongue to keep from making a wisecrack.

The man who was speaking looked like a humorless, no-nonsense type. Then again, thought Scott glancing quickly around, they all appeared pretty serious with their flat-top haircuts and neatly pressed, cookie-cutter clothes. They had immediately stripped Scott of his gun, then flashed some CIA credentials after Destini and Eli had been seated. Jasper, meanwhile, had been sent to the front of the train.

The man who was speaking sat in a small swivel chair directly across from them and actually looked like the youngest of the bunch. Scott wouldn't have figured that he'd be the one in charge. The other three remained standing as did Scott, for lack of seats, and still had their weapons aimed at all three of the new arrivals, including Eli. Although he found that a bit extreme and unnecessary, Scott opted to remain silent.

"I just can't decide," repeated the leader with a Boston accent after a short pause, "whether it's dumb luck or collective smarts that you all are still alive. Either way, it's damn impressive. I commend you on your ingenuity in the face of extreme crisis."

Scott couldn't tell by the man's impassive features if he was being sarcastic or not.

"Now then," he continued, "before we get to the matter at hand, there is the issue of a missing sheriff upon which I hope you can shed some light."

"He's in the back of an 18-wheeler headed east on I-40," Scott volunteered. "Some kind of refrigerated ice cream rig -- udderly smooth or something like that."

The man asking the questions raised an eyebrow. It took Scott a moment to realize what additional information he was after.

"Oh no, he's still alive," he added. "Heck, the truck's not even refrigerated. In fact, it's carrying a bunch of illegal aliens. You guys should probably be all over that."

One of the armed men holstered his weapon and then quickly relayed the information on his cell phone.

"Okay, see how simple that was?" The man in the chair asked. "I appreciate your cooperation and I have a good feeling that things will go ... udderly smooth ... if we can continue these lines of communication. Just so we're all comfortable, my name is Keith, by the way."

Scott noted that Keith didn't even give a hint of a smile at his own joke and for some strange reason that worried him more than the guns. He reminded Scott of a young and very intense Dennis Hopper -- someone who might change his demeanor in the blink of an eye and go over the edge.

"I don't think we should say anything else without a lawyer present," Destini interjected.

"That's rich," Keith responded. "I do believe that you, in fact, are an attorney, but the main thing to remember is that nobody has been accused of anything. We're just talking for the moment. Casual conversation. Let's keep it as such."

Keith paused again, then addressed Eli.

"Ma'am, are you feeling alright? Would you like some water or something?"

"I'm okay, thanks," Eli answered curtly.

Keith nodded, then reached inside his double-breasted blazer. He pulled out what at first glance appeared to be two long skinny straws and Scott couldn't help but wonder what kind of medieval torture this would entail. Then he saw Keith tear the top off of one and put the end in his mouth. Scott almost started laughing as he realized the man was sucking on a pixie stick, but then it made him question Keith's stability even more.

"Sorry, I don't mean to come across as some kind of freak," Keith said, as if he had read Scott's mind. "Just love these things. Very tasty. These have really helped me quit smoking.

"Of course that was two years ago," he added dryly, "so I guess I traded one addiction for another. Anyhow, not to get off track here … let's talk about the FBI agent you killed this afternoon. That's some serious shit my friend."

The sudden change of subject caught Scott off guard and he felt his face flush, but before he could even think to make some kind of reply, Destini spoke up.

"What are you talking about," she said, "I shot that arrogant little bastard."

The corners of Keith's lips raised ever so slightly as he seemed almost pleased by that admission. He leaned back as if considering the new possibilities this presented.

Scott, meanwhile, was dumbfounded. He looked back at Destini for some kind of explanation, but she avoided his eyes and kept her gaze directly on Keith.

"And, of course, I suppose it was self defense?" Keith asked her as he used his teeth to rip open the top of the other pixie stick. He spit the paper on the floor, tilted his head back and poured the stream of powdered sugar into his mouth.

"Considering that we'd all be dead if I hadn't shot him, then yes, it was," she answered coolly. "Besides, he was a double agent."

"Yes, he was," agreed Keith. "But we were monitoring him closely. He was our only link to your father's extensive drug cartel."

"Well, now you have a better link," Destini said.

"I was hoping you'd say that," Keith said, finally showing a trace of a smile. "I take it that you're willing to cooperate fully?"

"As soon as you let these two go," Destini replied. "They did nothing wrong but pick me up on the side of the road."

"That may be a little premature at this point..." Keith started to say, but was cut off by Destini.

"I can give you exact locations of homes, factories, delivery routes and names and bank account numbers. You've just hit the jackpot and all it's going to cost you is letting these two innocent people get on with their lives. Don't be stupid."

"You are correct," Keith replied after a slight hesitation, then motioned toward the two agents standing guard at the caboose door. "Get them out of here. Take them to the nearest bus depot and buy them tickets back home."

"No dammit," Scott said to Destini. "This is bullshit. I'm not just gonna walk out of your life and pretend this never happened. I love you. I'm staying here with you."

"Thank you Scott, just hearing that means a lot to me," Destini said, "but if you really, really do love me, then you'll do this for me."

There was a prolonged silence as the two of them stared unblinkingly into each other's eyes.

"No," Scott finally said. "I refuse to let it end like th…"

Before he could finish the sentence a sharp pain erupted across the right side of his temple. As his knees buckled and hit the floor he realized that one of the suits must have smacked him in the head with the butt of his gun. Geez, he didn't do a very good job, I'm still conscious, he thought amid a hazy swirl of pain and confusion. He heard Destini yell something, but her voice sounded distant and muffled, as if he were under water. Just as it seemed he was going to topple over face first, two hands grabbed him beneath his armpits from either side and dragged him toward the door. He could still hear Destini arguing, but couldn't understand why she refused to eat her cabbage. Wait, that doesn't make sense, he thought … and then everything went black.

He knew he hadn't been out long because a painful new sensation in his knees brought him back to reality. His vision was a little blurry, but he could see that they were dragging him toward the police cruiser they had just abandoned. His knees scraped against the hard desert floor as they went. He wanted to say something, but his mind couldn't quite focus on exactly what it was, plus his mouth felt like it had been stuffed with cotton. He closed his eyes and then felt himself being lifted and tossed into the back seat of the car. His head landed on something soft and then a hand started gently stroking his head.

"It'll be alright Scottie, it'll be alright," he heard Eli say.

But somehow, deep down, he knew it wasn't going to be alright. He knew he had to get back to Destini or he'd never see her again. He managed to shakily sit up and then fall against the door. He pushed against it but it didn't budge. He heard the car's engine start as if in a dream.

"Just rest Scottie," he heard Eli again.

He turned his body to look out the back window as the car pulled away. He watched the train fade and it seemed like he had no peripheral vision -- all he saw was the caboose in a circle of black, and it was getting smaller and smaller.

CHAPTER SEVENTEEN

He looked down at the large, metallic food cart in front of him.

Rows of small, white paper cups decorated with smiling daffodils were neatly lined up on a plastic tray, their individual contents seeming to undulate mockingly at him under the harsh fluorescent lights.

Orange Jell-O.

God, he loved that stuff.

Looking around to make sure nobody was watching him, Scott picked up one of the cups and took a plastic spoon out of his white, orderly's smock. He dipped the spoon into the wriggling mass, scooped out a large portion and put it in his mouth. Mmmmm, that stuff was good. He couldn't imagine ever having disliked it, but his tastes had changed along with his general outlook on life over the past year.

He greedily finished off the contents of the small container and discarded it into a trash bag attached to the end of the cart. Then he rolled the cart slowly down the well-lit hallway of the nursing home, pausing at each door to ask if any of the residents would like some of the soft, sweet desert.

Whenever one of the residents declined, he would move the cart a little further past the doorway and then eat their portion. No sense in letting it go to waste, he thought. Besides, even though he had his own little, one-bedroom apartment in the nursing home complex, they just didn't pay him enough to pass up any of the free kitchen food… that and the fact that his ex-wife was getting half his measly income as a result of the divorce settlement.

A couple of the more infirm residents needed help with the Jell-O, and Scott patiently spoon-fed them before going on to the next room. Finally he found himself standing in front of Eli's door. He knocked once and then, without waiting for a reply, he opened the door and rolled the cart inside.

Before he could say anything, Eli "shushed" him with a finger to her lip. He saw that she was watching some kind of reality show.

"No," she implored at the television, "don't trust that skinny little ho."

"Hey!" Scott said. "There are impressionable old people around here. Watch the language please."

He rolled the cart in front of the chair in which Eli sat, then pushed the few remaining cups of Jell-O to one side. He waited a few minutes until a commercial came on, then he reached underneath the cart and pulled out a small white cake decorated with tiny mandarin oranges. He placed it on the cart before her.

"Happy Birthday Eli," he said.

"Oh Scottie, thank you. That's so sweet."

He sat down slowly on the edge of her bed.

"Hard to believe it's been a year," he mused, staring absently at the TV. He hadn't watched any TV himself in several months -- ever since the trial ended. Destini's father had been easily captured in Guadalajara, Mexico, thanks to an insider's tip on where he usually spent the holidays and under what assumed identity. After his extradition to the United States on murder and drug trafficking charges, the court process was unusually speedy in his case and he had received a life sentence. Scott had taken out a loan to fly to New York where the trial had been held in hopes of seeing Destini. He had caught a glimpse of her just once as she was being herded into the courthouse, surrounded by an entourage of CIA agents, but she had not seen him.

After the trial ended, he had held out some hope that she would just one day turn up and they could start their life together -- but that day was fast becoming just a fantasy in his mind. He refused to believe that she had just discarded him so easily; rather, he figured that she was probably serving several years in jail herself on a reduced plea bargain, despite her cooperation. That's okay, he thought, he would just slop orange Jell-O and wait.

"You're looking pretty darn pathetic over there," he heard Eli say and it snapped him out of his reverie.

"It's not easy," Scott answered. "I don't know how you did it all those years after your husband was gone. Sometimes I just don't even want to get out of bed in the morning. Nothing seems to matter anymore."

"Yeah, it sucks," Eli replied.

Scott threw her a questioning look as if he was expecting some kind of moral support or words of encouragement instead.

"Well, it does," Eli stated. "However, I have some unfinished business that keeps me going."

"Oh yeah?" Scott remarked, only half listening.

"Yes," she said, clicking a button on the remote and turning the TV off. "Remember how I was going to visit Wendell for my birthday last year? Well, I saved up enough money and got us tickets to go see him this year instead. This time I want to make sure we get there, so you're not driving."

"What the hell are you talking about?" Scott asked, running his finger along the bottom edge of the cake and then sucking the frosting off.

"You have the weekend off, and I… well I have every day off… so we're flying to St. Louis tomorrow. The cab picks us up here at 8 a.m., so be packed and ready."

"Whoa, wait a minute," Scott said, "You've got to be kidding. Why didn't you discuss this with me sooner, and wait a minute, if I remember correctly, didn't Wendell live somewhere in Kansas?"

"He does," Eli replied, "but I've gotten pretty good searching on the Internet and I found us the best deal."

"Uh huh, and by 'best' you mean 'cheapest,' no doubt."

"I prefer the term least expensive," Eli replied. "Anyways, we fly into St. Louis, catch a bus to Kansas City, then take a cab down to Salinas Point. Total price, $570."

"Oh God, what can go wrong with this?" Scott asked, shaking his head and rolling his eyes for dramatic effect.

"Please Scott. You know how very badly I wished to see him last year. This could be my last chance. I need to do this."

"Where have I heard this before? Oh hell, save the spiel granny, I'd be honored to accompany you. Maybe we can do it right this time. At least one of us deserves the chance to be happy."

"Thank you Scottie," Eli said as she picked up a framed photo sitting on the night stand. In it, a soiled, torn, wrinkled and fading Ricardo Montalban peered out from a shiny, new frame. Scott noted that his teeth were still gleaming.

Bastard, he thought.

The following day's flight, bus trip and cab ride were uneventful except for one incident as they were boarding the plane out of San Diego. Eli had been pulled aside for a random search of her carry-on bag, obviously because she fit the profile, thought Scott. He feared the worst when the attendant asked what she was doing with "that thing" in her purse. It was Eli's response that made him catch his breath when she replied "I might be an old lady, but I ain't dead yet. Every woman needs something to keep her going."

Oh shit, oh shit, he thought, please God, don't let it be a vibrator. His face was already turning red as some of the other passengers filing by slowed down to watch the exchange.

"I'm sorry ma'am, but that could possibly be used as a weapon," the attendant had replied, not allying Scott's initial fears. Although he felt like saying "Look, we're not gonna ram it up the captain's ass and try to take over the plane," he was instead about to whisper that they'd be more than happy to take the batteries out, when the airline representative reached into Eli's bag and pulled out the ever-present photo of Ricardo.

"The glass on this frame could be broken and used as a weapon," the attendant continued. "I'm sorry, but you'll have to remove the photo from the frame ma'am."

Scott had let out a huge sigh then, and found himself doing the same now, but for a different reason. He was tired and dozing off a bit as the taxi pulled into the small town of Salinas

Point in the early evening. He sat up and watched the old, ramshackle businesses and white-painted homes drift by like some Norman Rockwell scene. Not much to this little place, he thought. To confirm that thought, he soon realized that they had gone through the downtown area, past the town's edge and were now on the outskirts. He was about to ask Eli about this when she instructed the driver to pull over.

"Sir," she said to the cabbie, "would you mind waiting here just about ten minutes or so?"

"Ma'am," he replied, "I will even turn the meter off."

Scott peered at the numbers on the dashboard device -- $163.75.

"Is this where we make a run for it?" He asked Eli after they had gotten out of the car.

She didn't reply, but walked toward a large wrought-iron arch that was covered in peet moss. Scott looked up. He couldn't make out what the letters spelled underneath nature's green camouflage, but then again, he didn't need to be able to read it as he could clearly see the rows of gravestones spreading out beyond the entry.

"Holy crap, please don't tell me that Wendell died?" He blurted out and immediately regretted doing so.

Eli turned back to him and smiled. She held out her hand for Scott, who, despite his bewilderment, took it and let her lead him into the still sanctuary. They walked in silence for a long time and Scott found himself thinking there were more people in here than there were back out there.

They stopped in what was obviously an older section of the cemetery -- evident by some of the crumbling markers and the fact that there weren't any signs of recent flowers at the sites. Scott was completely bewildered.

"Silly boy," Eli said by way of explanation, "your grandfather's middle name was Wendell."

Scott's eyes widened and he looked down at the headstone they had stopped before -- Robert Wendall Frost.

It took him a moment to find his voice. "You mean there never was a Wendell? I mean, this is Wendell? I'll be damned."

Eli nodded in confirmation, then addressed the granite marker -- "I'm sorry that it's been such a long time dear. It's so good to be near you again."

Scott felt a lump the size of a golf ball form in his throat and his eyes started to tear up.

"I'll leave you alone," he whispered and slowly backed away. He could hear Eli continue to talk as he made his way to a large oak tree nearby. There, he leaned against the wide trunk and watched as Eli caught up with her long-gone husband.

My God, he thought, now that is true love. He felt the tears stream down his cheeks and made no attempt to wipe them away. His heart ached for Destini and he wondered if he was doomed to live only with a memory, as Eli had done for so long. He looked up to the sky, but the setting sun gave no answer.

After a few minutes, Eli walked over to join him.

"I'll have to come back tomorrow and bring some flowers," she said matter-of-factly.

Scott put his arm around her shoulder and led her back down the path toward the arch. He could see the cab still waiting off the main road and was surprised that the taxi driver hadn't taken off with their meager possessions in his trunk. Maybe he had rifled through their belongings and realized there wasn't $163.75 worth of stuff to be had.

As they passed beneath the arch, Scott turned and looked back into the cemetery and literally felt his chest tighten with a sudden realization. I might as well go lay down in there too, he thought. I'm dead already. He stood there for a long time and Eli didn't question him.

"I'm not gonna let this happen to me," he said, thinking out loud.

Eli waited for him to go on.

"I mean, I'm not going to let go. It's just way too much to lose. I have to start looking for her. I have to start finding her. I have to start…"

"Scottie," Eli interrupted, "would you mind if we started after breakfast tomorrow?"

He laughed at that and gave her a hug. "That sounds like a plan."

As they drove back through the small town, Eli pointed the driver toward a faded, two-story pink house with a crooked, hanging sign that read "Bed and Breakfast."

"We may be out of luck here," Scott cracked. "It's after six and we didn't confirm our reservation with a credit card. They're probably all booked up by now since it's the middle of Peet Moss season."

"What's that?" The cab driver asked.

"You know..." Scott replied, "I'm really not too sure."

"There's a little sign in the window that says 'vacancy,'" Eli said.

"Isn't this how that Stephen King vampire story starts?" Scott asked rhetorically.

"Which one's that?" The cab driver asked.

"You know... I'm really not too sure," Scott repeated.

"There was a bigger motel a few miles down just on the other end of town as we came in," the cabbie volunteered.

"Oh no, this is perfect," Eli said. "Please let us out here."

Scott was flabbergasted when Eli pulled out a huge wad of cash and paid the driver in 20's. She must have given him a hefty tip, because the driver shook her hand vigorously and then said to Scott "You take care of this little lady."

"Uh, yeah," he replied, still curious about the large sum of money, "and you, uh, beware that they travel by night. May God be with you."

Scott chuckled as the cabbie's expression changed to a serious look and he quickly got back in his car and sped off.

"Um, I just thought of something," he said as they walked toward the front door of the boarding house. "How are we getting out of this town?"

"Nobody gets out of this town…alive," said Eli in a hushed tone. They both started to laugh and then quickly stopped.

"That wasn't funny," Scott said.

"No, not funny," Eli agreed.

There was nobody in the front foyer of what could barely be called a lobby, although a big TV set in front of an empty couch was on and playing some old black-and-white movie. There was a small counter on the left side of the room by the entrance and in the back center of the room were some stairs that led to the second floor. Scott could smell something sweet cooking from in the back somewhere and his stomach growled.

"By the way, what's with all the cash, did you empty your savings account or something?" Scott asked.

"Yes I did," Eli replied. "I have no intention of returning to that depressing damn nursing home. I think I may settle down here."

"Are you kidding me?" Scott asked.

"Isn't that Humphrey Bogart?" Eli asked in return, looking at the television.

"Hey, don't try changing the subject, are you… wait a minute, that is Bogey. Holy shit, do you know what that movie is?"

He went on without giving her a chance to answer. "It's 'The Petrified Forest.' Son of a bitch. That's a sign. It's a sign or something, I tell you."

Scott walked excitedly over to the counter and was about to ring the small bell for some service when his hand froze halfway down. There next to the bell was an Indian figurine that looked remarkably familiar.

His mouth fell open as his outstretched hand slowly reached for the kachina doll.

"What the fuck?" He said as he picked it up.

"Hey, careful with that, it has sentimental value," he heard from the top of the stairway.

The sound of Destini's voice caused him to drop the doll as he spun around. In a last-second effort to keep it from hitting the floor, he extended a foot to try and stop it, but wound up kicking it up and across the room instead. It flew just past Eli's head and bounced off the wall.

"It's okay, just come in here and kick my shit around why don't you," Destini said as she came down the stairs with a huge smile.

"Oh my God," Scott managed to say and then ran to her and took her in his arms. "I can't believe this. How did you… why are you…"

"Easy there," Destini said. "It was Eli who told me to meet you in this town one year from the day after I last saw you. I think you had just been knocked silly, but before they took you two away, she was able to tell me that much at least. Anyhow, the government has set me up real nice here. By the way, my name is Annemarie now, so get used to calling me that. You're my hired help and all-around handyman, so you'll be doing as I say. Understand?"

"Yes ma'am," Scott replied enthusiastically.

"Well good then, welcome to your new home. Let's go eat," she said.

"I just have to know one thing…" Scott said as they walked toward the kitchen.

"Oh Jesus Christ, fine then," Destini said with some agitation, "yes, I did kill my husband. I… shot… Jerry. There, are you happy now? Can we move on?"

"Um, I just wanted to know if you knew how to make orange Jell-O," Scott finished.

"Oh," Destini replied. "Hmmmm… no, I don't think so. Is that a problem?"

"No, no problem at all," he answered quickly. "I hate that fucking stuff."